Date: 1/8/20

LP MYS DUNNETT
Dunnett, Kaitlyn,
Clause & effect

CLAUSE & EFFECT

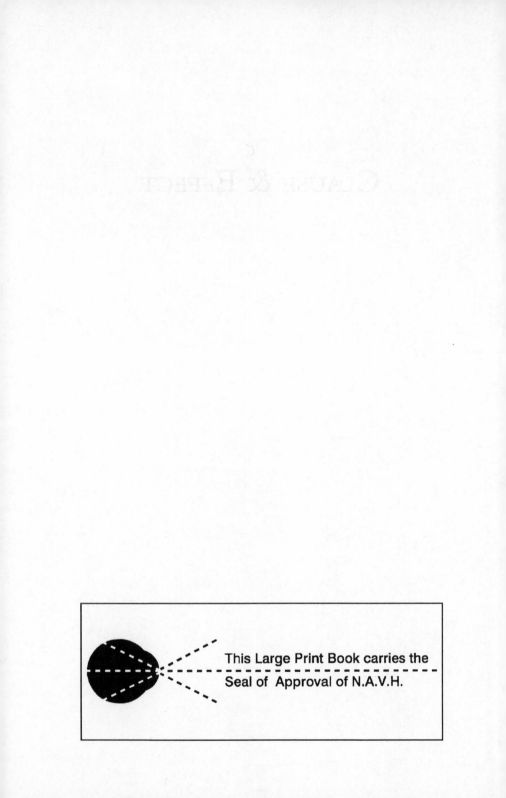

This Large Print Book carries the Seal of Approval of N.A.V.H.

CLAUSE & EFFECT

KAITLYN DUNNETT

THORNDIKE PRESS
A part of Gale, a Cengage Company

Farmington Hills, Mich • San Francisco • New York • Waterville, Maine
Meriden, Conn • Mason, Ohio • Chicago

Copyright © 2019 by Kathy Lynn Emerson.
A Deadly Edits Mystery.
Thorndike Press, a part of Gale, a Cengage Company.

ALL RIGHTS RESERVED
Thorndike Press® Large Print Mystery.
The text of this Large Print edition is unabridged.
Other aspects of the book may vary from the original edition.
Set in 16 pt. Plantin.

LIBRARY OF CONGRESS CIP DATA ON FILE.
CATALOGUING IN PUBLICATION FOR THIS BOOK
IS AVAILABLE FROM THE LIBRARY OF CONGRESS

ISBN-13: 978-1-4328-7145-1 (hardcover alk. paper)

Published in 2019 by arrangement with Kensington Books, an imprint
of Kensington Publishing Corp.

Printed in Mexico
1 2 3 4 5 6 7 23 22 21 20 19

CLAUSE & EFFECT

CHAPTER 1

"Oh, no. You're not roping me into this."

Neither my best friend from high school nor my oldest enemy paid a bit of attention. The friend, Darlene Uberman, widened her big cornflower-blue eyes at me as if she couldn't believe what she was hearing. True to form, Ronnie North pursed her thin lips and glowered.

We were sharing a table in Harriet's, a popular café on North Main Street in Lenape Hollow, New York, the small, rural village where all three of us were born nearly seventy years ago. There is no Harriet. The place is owned and operated by Ada Patel, a New Jersey native who drifted into town a couple of years ago and set herself up in the business of dispensing coffee and pastries in the morning and soup and sandwich combos from noon until two. She also makes a mean French fry. I popped one into my mouth in a futile attempt to show that I was done talking about the project Darlene and Ronnie had lured me to Harriet's to discuss. It was Friday the thirteenth. I'm not normally a superstitious person, but I should have known better than to accept their invitation.

"C'mon, Mikki," Darlene wheedled. "You're the perfect person to tackle this."

"I already have a full-time job," I reminded her, "not to mention a cat who goes into a decline if I don't spend the majority of my free time at home."

Since late last year, I've been self-employed as a freelance editor . . . a "book doctor" if you will. After I was widowed, although it had been some fifty years since I last lived in New York State, I moved back to my old home town in the foothills of the Catskill Mountains. Why? Because the house I grew up in came on the market. On impulse, perhaps overwhelmed by nostalgia, but more likely due to temporary insanity, since New York is an even more expensive state to retire to than Maine, I bought it. The next thing I knew I was faced with a host of necessary but pricey repairs and had to come up with a way to pay for them. Since my retirement income from decades of teaching junior high English wouldn't stretch that far, I set up shop as "Michelle

Lincoln, The Write Right Wright."

My business is not a hobby that can be set aside at will. Even though the most pressing of the renovations were completed last fall, I still need the income to pay for upkeep and one or two additional home-improvement projects that can't be put off much longer.

"Where's your civic pride?" Everything about Ronnie — her tone of voice, her superior attitude, her narrowed eyes — was geared to taunt. "Don't you want the quasquibicentennial to be a success?"

"Did you practice saying that in front of a mirror?"

I was inordinately pleased to have a comeback, even if it wasn't exactly a zinger. In high school, when Ronnie was the bane of my existence, I had a tendency to shrink into myself or scuttle away rather than stand up to her bullying. An hour or two too late, I'd come up with the perfect response to whatever rude thing she'd said to me.

Quasquibicentennial? That's the name given to a 225th anniversary celebration, in this case the anniversary of the arrival of the first settlers in what is now the village of Lenape Hollow. I know how to pronounce the word inside my head, but I'm not about to attempt it out loud. It's right up there

9

with Worcestershire sauce on my list of tongue twisters to avoid.

When Ronnie reached for her water glass and took a sip, looking miffed, I suspected I'd hit the nail on the head with that crack about the mirror. *Right in character,* I thought. *It's all about image with Ronnie.*

The contact lenses she wears to compensate for being nearsighted also brighten the color of rather plain brown eyes and it's glaringly obvious that she's had more than one facelift. She can afford it, which makes it hard to understand why she doesn't spring for a better dye job. Her hair, which at our age should be gray like mine or a fluffy white mop like Darlene's, is still the unrelieved black of her youth.

Each to their own, I guess. I choose to be proud of my age. I was never a great beauty, and five minutes after dressing in my best, my clothes tend to look like I've slept in them, but I lucked out in the gene pool. Although I was a brunette when I was younger, my hair is now that shade of gray that appears blond in some lights. Though I say it that shouldn't, it doesn't look half bad on me, and it complements my pale, relatively unlined skin and light blue eyes.

I let the silence stretch, concentrating on my grilled cheese sandwich. I chewed slowly, happy to let Ronnie stew. Yes, it was petty of me to enjoy having her at a disadvantage, but I didn't feel a bit guilty about it. She tormented me throughout my vulnerable teen years. She deserved a little payback.

Across the table from me, Darlene was struggling not to laugh. She knew exactly what I was thinking. She also knew that I wouldn't turn down their request just to spite Ronnie. It remained to be seen if my other objections would hold up.

To avoid locking eyes with either of them, I shifted my attention to what was going on around us. Inside the café, Ada was waiting on a foursome of local businessmen. A young woman sat alone in a corner reading a book. A middle-aged couple occupied one of the tables for two, engaged in an intense conversation. Delicious smells filled the air — the ever-present aroma of fresh ground coffee mingled with scents from all my favorite comfort foods. I try to eat sensibly. I do. But I have a weakness for homemade pastries and deep-fried potatoes and innumerable other things that are bad for me.

I'd finished my sandwich and my fries. To quell the impulse to order seconds, I concentrated on the view through the plate glass·window beside me. Although it was a

11

sunny and pleasant afternoon in mid-July, there wasn't much to see. The sidewalk was empty and even though Main Street is the main route through downtown Lenape Hollow, only a few vehicles passed by.

Directly across the street from Harriet's is the Lenape Hollow Police Station, a relatively new addition to the landscape. As I stared at the front entrance, Detective Jonathan Hazlett emerged and headed for his car. He glanced toward the café, recognized me at our table beside the window, and lifted a hand in greeting. I returned the wave and added a smile. How could I not? The man is seriously good-looking. If I were forty years younger . . .

Squelching that thought, I turned back to my companions. Darlene, a frown emphasizing the lines chronic pain had etched in her face, was just polishing off her turkey club. Studiously ignoring me, Ronnie rummaged through her designer handbag.

I repressed a sigh. That dig about civic pride had stung. For months I'd been trying, bit by bit, to become more active in the life of the community. I wanted to do my part, but there were limits. I'd be a fool to let myself be talked into taking on more than I could reasonably manage.

"I'm willing to proofread and edit," I said,

"but someone else will have to handle any rewrites."

"How hard can doing a few updates be?" Ronnie asked. "It isn't as if you have to create an entirely new script for the pageant. The one that was performed for the bicentennial just needs a little tweaking."

Hah! I'd heard similar logic in the past. It invariably meant *Give up all your free time for the foreseeable future.* True, I hadn't seen the actual text, but the mere fact that it dated from the early 1990s was enough to set off warning bells. Back then, the Internet was still a new phenomenon. Home computers existed, but they were oversize and expensive. Were there laptops? I wasn't sure, but I didn't think so. There were definitely no tablets or smartphones.

"Do you have a copy of the script with you?" I asked.

Ronnie and Darlene exchanged a look.

"There's only one," Darlene admitted. "It's kept in the archives at the historical society."

"Let me guess — typewritten?"

"Hey, it could be worse." Darlene's eyes twinkled, giving her the look of a mischievous elf. "This is the original, with black ink on nice white bond paper. You should be grateful it isn't a carbon copy or a photocopy or . . ." She lowered her voice to a sepulchral whisper. "Mimeographed!"

I repressed a shudder.

Ronnie looked disgusted with both of us. "This isn't a joking matter, Darlene. We must move forward on this project without delay. We have a script, Mikki. It isn't as if you'd be starting from scratch."

And if I believe that, I bet you have a nice bridge in Brooklyn you'd like to sell me.

I kept this sarcastic response to myself. All I said aloud was, "Have either of you read it?"

"Gilbert — that's Gilbert Baxter, director of the historical society — summarized the content for us at last night's meeting of the board. Aside from a few instances where the text needs to be adjusted for political correctness, he didn't seem to think there was much that requires changing. History is history, after all."

"Political correctness," I repeated, feeling my heart sink to my toes. "That's the literary equivalent of a field full of land mines." And another excellent reason to decline the honor they wanted to bestow upon me.

Ronnie fiddled impatiently with the slim leather wallet she'd pulled out of her purse. "It's no big deal. Just a few places where references to savages and Indians should be

14

changed to Native Americans."

"Oh, that's rich. Correct me if I'm wrong, but aren't all our high school teams still called the Indians?"

The logo is the profile of a chief in a war bonnet. Can you say *stereotype*? That portrayal isn't even accurate for this part of the country. As far as I know, the Lenni Lenape and other East Coast tribes never wore war bonnets.

"That's neither here nor there," Ronnie said in a snippy tone of voice. "What's important to remember is that the quasquibicentennial is Lenape Hollow's opportunity to take advantage of the resurgence of tourism in Sullivan County. The village board of trustees and the town council both support the decision of the board of directors of the historical society to produce the historical reenactment of our founding."

She went on, giving a little lecture on our duty to give back to the community and blah, blah, blah. I listened with only half an ear to this familiar refrain. Ever since Lenape Hollow lost its bid to become the site of Sullivan County's new casino, everyone and his brother has been coming up with schemes to lure some of the new crop of tourists our way. Once upon a time,

15

resort hotels were the key to prosperity throughout the area, at least during the summer months. Lenape Hollow was desperate to bring back the good old days. They called it "revitalizing" the town.

"In addition to the pageant, there will be a parade and other events," Darlene chimed in when Ronnie paused for breath. "People will see that Lenape Hollow is coming back to life and that it's a good place to live, to work, to play —"

She broke off when I rolled my eyes at her. "Do you really think there's going to be much crossover between gamblers and history buffs?"

"Would it kill you to pay a visit to the archives and take a look at the manuscript?" Ronnie demanded.

"Maybe it really doesn't need much work," Darlene coaxed. "You can't tell until you take a look at it."

Ada chose that moment to bring our bill. Ronnie snatched it up, although she did so with a sour look on her face. After a quick review of the charges, she handed over a credit card.

"I couldn't help but overhear," Ada said. "You should do it, Mikki. Who else are they going to find who can whip a script into shape at this late date? The big day is less

16

than a month away."

I glanced at Darlene for confirmation.

She shrugged. "August eleventh. We lucked out though. One of the other board members is the guy who directs the junior class play at the high school every year. He's volunteered to take over that end of things. He says he needs two weeks for rehearsals, so you'll have nearly that long to doctor the script."

"So, no pressure, right? Just drop everything and get busy?"

"Two days' work, max."

I didn't believe that for a minute, but I could feel myself weakening. Let's face it. It's nice to be needed, and I did want the quasquibicentennial to be a success.

"I'll think about it," I said, "but I'm not making any promises."

"I don't know what there is to think about. Either you're up to the task or you're not." Snatching her receipt from Ada, Ronnie got to her feet in such a flurry of movement that a whiff of her pungent perfume eddied my way.

I wrinkled my nose. I've never cared for Emeraude.

"We do need to have your decision soon," Darlene said in a tentative voice. "Tomorrow?"

17

Ronnie gave a disdainful sniff. "Your *sister* would already have convinced Mikki to agree. I don't know why I thought *you* would be any help."

With that parting shot, she left the café. In silence, Darlene and I watched through the window as she got into her obscenely expensive Rolls-Royce and drove away.

"I used to wonder why she didn't employ a chauffeur," Darlene said, "but then I remembered how much she likes to be in control. Put someone else in the driver's seat? Never!"

It was a nice stab at distraction, but I heard the unsteadiness in Darlene's voice.

"Why did she bring up your sister?"

"That was just Ronnie being Ronnie." But Darlene didn't meet my eyes. "She likes to issue challenges."

That much was certainly true. Ronnie wanted me to rise to the bait and prove I could handle the job. It followed that she'd try to motivate Darlene by turning this into a competition between her and her older sister.

I had almost forgotten that Darlene *had* a sister, and for the life of me I couldn't remember her name. I did recall that she was five or six years our senior and had been a cheerleader. When she was a senior and

Darlene and I were still in junior high, she'd wanted nothing to do with either of us.

Darlene reached for her cane as she eased herself out of her chair. So far, this had been one of her good days. On the not-so-good days she used a walker. On the bad ones, she alternated between a wheelchair and a scooter. Near-crippling arthritis all too frequently drained her energy. It had forced her to take early retirement from her job as head librarian at the Lenape Hollow Memorial Library, but she'd refused to become housebound. She served with Ronnie on the historical society's board of directors and belonged to two or three other local groups as well.

I collected my shoulder bag from the empty chair on my side of the table, but I wasn't ready to let the subject drop. "If your sister is so devoted to the historical society, why isn't she working on this project?"

"Judy has moved on." Darlene's words were clipped. Briefly, she closed her eyes. When she opened them again, she sent me an apologetic look. "It's a long story, and not one I want to get into right now. Besides, I really need to head home. Who knows what trouble the puppy has gotten into since I've been gone?"

At the mention of this newest member of

her family, she got a goofy pet-lover look on her face. Her longtime companion, an elderly schnauzer named Edmund, had gone to his reward a few months earlier. It had taken a while for Darlene and her husband, Frank, to talk themselves into adopting another dog, but ever since they'd taken the plunge, she'd been like a mom with a newborn. There were at least two dozen pictures of Simon on her phone, and she'd made me look at every one of them while we were waiting for Ronnie to join us at Harriet's.

"You really have to come by and be introduced," Darlene said as we left the café. "How about tomorrow morning?"

"I can see right through your devious plot, you know. The puppy is just an excuse to get me over to your house so you can badger me into tackling a full-scale revision of that manuscript."

"Maybe. Does nine work for you? I'll make one of my famous brown-sugar-topped coffee cakes."

My mouth was already watering but I waited until we reached her van to answer, standing by the open passenger-side window while she settled herself in the driver's seat. "Yes to the coffee cake and the dog."

"And the pageant?"

"That's still a maybe. Ask me again tomorrow."

CHAPTER 2

Walking home from Harriet's, I took the scenic route. Nowhere in Lenape Hollow is all that far from anywhere else in the village, but the hills will kill you if you aren't in shape. I'm no spring chicken, but aside from my need to wear hearing aids and glasses, I don't have much that's wrong with me. Even so, I was winded and unflatteringly sweaty by the time I started up my short and blessedly flat driveway.

"Hey, Mikki!" my next-door neighbor called out as she trotted down her porch steps. With the athletic stride of a long-distance runner, she headed for the station wagon parked across the street, car keys at the ready.

"Hi, Cindy." I had to look up to talk to her. Our front lawns dip down on either side of my driveway and I was standing in the valley between the two. "Going to pick up the kids?"

"Nope." With a toss of her ginger curls she stopped to grin at me. "They're with my mother. You are looking at the newest employee of Fast Foods."

"Congrats. I think."

Contrary to what the name implies, Fast Foods is a small local grocery chain. In March, they opened a store at a new location just outside the village limits but still within the town.

I should probably explain that Lenape Hollow the town consists of one village, also named Lenape Hollow, and six hamlets: Lenape Falls, Muthig Corners, Lakeville, Steenrod Springs, Dutch Flats, and Feldman. The latter was created when, as the site of the world-renowned but now defunct Feldman's Catskill Resort Hotel, it was awarded its own post office.

"It's only part-time," Cindy said, "but it will help pay the bills. And it will get me out of the house."

I couldn't help but smile back at her. Cindy Fry is one of the most upbeat, enthusiastic, buoyant people I've ever met. There are times when just watching her with her three boisterous young children wears me out. Then again, she's more than forty years younger than I am. At her age, I had boundless energy too.

By the time she drove away, I'd gone up the three steps cut into the side of my lawn and was halfway along the paved path that runs the width of the front porch. Ahead of me was the chest-high picket fence that separates my property from my other next-door neighbors. I wasn't surprised to see movement through the wooden slats. Marie O'Day loves her garden and spends almost as many hours a week tending it as she does working at O'Day Antiques, the family business. When I got closer, I could see that two people were hard at work. Marie had roped her husband into helping with the weeding.

I don't have much of a green thumb and I can't identify most flowers, let alone tell one floral scent from another, but I appreciated the fragrance wafting my way on a gentle breeze. There have always been flowers on that side of my house. Back in the 1950s and '60s, when Cora Cavendish lived there, she even managed to coax a magnolia tree into flourishing. That's a real feat this far north. I can remember collecting the petals that fell into our yard and holding them up to my nose to inhale that delicious smell. The tree is long gone, but thanks to Marie there are still plenty of gorgeous, colorful, fragrant blooms to enjoy.

Just as I started to mount my porch stairs,

two heads popped up on the O'Day side of the barrier, staring at me with disconcerting intensity through identical pairs of oversize sunglasses. My steps faltered, but only for an instant. I thought I knew what was coming, and since I finally had an answer the O'Days would like, I plunged into the conversational pool before either of them could get a word out.

"Good news," I announced. "The trees are coming down next week."

The people who lived in my house before I bought it had let a virtual forest spring up in the backyard. I wasn't sure which of the previous owners had planted so many trees, mostly evergreens and ash with a few maples and birches mixed in, but this mini-forest had been allowed to flourish unchecked for decades. The O'Days rightfully saw it as a fire hazard, as well as a potential breeding ground for the ticks that cause Lyme disease. The growth was also unsightly, since no one had bothered to prune or cut back the underbrush.

While I'd known from the moment I moved in that I'd have to do something about all those trees, I'd had to have much-needed repairs on the house completed before I could even think about tackling the backyard. I'd also needed to replenish my bank account before embarking on another home-improvement project. My freelance editing business had not yet generated enough income to cover the cost, when I lucked out and met someone willing to barter. A local custom woodworker has arranged for an arborist to cut down all but a few of my trees in return for the wood. Win-win, right?

I explained all this to the O'Days and got nods of approval in return. Then they exchanged one of those silent husband-and-wife communications before Tom spoke.

"Someone was here looking for you earlier. A young man. He didn't give his name."

"Or state his business," Marie put in.

"Were you expecting company?"

I shook my head. A door-to-door salesman seemed unlikely and religious groups send their representatives out in pairs. It was the wrong season for politicians. That left walk-in client or delivery person. "Did he have a package with him?"

Tom thought for a moment. "He wasn't carrying anything that I could see."

"Not a process server, then," I quipped.

"I should hope not!" Marie looked offended by the very thought.

I resisted the urge to remind her that, given the number of times the police had been called to my house the previous autumn, it was only to be expected that, at some point, I would be summoned to court to give testimony.

"Well," I said instead, "if he has business with me, I'm sure he'll come back." With a wave in farewell, I continued on into the house.

Calpurnia met me just inside the door to lead me straight down the hallway to the kitchen. She stopped in front of her food bowl and sent me a pointed look.

"Fine," I said. "I'll open another can of cat food, but in return you have to listen while I tell you about my morning."

I wrinkled my nose at the pungent aroma as I dished up her favorite ocean whitefish and tuna combo. While she scarfed it down, I recapped the highlights. She did not comment or offer advice. Those are but two of the positive aspects of using a feline as a sounding board. It isn't that she doesn't express opinions, but since she only speaks cat, I can interpret her remarks as I choose.

"So, I'll be going to Darlene's tomorrow and she'll make another pitch to try to get me to commit to this historical society project," I concluded as Calpurnia abandoned the nearly empty food bowl and began to clean her whiskers. "I'll probably be gone most of the morning."

She gave me the hairy eyeball.

"I'll leave you plenty of kibble and water. It's not as if I'm going away for the entire weekend."

Back when my husband was alive and Calpurnia was a kitten, he and I once took a three-day trip and left her on her own in the house. We thought she'd be fine. She had a clean litter box, food, water, plenty of comfortable places to sleep, and dozens of toys. We came home to find kitty litter scattered all over the house, a spare bag of kibble chewed open and ditto, and an unspeakable mess right in the middle of the good bedspread on our bed. The stain never did come out.

I was furious with her at first, but my anger only lasted about five minutes before I put myself in her place. If I'd been abandoned with no idea if my people were ever coming back, I'd have been pretty upset, too.

Remembering that incident, I gave her an extra cuddle before going upstairs to my office. I had work waiting for me — editing I would actually be paid to do. With only a short break for a light supper, I kept at it until nearly ten.

I was yawning by the time I finished going

through a manuscript I'd promised to return to its author by the end of the week. In the morning, I'd check my corrections and the comments one last time before sending the file to my client, along with his final bill.

Tempted as I was to shut down the laptop and head straight to bed, old habits die hard. I checked my email. I immediately wished that I hadn't. Along with the usual spam and a confirmation that my online order of three new mystery novels had shipped, I found two messages I couldn't put off answering. One was from my sister-in-law in Maine. The other came from a new client who had a project that was a little different from most of those I take on.

I skimmed Allie's email first. She still thought I was crazy to have moved so far away, but she dutifully brought me up-to-date on what everyone in her immediate family had planned for the remainder of the summer. In addition to Allie, my late husband's sister, this meant her husband, their two kids and their spouses, and Allie's three grandchildren. Since I was an only child and both of my parents had been, too, Allie and company were all I had by way of close kin. I missed them . . . but not enough to consider moving back to Maine. Without

James, I no longer wanted to live there.

Our home had been out in the country, where we had no close neighbors. Since my husband was also my dearest friend, I'd never felt the need for other people to pal around with. I left behind plenty of acquaintances when I moved, but no one I was particularly close to.

I stood, stretched, and wandered over to the bank of windows that overlooked Cindy's house. There wasn't a lot of distance between the two structures. When I looked down, I could see right into her kitchen. If she was standing at her sink, she had a clear view of whatever was going on in my dining room. Living so close to other people had taken some getting used to, but I'd soon discovered it had definite advantages. Here on Wedemeyer Terrace, we looked out for one another.

I'd loved this house and this neighborhood when I was a kid. I was happy to be living here again, especially when I turned away from the window to study the room I'd made into my at-home office. As a teenager, it had been my bedroom. It had been barely large enough to accommodate a double bed, a dresser, and a student desk, but the small size had been offset by two great assets, a walk-in closet and an attached balcony.

At the same time I had the obligatory home repairs done, I splurged a bit and asked the carpenters to take down one wall and erect a new one a few feet farther out. This gave me a third more space in my new office than I'd had when it was a bedroom. Where once the upstairs hall had been overlarge and oddly shaped, it was now a neat rectangle with five doors opening off it. Circling from the southeast-facing corner at the front of the house and moving clockwise, they led to the master bedroom, the stairs to the attic, my office, the bathroom, and, after one passed by the top of the down staircase, the small room where I slept before moving into the larger one at age twelve.

Sometime in the last fifty years, a previous owner had closed off the door that once connected this little room to the master bedroom. I applauded that change. Whoever built the house apparently hadn't cared about privacy. There had also been another door, one that led from my parents' closet into the back bedroom. Since they took in a roomer every summer for the first few years they owned the place, that door was one of the first things they got rid of, walling it in on both sides.

Lots of people rented out rooms in the good old days when the foothills of the Catskills were a tourist mecca. Not every summer visitor wanted to stay in a hotel or a bungalow colony.

Back at my desk, I answered Allie's email with a bright cheery note telling her I was keeping busy and had just been offered an interesting new challenge. I didn't go into detail. I'm not sure I was entirely clear in my own mind which project I was referring to, the one Darlene and Ronnie had offered me, or the book I'd agreed to work on with Valentine Veilleux. She was the client who'd sent the other email currently awaiting my attention.

When I opened it, an image came up with the message. It was a photograph of cats, dogs, and kids playing together on an emerald-green lawn under puffy white clouds in a cerulean-blue sky. The text was a two-word question: Cover art?

I smiled. Val hadn't hired me to make decisions about her photographs. My job was to smooth out the prose that went with them. That said, she had a tendency to toss random ideas my way, some of them serious and some not. I was 99 percent certain that this was one of her not-so-serious suggestions.

The coffee-table book she's putting together is a new venture for us both. As a professional photographer, her regular gig is taking pictures for groups who want specialty calendars. She does the photo shoots and creates the finished product. For the most part, they're used to raise funds for charitable or civic organizations. Val also does magazine work and has shot more than a few weddings, but well over half the photos she's taken during her career are of dogs, cats, and other animals. It was a no-brainer to decide to collect the best of the best and market the result to pet lovers.

Since I knew from our previous correspondence that Val had a good sense of humor, and because I was a bit punchy after a long day, I typed: It's okay, but I like this one better. I attached a recent snapshot of Calpurnia, taken without much skill with my iPad, and hit the SEND key.

Then, at long last, I went to bed.

CHAPTER 3

The next morning I was up early. I spent an hour reviewing the work I'd done the previous night and then sent the file to my client. After I shut down my laptop and changed from ratty-looking sweats into jeans and a clean L.L. Bean long-sleeved tee, I headed for Darlene's house.

Darlene and Frank live on a quiet, tree-shaded street that's just barely within the village limits. What difference does that make? Not much unless you're reporting a crime. The village is patrolled by the Lenape Hollow Police Department. The rest of the town of Lenape Hollow is the responsibility of the Sullivan County Sheriff's Department.

I was greeted at the kitchen door by an enthusiastic bundle of black fur. Yipping in excitement, it raced toward me, stopped just short of the toes of my shoes, and did one of those wriggle-all-over moves that only dogs can do. Tongue hanging out, eyes bright, he was about to attempt a leap into my arms when I squatted down to his level and held out my hand to be sniffed.

"Simon, I presume?"

Before Darlene could answer, Simon pounced, toppling me backward onto the tile floor. The puppy landed on top of me and a warm wet tongue lapped at my face. Laughing, I started to push him aside, then changed my mind and gave him a hug. He might not have learned his manners yet, but there was no denying he was loveable.

"Are you okay?" Darlene caught Simon by the collar and hauled him to one side, allowing me to maneuver myself upright. She looked more amused than concerned.

"I'll live."

Darlene was using her walker for balance, the middle stage between cane and scooter. We had been friends a long time, so I didn't hesitate to ask how she was coping with Simon's energy.

She shrugged. "We're doing okay." She released her grip on his collar. "Sit, Simon. Stay."

He obeyed, but his eyes followed us to the table where Darlene had already set out the freshly baked coffee cake, two plates, utensils, and cream and sugar. I didn't offer to help her pour boiling water into her French press, but I did carry it from the counter to the table for her, inhaling the rich aroma of freshly brewing coffee as I walked the short distance.

"So," I said as she cut into the coffee cake and served me a generous portion. "What's up with Judy?" It had taken a while, but I'd finally remembered her sister's name.

She grimaced. "Do we have to talk about her?"

"Of course not, not if you don't want to." Belatedly I twigged to a possible reason for her reluctance. At Harriet's, Darlene had said her sister had "moved on." "Oh, Darlene. I'm so sorry. I didn't think. Is Judy still with us?"

Ordinarily I avoid using euphemisms, but for some reason I was hesitant to come right out and ask if Darlene's sister was dead. I wouldn't have known. Although we were close in high school, we lost touch after I went off to college in Maine. A few months later, my parents sold their house and left Sullivan County for good, taking with them the likelihood I'd reconnect with former classmates during holidays or over summer vacations.

An amused chuckle reassured me. "She's fine, as far as I know, but we don't see much

36

of each other. She remarried and moved away from Lenape Hollow about ten years ago."

"Where is she living now?"

I expected Darlene to name some far-away location. California, maybe, or Florida, or Arizona — one of those spots popular with retirees who no longer want to deal with snow in the winter. She made me smile by naming the nearby town of Monticello, a traditional Lenape Hollow rival when it came to high school sports.

"I'm surprised she didn't continue her work with the historical society."

"She could have if she'd wanted to, but no matter what Ronnie thinks, she wasn't all that dedicated, and she'd have had to give up her seat on the board of directors once she no longer lived in the village."

"Have you been involved with them long?"

"I suppose I have, one way or another, but when Judy was active, I was still working at the library and didn't have much time for volunteering."

I nodded encouragingly and took another bite of a coffee cake to die for.

"Long story short, a couple of years ago there was a vacancy on the board, I agreed to be nominated, and I was voted into office." She pushed her coffee cup aside and folded her arms, giving me a direct stare that rivaled Calpurnia's hairy eyeball. "Now let's talk about what the board wants *you* to do."

Two front paws landed on my thigh, saving me from having to give an immediate answer. I stroked Simon's soft head, which encouraged him to do a little dance on his hind legs. "What kind of dog is he?"

"Purebred mutt. Don't change the subject. Simon — down." At the hand gesture that went with the command, the puppy obeyed.

"How can you resist that sad-eyed look?"

"Practice. Don't you dare sneak him any food."

I held up both hands to prove they were empty. Satisfied, Darlene refilled our cups.

"Was it your idea to have me edit the pageant script?"

"No, but I thought it was a good one." She took a sip of coffee. "It's a bit complicated. Shall I give you some backstory?"

"Why not?" Listening didn't mean I had to accept the job.

"As Ronnie mentioned in passing, there were actually three boards involved in the decision to resurrect the pageant performed at the bicentennial."

She lifted her hand, arthritic index finger extended.

"The town is governed by a town supervisor and four councilmen. They'd have loved to take charge, but the town of Lenape Hollow wasn't incorporated until 1807. It's only the village that's coming up on its 225th anniversary, so that put the mayor in the driver's seat."

Her middle finger came up.

"The village is run by his honor and a four-member board of trustees. I don't think you've met Tony Welby, but you do know all the board members. Your next-door neighbor, Tom O'Day, is one of them. So is Frank."

"Your Frank?"

"None other." Darlene had married Frank Uberman, her high-school boyfriend, while they were still in college. "The other two are Ronnie North and Joe Ramirez."

Joe owns the gas station on Main Street and is a real sweetheart. He regularly saves me the trouble of pumping my own gas by coming out and lending a hand. This is not to be sneered at. Full service doesn't mean the same thing in New York State as it does in Maine.

"They voted in favor of holding a quasquibicentennial," Darlene continued, stumbling a little over the word. She glared at me when my lips twitched in amusement.

"They tossed around ideas and that was when Frank remembered seeing the pageant when it was performed for the bicentennial. He suggested doing something similar. The mayor wasn't terribly enthusiastic, but the rest of them thought it was a great idea, especially Ronnie."

She lifted finger number three.

"Since she's also on the board of directors for the historical society, she assured the mayor and the other trustees that we'd be happy to take charge of that part of the festivities. It was a sensible suggestion. The historical society sponsored the original pageant twenty-five years ago."

"Too bad Ronnie didn't also volunteer to revise the script."

Darlene fought a grin. "She prefers to delegate. Now hush. I'm not through giving you the backstory. The original idea was for someone to write a new pageant, but by the time the historical society board got together to discuss the project, the society's librarian had found a copy of the old script in the archives and shown it to Gilbert Baxter, the director. Since we were already working with a tight time frame, he decided that updating it would be a better plan than starting from scratch."

"And Ronnie just happened to know

someone who edits manuscripts for a living."

"Your name did come up, but it wasn't Ronnie who mentioned you. It was Greg Onslow."

I nearly choked on my coffee. "Onslow? What's he doing on the board of the historical society?"

Darlene's lips quirked into a wry smile. "Our local entrepreneur, although he has his fingers in a lot of pies, is not a member of the board. He was invited to the meeting by the director because Baxter hoped to convince him to provide the venue for the pageant."

"Local entrepreneur?" I muttered. "Try local crook."

"You won't get any argument from me, but the fact remains that he's a mover and shaker in this community, and I expect he's trying to improve his image, given what happened last fall. Anyway, he agreed to let us use his property on Chestnut Mountain, and then he suggested that you would be the ideal person to take on the challenge of revising the script."

I shook my head in disbelief. When I first met Greg Onslow, CEO of Mongaup Valley Ventures, he'd been trying to launch a project called "Wonderful World." He'd bought the grounds that formerly surrounded a hotel, long since burned to the ground, and the adjacent village-owned recreation area, with the idea of turning the whole area into an amusement park. Even before his company's involvement in some shady activities came to light, there was plenty of opposition to this idea. The undertaking is currently in limbo. Now that someone's actually building a huge water park next to the new casino, it's probably dead.

Darlene shrugged. "Everyone seemed to take it for granted that you'd agree. We spent the rest of the meeting debating how much money to allocate to sprucing up the historical society building, in particular the area where our larger exhibits are displayed."

"Everyone? Who else is on the board besides you, Ronnie, Baxter, and the guy who volunteered to direct the pageant?"

"There are three others. Two are automatic members — the mayor and the Lenape Hollow town historian. The third is Sunny Feldman."

"Feldman? As in the hotel?"

"The last of the dynasty. Since she picked just the right time to sell out, she has no money worries. She made a bundle before

Sullivan County's tourism industry collapsed."

I'd never met Sunny, but Feldman's had been a major employer in the community when I was growing up. Once a landmark, it had been going downhill for decades. It was sad to see what had become of the place. I drove through the property shortly after I returned to the area. The buildings are condemned, the land overgrown, and no one seems to care. Now that I thought about it, I was surprised Greg Onslow hadn't decided on that location for his theme park. True, Feldman's Catskill Resort Hotel, to give it its proper name, didn't have a lake, but it did boast the remains of a small airport, a golf course, and a ski slope of the bunny variety.

"So anyway," Darlene continued, "Ronnie recruited me to help her talk you into volunteering and you know the rest, except that there's one detail in the script that may pique your interest."

I narrowed my eyes at her. "Oh?"

"According to what Baxter told us, John Greenleigh plays a key role in the pageant." She grinned at me. "Your ancestor, right?"

"John Greenleigh was one of the first settlers in what's now Lenape Hollow." I helped myself to another sliver of the coffee cake. "He came from Connecticut, as most of them did, bringing his wife and young children with him. When the town was incorporated, he was elected fence viewer." My grandfather, who'd filled my young head with tales about our family, hadn't known anything more than that about him. "I can't imagine what the author of the pageant could have had him doing. To tell you the truth, I'm having a hard time envisioning much action at all. Most of those early settlers spent every minute of their time planting crops and building houses and barns. Important, but boring."

"Admit it. You're curious."

I drained the final drop of coffee from my cup and stood, nearly tripping over the puppy sleeping next to my chair. When I'd recovered my balance and given Simon a tummy rub to apologize, I made an attempt, most likely futile, to keep my options open.

"I'll take a look at the script," I said, "but beyond that, I'm not making any commitment."

44

CHAPTER 4

That afternoon I walked to the historical society headquarters on Blake Street, a journey of less than twenty minutes door-to-door. The building has been there forever, so much a part of the landscape that I'd never paid much attention to it before. It started life as the Lenape Hollow Normal School, an institution dedicated to training teachers back when an eighth-grade education was considered more than adequate for the average youngster.

I thought I remembered the building as a private home during my youth, but since that was over fifty years ago, I was a little hazy on the details. Sometime between then and the present, it had been taken over by the historical society, renovated to meet their needs, and opened as a combination museum and research center.

The sign mounted next to the door told me that the premises were open to the public from twelve-thirty to six on Tuesday through Friday, and from nine to five on Saturday. Apparently, if the only time you had to research your family history was in the evening, you were flat out of luck. Fortunately for me, this was Saturday and it was not yet two o'clock.

When I stepped into a generously sized vestibule that doubled as a gift shop, the first thing I saw was a rack containing postcards showing old-timey scenes of Lenape Hollow and the surrounding area. Another showcased books and pamphlets, both fiction and nonfiction, with a connection to the village. The majority of them seemed to be self-published. A small table holding a guest book and a donation box was angled into a corner. A small, neatly lettered sign informed me admission was free but a contribution of any size would be greatly appreciated.

The door to my left was closed, although a light showed from within. GILBERT BAX-TER, DIRECTOR had been etched into the glass panel, but I couldn't tell if he was in there or not. The lettering on the door to my right read: SHIRLEY MARTIN, LIBRAR-IAN. It stood open to reveal a small office and a middle-aged woman sitting behind a desk overflowing with books and papers.

More books were stacked on shelves, sharing the space with assorted framed photographs of two cats, a Siamese and a domestic shorthair.

She didn't smile when she caught sight of me, but neither did she regard me with disfavor. She stood and held out her hand. "Shirley Martin." Her grip was firm and brief. "How can I help you?"

"Mikki Lincoln. I've agreed to take a look at the script for the pageant, although I've not yet agreed to work on it."

Her nod indicated that she recognized my name. "Fair enough," she said. "It's upstairs in Archives."

Assuming I'd follow her, she set off at a brisk pace. We were both dressed for the warmth of an afternoon in July. The loose, colorful caftan she wore billowed out behind her. I'd changed from my jeans and long-sleeved tee into casual slacks and a short-sleeved, emerald-green top. These were my go-to-town clothes, as opposed to the two levels below that — visit-with-old-friend-who-has-a-new-puppy, and work-at-home.

We left the vestibule by a door directly across from the entrance, moving into an open section that appeared to run from one side of the building to the other. Straight ahead, a brass railing separated this level from a lower one that was two stories in height. On an old-fashioned wooden signpost, arrows pointed the way to various displays and resources. Archives were up the stairs to the right. Newspapers on microfiche and the obituary files were down the stairs to the right. Current exhibits and a meeting room were down a short flight of steps to the left.

Shirley gestured toward the railing. "From here you can get a bird's-eye view of our larger, semipermanent displays. We've recreated rooms from three local businesses in days gone by."

I stepped closer and stopped in my tracks. I didn't need signage to identify the middle scene. A mere glance took me back a good sixty years and still had the power to make me cringe. I stared, feeling shaky, at the inner room of the dentist's office I'd been taken to as a child. It was all there: the hard leather chair, the spit bowl, and the ominous-looking drill suspended from the ceiling. A small placard gave credit to Dr. Badham's children for donating the equipment their father had once used to torture his patients.

I do not use the term lightly. Dr. Badham did not believe in Novocain or laughing gas. He drilled, filled, and extracted without offering his patients any means to alleviate their pain. No matter what their age, he advised them to tough it out. I can't imagine why my parents bought into that philosophy, or why I tolerated it, even as a child, but an entire generation of patients grew up thinking that dental work had to hurt like hell. I can still remember my astonishment when, at the age of twenty or so, I went to a new dentist to have a tooth filled and the worst pain came from the needle that injected the anesthetic.

With an effort, I shook off a slew of unpleasant images and forced myself to examine the other exhibits, a drug store and a millinery shop. Both brought back much more pleasant memories. I'd tasted my first root beer float at the counter in the former and shopped at the latter with my mother for a hat to wear to church on Easter Sunday. I miss fancy, frivolous hats. They serve no useful purpose, but they were fun. The last time I wore one was as part of my going-away outfit when I got married. Ball caps, sun visors, and winter woolies don't count.

Two men were moving around among the displays of pillboxes, cloches, and wide-brimmed hats decorated with feathers and fruits. The fellow carrying a clipboard looked familiar, but at first I couldn't place him. He was in his thirties, short and stocky but not fat. He wore a T-shirt and jeans, and what I could see of his skin on arms and face was darkly tanned. Then he turned slightly and I got a better look at his face — thin brown hair with a receding hairline, a large, slightly flattened nose, and a perpetual squint. The name that had been eluding me abruptly popped into my head — Charlie Katz, a local carpenter. The previous autumn, he and his crew had spent several days working on renovation projects at my house.

I did not recognize his companion, but based on his three-piece suit, I could make an educated guess at his identity. "Is that Gilbert Baxter?"

Shirley agreed that it was, but did not suggest we interrupt them in order to introduce me to him.

Baxter appeared to be in his mid-fifties, with salt-and-pepper hair and a little goatee of the same shade. He was taller and thinner than Charlie and considerably more animated, using elegant, long-fingered hands to emphasize some point he was trying to make.

Following Shirley, I continued on up to the second floor. As I was climbing the stairs, it suddenly struck me that the building was not air-conditioned. The higher we went, the more obvious that lack became.

"Isn't heat and humidity bad for documents?" I asked.

"You've got that right. We have a window unit in Archives. The board keeps promising to allocate funds to make the whole place climate controlled, but there always seems to be something else that takes priority. The work that's being done now couldn't be put off — structural issues, or so they tell me."

It seemed to me that protecting documents ought to be the first priority of any historical society, and clearly Shirley agreed with me, but I could also understand how being strapped for cash might delay all but the most essential building improvements. I assumed the historical society was a non-profit, dependent on donations. To lure in new patrons, the board of directors had to give the display area precedence over places a casual visitor wouldn't see.

Shirley wasn't the least bit winded by the climb. While I paused on the landing to catch my breath, she continued on down a hallway lined with memorabilia. She moved at such a fast clip that I didn't catch up with her until she'd unlocked a wooden door

51

with the word ARCHIVES painted on it.

I stepped into a long, narrow room that ran from the front of the building to the back. It was noticeably cooler inside than in the hallway. The ancient air conditioner in one window hummed loudly, its steady rumble occasionally broken by an ominous rattling sound.

"Sit," Shirley said.

I wasn't sure if that was an invitation or an order, but I pulled out one of the plain wooden chairs drawn up to a mission-style table and plunked myself down. She went straight to the row of metal file cabinets that lined one side of the room. They were a match for gunmetal gray shelves, map cases, and another storage unit I couldn't give a name to. It took only a few seconds for her to find what she was looking for.

The pages were held together by a cardboard binder. I hadn't seen one like it in decades. Metal strips were threaded through holes punched in the sheets, folded over, and secured by little metal bands that slid over the strips. Paper cuts are painful, but slice a finger on one of those babies and you're in a world of hurt.

"Is this the only copy?" Even though I already knew the answer, I clung to a sliver of hope.

"Sorry," Shirley said. "I'm sure there must have been more once — the pageant had a large cast — but I was only able to locate the one."

"I suppose it doesn't really matter. Once the script is updated, new copies will have to be made anyway."

I flipped open the cover and looked at the title page. The pageant had been written by someone named Grace Yarrow. The name didn't ring any bells, and since the board had decided to tap me to do an update, I assumed she was no longer available to do it herself.

The first thing I noticed was that the script had been typed on a typewriter with a wonky key. Every uppercase *A* was slightly elevated above the other letters. The binder contained ninety-eight slightly yellowed pages. I had no idea if that was long or short for a pageant. I had a vague recollection from somewhere that it took three to four minutes to read a page aloud, but these seemed to be heavier on stage directions than dialogue.

John Greenleigh's name leapt out at me. Darlene had been correct about his role in the pageant. That wasn't the deciding factor, of course, but why kid myself? In the days to come, I'd undoubtedly regret being

53

such a pushover, but in my heart, I was already committed to doing my bit for Lenape Hollow. If I learned a little more about my own family history in the process, so much the better.

I closed the cover and looked around for Shirley. A scowl on her face, she was briskly wielding a dust cloth. I couldn't tell if the sour expression came from her dislike of the chore or from her obligation to stick around to keep an eye on me when she undoubtedly had better things to do.

"I'll need to take this manuscript home with me," I said.

"Sorry. Archive materials do not circulate."

"Surely you can make an exception."

"Not unless I want to give Gilbert Baxter an excuse to fire me. He's very particular about our holdings staying in the building."

I knew better than to try to fight that battle. Petty bureaucrats just dig in their heels when you try to make them use common sense. "Do you have a copier?"

"No copying is allowed, either. The director says it damages the originals."

I hadn't formally met Gilbert Baxter yet and I already disliked him. "I can understand the reasoning behind such a rule if we're talking about an eighteenth or nineteenth century book or document, but this script is hardly an antique."

"Sorry. If it were up to me, I'd say go ahead and take it, but he'll insist it's irreplaceable because it's one of a kind."

"I suppose that logic also prevents me from using a scanner?"

"I'm afraid so, but there's nothing in Baxter's rulebook to keep you from bringing a laptop or tablet in with you when you come back. You can type up your own copy and make changes as you go. Didn't you just say you'd have to do that in any case?"

The thought of that much keyboarding nearly made me change my mind about tackling the project. I repressed a sigh. With a copy, I could have scribbled on the pages to my heart's content, making corrections and marking places that needed more attention — work that could then be done by some other lucky volunteer. I might even have been able to rope someone else into doing all the typing.

"I suppose I can come back tomorrow —"

"We aren't open again until Tuesday afternoon."

I leveled my stern "teacher stare" at her. "You *do* know there's a deadline for this project, right? And that the historical society is the entity that's sponsoring the pageant?"

Shirley looked thoughtful. "Well, I'm here on Mondays. And the carpenters will be starting work that morning. I guess you could come in then, too."

I feigned enthusiasm. "Great. What time?"

"Eight o'clock too early?"

I was always up by that hour, although not necessarily in a fit state to interact with other people. I swallowed my automatic objection and agreed that eight would be fine.

It was going to be a long week, no matter how early in the day it started.

56

CHAPTER 5

I was waiting at the front door, laptop case in hand, ten minutes before the time Shirley had told me to meet her on Monday morning. The small parking lot at the back of the building was empty when I arrived, but not for long. Shirley showed up first, driving a zippy red sports car. It was joined almost immediately by Gilbert Baxter's dark blue sedan and Charlie Katz's white panel truck. All three drivers entered by a rear door. It took Shirley a couple of minutes to come and let me in, and when she did, the historical society's director was right behind her, looming in the vestibule and looking peevish.

"Who is this, Shirley? We're closed to the public today." He spoke with a slight lisp, as if he had recently acquired dentures and wasn't yet used to wearing them.

I stuck out my hand. "You must be Gilbert Baxter. I'm Mikki Lincoln, the person you and the board of directors recruited to whip the pageant script into shape."

"Oh, yes. The, er, celebration of our 225th."

I hid a smile. It appeared that I wasn't the only one who went out of my way to avoid saying "quasquibicentennial" out loud. For some of us, the syllables simply refuse to flow trippingly off the tongue.

"I don't know about this. With all the construction going on, it's not a good idea for anyone to be wandering around unsupervised."

"You could let me take the script home with me," I suggested.

He fussed with his goatee, alternately ruffling and smoothing it. "I don't see how that's possible. It would set a bad precedent."

It had been worth a shot.

In the exhibit area, Charlie had already started work. This seemed to involve a lot of banging and scraping, but I didn't think it likely the construction would interfere with my access to Archives.

"I don't know what you're worried about," Shirley said, echoing my thought. "Ms. Lincoln will be working upstairs, well out of Charlie's way."

Baxter frowned at her. His features

smoothed out only slightly when he turned to me. "I want it clearly understood that you aren't to wander into the work area."

"I wouldn't dream of it." I resisted an urge to salute.

Satisfied that I'd obey his orders, he turned his back on us, strode the few steps necessary to enter his office, and closed himself inside.

Shirley rewarded me with a conspiratorial grin. "He'll leave you alone now that he's asserted his authority, such as it is. In any case, he'll go out again in an hour or so. He never sticks around here very long at a time."

"Good." I was unimpressed by the director, and glad he wouldn't be hanging over my shoulder while I was trying to concentrate.

"You know how to find Archives." Shirley handed me a key. "In addition to the rules you already know about, food, drink, pens, and smoking are strictly forbidden."

"No problem."

Since it was only a little after eight in the morning, I'd recently consumed my usual breakfast of toast, coffee, and juice. I was good for two or three hours of typing before I'd need to take a break. With luck, I could transcribe a healthy chunk of the manuscript before I ran out of steam.

I set to work with a will, but my pace was abysmal. In order to copy the text, I had to read it. I suppose a professional typist can make a duplicate without giving any thought to the words on the page. Court stenographers seem to be able to record testimony without really hearing it. I'm not that focused.

Right off the bat I realized that the pageant had an enormous problem. Grace Yarrow, whoever she was, had chosen to use a voice-over. Her narrator literally told the audience what they were seeing.

Boring!

As I typed, I couldn't help but think how much more lively the scenes would be if the characters spoke for themselves. Unfortunately, that would mean doing a major overhaul of the script — a total rewrite. So far, I'd made only small, copy-editor-style corrections, but my resistance was weakening.

"Don't even *think* about taking on a job like that," I muttered to myself.

Did I want to write dialogue? No, I did not. But I knew in my heart that if this pageant was performed as written, no twenty-first-century audience would sit still for it. In today's world, like it or not, a successful production has to take into account the shorter attention span of people under the age of forty. In the parlance of the theater, this show was a turkey.

Perseverance is one of my few virtues. I soldiered on, and before long several other things began to bother me about Grace Yarrow's script. Ronnie had mentioned the political correctness issue. It didn't take me long to find the first instance of that problem.

Historically accurate speech is sure to offend some people, but it galls me to use anachronisms. If the speaker was a settler in the 1790s, he'd use the word *savage,* or maybe *redskin* or *red man.* Were either of those any less problematic? Was *Indian*? The English language is littered with linguistic traps, no matter how sensitive its speakers think they're being.

At least the legendary Tom Quick did not appear in the bicentennial pageant. He might have. He lived in this part of New York State at about the same time as the founding of Lenape Hollow. Who was Tom Quick? He was a pioneer who was notorious for his hatred of Indians. He went out of his way to hunt down and slaughter them, and the killing didn't end with his death. After he died, vengeful natives hacked

61

his body to pieces and distributed them among their villages to prove their great enemy was really dead. Unfortunately, since he had succumbed to smallpox, he ended up killing more Indians in death than he had in life.

I thought about that as I once again typed *Native Americans* instead of *savages.* I backspaced and changed the word to *Indians.* A few pages on, I stopped and used FIND AND REPLACE to substitute *indigenous peoples.* I stared at this word choice, still not satisfied.

Oh, the hell with it, I thought, and made a mental note to do more research on the issue. Beset by the sneaking suspicion that I would find lots of controversy and no definitive answer, I went back to copying the text word for word.

A little farther along, I stopped again, this time to wonder what Ms. Yarrow's qualifications had been as a historian. There was no author bio at the end of the manuscript. Neither had she included a bibliography of her sources.

Well, what did I expect? I felt my mouth twist into a wry smile. If the way I'd been selected was any indication, poor Grace Yarrow had probably been pressured into writing the pageant because no one else wanted the job. I envisioned her sitting at home with her typewriter — the one with the wonky key — banging away on deadline. Had she even had time to do research? Probably not.

I'm no expert, either, but we were required to take New York State history in seventh grade. Parts of what we were taught have stuck with me, and I have the added advantage of having heard, firsthand, my grandfather's stories about our family. I took a break from typing to flex my fingers and reread the part of the narration that was bothering me.

Josiah Baxter was one of the earliest settlers in Lenape Hollow and the following year he persuaded his father, Joshua Baxter, who was formerly from Scotland but for some time a resident of Connecticut, to move west. Joshua, his wife, and his sons Ephriam and Nathan, stopped first at Thunder Hill and then settled in Lenape Hollow. His son William joined them in 1796. Josiah's wife brought apple seeds with her, which she planted promiscuously among the logs.

No, I thought. *That's wrong. I'm certain of it.*

My grandfather had been proud of his ancestor, John Greenleigh. One day when I was ten or eleven, he showed me several passages in a very old book. The first had to do with the founding of Lenape Hollow. The second, in another section, related how John Greenleigh's cousins settled in nearby Falls-burgh.

I stood up, stretched, and scanned the shelves of the long, narrow room where I'd been working. It would have been useful to know the title of the book I was looking for. I could picture it in my mind, but "medium-sized with a black cover" wasn't much help. I wondered what had happened to the copy Grampa showed me. I couldn't remember seeing it among his effects. Had he borrowed it from the library or from a friend? After all this time, there was no one left in my family to ask.

Even though I'd only been working for a little over an hour, I decided this was as good a time as any to take a break. I opened the door to a screech that ranked somewhere between a cat being strangled and the scraping of fingernails on a blackboard. It took me a moment to recognize it as the sound of nails being pulled out of a thickness of wood.

So long as I was shut inside the archives

64

room with the noisy air conditioner turned on, the racket Charlie was making had been muffled. It grew louder with every step I took along the hallway. He was ripping down a section of wall. Puffs of plaster dust drifted up to meet me as I descended to the main floor of the building. It was a good thing someone had thought to cover the displays with drop cloths. They'd have been a bear to clean.

Skirting the construction area, I headed into the vestibule and poked my head into Shirley's office. "Got a minute?"

"Sure, but you'd better close the door behind you. It won't shut out the crashing and banging, but if we talk very loudly we might be able to carry on a conversation."

I wasn't so sure about that. It was a challenge just to hear myself think.

"I didn't realize sprucing up the place would involve quite so much tearing down."

She laughed. "Neither did the board of directors, but it turns out that there's considerable water damage in a couple of places. It warped the cheap paneling a previous board put up to cover walls that had seen better days. Charlie will have to install new Sheetrock before he can plaster and paint. But you didn't come down here to ask me about the renovations. What can I do for you?" She waved me into the visitor's chair in front of her desk.

"I'd like to consult a book. An old one. I haven't had any luck remembering the title but it contained short histories of each of the towns in Sullivan County and had lists of local businesses at the back." I smiled, remembering another tidbit. "My grandfather proudly pointed out his grandfather's entry — George Greenleigh, farmer, twenty-five acres."

"I expect that would be the *Gazetteer and Business Directory of Sullivan County, N.Y. for 1872–3,*" Shirley said. "Compiled and published by Hamilton Child and including excerpts from James B. Quinlan's *History of Sullivan County.*"

"That sounds about right." I was impressed by how quickly she'd identified it. "Do you have a copy?"

"We have three, which is the only reason I'm allowed to keep one in my office." She didn't come right out and say she thought the director's petty rules were stupid, but I had no difficulty reading between the lines.

Copy three of the *Gazetteer* was shelved on the bookcase behind her desk. Plucking it out of a pile of similar volumes, she handed it over with a flourish. At first I thought there had been some mistake because the book was bound in green and looked almost new, but when I opened it, I saw that the pages inside were spotted with age. That distinctive "old book" smell drifted up to me. Everything but the binding dated from the nineteenth century.

It took me only a few minutes to locate what I was looking for in the section on Fallsburgh's history. As I'd remembered, my ancestor's cousin settled there in 1789. His name was Thomas Grant. The following year his father, Joshua, "who was formerly from Scotland but for some time a resident of Connecticut," had also moved west. According to this account, written less than a hundred years afterward, Joshua, his wife, and their sons Joshua Jr., Ephriam, and Nathan, stopped first at Thunder Hill and then settled in Hasbrouck. Joshua's son William joined them there in 1796, having previously lived for a time with his brother Thomas in Fallsburgh. Although the given name of Joshua's wife was not recorded, a story about her was. She brought apple seeds with her to her new home and planted them "promiscuously among the logs."

"Bingo," I said aloud. "The woman who wrote the pageant for the bicentennial appropriated one section of her script from the history of another town."

Shirley frowned. "That's not good. It means we can't trust the accuracy of other details, either. What do you suggest we do?"

"It might be best if the board hired someone to write an entirely new script."

"Can't you — ?"

"I'm a freelance editor, not a writer. I'll be happy to make suggestions and proofread the final version, but I don't have time to do a complete rewrite." I lifted my hands in a "what can I say?" gesture. "The number of hours I can volunteer is limited. I'd like to help. I really would, but my first obligation has to be to my paying clients."

"There must be a way to work something out." Shirley toyed with a pencil, brow furrowed in thought.

I leaned forward, curious to hear what she would propose, but before she could make any suggestions there was a tremendous crash from the direction of the display area. Shirley and I sprang to our feet at the same time, but I was closer to the door. I reached the brass railing seconds later.

At first all I could see was a great cloud of dust. It had begun to settle by the time I reached the lower level with Shirley at my heels. By then I could make out two vaguely human shapes amid the rubble. One thrashed about. The other lay still, partially

68

covered by a large piece of wallboard.

Coughing and swearing, Charlie pushed aside Sheetrock, paneling, and what looked like broken bricks as he attempted to stand. Smaller chunks of building material fell from his clothing once he made it to his feet. Dust and cobwebs coated his face and hair.

Shirley was right beside me as I waded into the debris. Charlie didn't look too badly injured, but he was swaying in an alarming manner. It appeared that most of the wall he'd been working on had collapsed on top of him. The other figure still wasn't moving.

While Shirley caught hold of Charlie to keep him upright, I shoved aside more fallen building material in an effort to reach the second victim. It wasn't until I moved the wallboard out of the way that I got a good look at what lay beneath.

Shock held me motionless. I wanted to scream, but was unable to produce so much as a squeak. I wanted to believe I was hallucinating. I tried to convince myself that I'd fallen asleep in the archives and that this was all a dream. Any explanation was preferable to accepting the truth of what was right there in front of me.

As if from a distance, I heard Charlie's voice.

"Who's that? I was working alone. No one else is supposed to be down here." He took a step closer. "Oh, my God!"

Shirley came up beside us. For a moment longer, all the three of us could do was stare at the grisly sight before our eyes. Then Shirley cleared her throat.

"Huh," she said. "That's not something you see every day."

Her matter-of-fact words snapped me out of my trance. I backed away, slowly at first and then more rapidly. As I retreated, I stumbled over some of the rubble. If Charlie hadn't grabbed my arm, I'd have gone sprawling. He kept hold of me until he and I and Shirley were safely back up the stairs and heading into the vestibule. Only then did he release me, leaving behind a ghostly handprint that unnerved me nearly as much as what we'd just discovered.

Shirley headed straight into her office. "I'll call the cops."

That sounded like an excellent idea to me. I was more than willing to let the police take charge.

What I'd found under that wallboard was going to give me nightmares, and yet I couldn't stop myself from turning around and walking back to the brass railing. I braced my hands on the cool metal, dimly aware that it felt gritty beneath my palms. The scene below looked like something out of a disaster movie . . . right down to the human remains that had fallen out of the wall when it collapsed.

CHAPTER 6

It didn't take long for the police to arrive. The EMTs showed up a short time later and hustled Charlie off to the hospital. Even though he'd seemed fine at first, they thought there was a good chance he'd suffered a concussion.

"Better safe than sorry," Shirley said, and I had to agree.

Detective Hazlett, he of the six-foot frame, muscular build, and piercing dark brown eyes, ordered us to stay put in Shirley's office. "Someone will be in to talk to you shortly," he promised.

When he had shut us in and gone to take his first look at the body, I sank into Shirley's visitor's chair and closed my eyes. "This is not how I'd expected to spend my day."

"Curious," Shirley said.

I opened my eyes into the merest slits. She had circled her desk but was still on her feet. The faint clicking of her keyboard sounded extraordinarily loud now that Charlie was no longer breaking the sound barrier at the back of the building. Police personnel were on the premises, but whatever they were doing, they were being quiet about it. Taking photographs of the scene, I supposed, and waiting for a medical examiner to declare the victim dead. Since most of my knowledge of police procedure is gleaned from cop shows and mystery novels, I was only guessing.

"Huh," Shirley said as she used her mouse to scroll down a web page.

"What —" I had to stop and clear my throat. "What are you looking for?"

After a moment, she turned the monitor around so I could see the screen. The headline read 400-YEAR-OLD MUMMIFIED CAT FOUND IN WALLS OF COTTAGE. A photograph showed the owner holding up his grisly discovery.

"That's a cat?" True, it resembled one, eerily complete right down to its long thin tail. At the same time, there was something "off" about it, and I don't just mean the fact that it was dead.

Although she was clearly a cat lover herself, witness the photographs on her shelf, Shirley studied the creature with more detachment than I could manage. "I guess it's real, although it looks pretty big for a housecat. The article says that people used to wall up cats to ward off witches. Sort of a protection spell for the house." She read on. "Huh! According to the report, this wasn't the first time this mummy was found. The people who owned the cottage before the guy in the picture put it back inside the wall. He's planning to do the same thing." She cracked a small smile. "His wife isn't happy about the idea. For some reason she thinks living so close to feline remains will give her nightmares."

I shuddered. "That thing looks like it's made out of papier-mâché."

"Oh, it's a mummified cat, all right. If conditions are just right, the same thing can happen to any body that's been walled up for a while."

Can? Try *had*. What we'd just discovered had been dead for a very long time but it still retained its human form.

I rose and went to stand beside Shirley as she clicked back to the list of results in her search string. The next article she brought up bore the title SKELETON FOUND IN CHIMNEY 27 YEARS AFTER MAN DISAPPEARED. Heads close together, we skimmed the text. Police had used DNA to identify the victim. Although no one had any idea how he'd gotten into the chimney, there was apparently no suspicion of foul play.

"Hmm," Shirley said. "Strange." She had a speculative gleam in her eyes. "Did what we saw look like a skeleton to you?"

"I don't want to think about it."

As soon as the words were out of my mouth, my subconscious made a mockery of them. A screen shot of what I'd uncovered was as vivid in my mind as if it had been live and in color. Worse, the picture refused to be dislodged. Feeling a bit sick to my stomach, I shot Shirley a baleful glare. "Thank you so much for that indelible image."

She shrugged. "The cops are going to ask us what we observed. Besides, it's good therapy to talk about things that disturb you."

"Read that somewhere, did you?" Just at the moment, I resented both of the librarians in my life — Shirley for making me dwell on those human remains, and Darlene for getting me into this mess in the first place.

"I did," Shirley agreed, "and despite the fact that the last few minutes don't amount to much in the way of in-depth research,

75

I've reached a couple of conclusions. I want to know if your observations match mine. What did you see?"

"A dead body fell out of the wall."

I considered the image frozen in my mind's eye. That *thing* had once been a person. Although the ghoulish remains bore little resemblance to a living man or woman, I had glimpsed a skull. I'd also seen a hand and arm. The latter two body parts had not been skeletal. They'd had a leathery look . . . similar in appearance to the limbs of the mummified cat.

Bile rose in my throat. I forced it back and I took deep breaths. Shirley was right. What we'd seen had not been anything so simple as a skeleton. Bones would have scattered hither and yon when the wall came down. I frowned. Something had kept the body more or less in one piece. When I concentrated on the picture in my head, more details rose to the surface.

"It was wrapped in clear, heavy-duty plastic," I whispered.

"Plastic fastened with duct tape." Shirley's gaze sharpened as she met my eyes. "You're looking a bit peaked. I'll make coffee."

A few minutes later, I was back in the visitor's chair and holding a bright yellow ceramic mug in both hands. I'd hoped the warmth would chase away the coldness that had seeped into every muscle in my body. It didn't, but the infusion of caffeine seemed to stimulate my brain.

"We just found a murder victim," I said.

"Yes." Shirley drained her mug and refilled it.

I shook my head when she held up the pot. My nerves were jangled enough. I couldn't seem to control a twitch in my left foot. Truth be told, I felt shaky all over.

"There must have been an old chimney behind that wall," Shirley mused. "There were bricks in the debris."

"That makes sense. This building dates back to the time when people used fireplaces for heat."

"It was a solid wall by the time I started working here."

I grimaced and took another sip of my coffee. At some point before that, the victim had been stuffed up the chimney. Then the fireplace had been closed off and covered with wallboard. Mystery writers joke about coming up with "a great place to hide the body," but I wasn't finding anything amusing in this real-life situation.

"I've had my job here for nearly twenty-three years," Shirley said. "I moved to Lenape Hollow with my husband when he took a position teaching at the local community college." She reached behind the framed cat photos to bring out one of herself standing next to a tall, gray-haired, distinguished-looking gentleman in a lab coat. "Chemistry. Are you married?"

"I'm a widow."

Strangely, given the situation, I found myself telling her all about James, and from there I segued into the story of how I'd returned to my old hometown on a whim, and why I'd then been obliged to start a new career at the age of sixty-eight to pay for the repairs necessary to make my new/old home livable.

"More than you wanted to know, right?" What I'd intended as a self-deprecating laugh came out sounding hollow.

"Less. You haven't yet told me about your cat."

"How do you know I have one?"

She made a snorting noise, and I felt my cheeks warm. As usual, even though I'd put on clean clothes just before heading for the historical society, they'd magically acquired a full complement of cat hairs.

"She's a calico," I said.

We were exchanging cat stories to pass the time, and to take our minds off what was going on in the other room, when

Detective Hazlett finally returned. He brought renewed tension into Shirley's office with him.

"Ladies. Sorry to keep you waiting. I just have a few questions and then you can go."

If his deep, pleasant voice was geared to soothe the frazzled females, it fell short of its goal.

"Go?" Shirley stood, flattening her hands on the surface of her desk. There was a mulish expression on her face. "Go where? This building and its contents are my responsibility."

"I promise you that we'll lock up when we leave, but right now your building is my crime scene."

"How long before I can get back in? I have work to do." She didn't sound even remotely mollified by his assurances.

"We'll finish up here as quickly as possible, but the whole process will go much faster if you'll just sit back down and let me take your initial statement."

Shirley dropped into her chair and folded her arms across her thin chest. "Go ahead."

True to his word, the detective finished with us in a matter of minutes. Neither Shirley nor I knew anything about the remains — not how they'd come to be in the chimney or to whom they belonged.

79

That last point intrigued me. "Do *you* have any idea who the victim is?"

Detective Hazlett closed the small spiral-bound notebook in which he'd been recording our answers. "That will take some digging. That wall has been in place for decades."

"A quarter of a century by my reckoning," Shirley said. "The last time any work was done on that part of the building was twenty-five years ago, just before the bicentennial."

"Someone took sprucing up to a whole new level," I said, not quite under my breath.

Hazlett gestured for us to precede him into the vestibule. It was only when I saw Shirley gathering up her tote bag and a sweater that I remembered I'd left my laptop in Archives.

"I hate to trouble you, Detective, but I need to go back upstairs for my things." I sent him my sweetest little-old-lady smile. "If I can't retrieve my laptop until later in the week, I'll have a hard time getting any work done."

To my relief, he agreed to escort me to Archives. I have backups of all my files, but if he'd refused, I'd have had to borrow a computer, or use one of the ones available to patrons of the Lenape Hollow Memorial Library. Doable, but a royal pain.

Shirley slipped back into her office and returned with the third copy of the *Gazetteer and Business Directory of Sullivan County, N.Y.* "You may need this when you do the rewrite. You'd better take the pageant manuscript home with you too, since it's clear no one has any idea when we'll be allowed back inside the building." She thrust the book into my hands, winked to let me know that I'd heard her correctly, and left before I could thank her for bending the rules.

Detective Hazlett took my arm. "This way."

He sped up as he escorted me past the activity around the body and the fallen wall. He needn't have worried. I had no desire for another look.

While I packed up my laptop and the book and hesitated over taking the script, Hazlett strolled around the room, giving a cursory once-over to the cabinets and shelves. He was unaware of my quandary. If I took the binder with me, it might be viewed as my tacit agreement to do more than just edit the text. With less than two weeks until the start of rehearsals, rewriting the whole thing would be a daunting, time-consuming task, but what was the alternative? The pageant was scheduled to be a big part of the quasquibicentennial. Somebody had to do it.

"Ready to go?" Hazlett asked.

"I guess so." Resigned to my fate, I added the manuscript to my laptop case. Only after I'd done so did I notice the morose expression on his face. "You don't look all that anxious to get back downstairs yourself."

My observation prompted a rueful chuckle. "This is what you call a no-win situation, Ms. Lincoln. The public is going to want answers and I don't have any." He ran a hand through his short, thick, rust-colored hair, leaving a few stubbly bits standing on end. "After all this time, we may never be able to identify the remains, and if we don't, then figuring out who hid them behind that wall will be next to impossible."

CHAPTER 7

By the time I walked home, word that something extraordinary had happened at the historical society was already out. Tom O'Day was waiting for me on my front porch. Instead of letting myself into the house, I joined him in the little conversation area I'd created with wicker furniture. When the weather is fine, I sometimes work in this space, using the coffee table as a desk.

Wearily I sank down onto a soft seat cushion. "I was hoping to come home and collapse. It's been a wretched morning."

"So it's true then? You found a body?"

"Close enough. Human remains fell out of a wall when it collapsed."

He gave a snort of laughter before he realized I wasn't kidding. "Seriously?"

"I'm afraid so."

He removed his glasses and concentrated on cleaning them with a pristine white handkerchief he'd pulled out of the pocket

83

of his dress slacks. I assumed from his attire that he'd been at O'Day Antiques when he heard what happened. I wasn't certain why news of the discovery should have provoked a rush to question me. Then again, maybe he'd just come home for lunch. I'd lost track of the time, but the empty feeling in my stomach told me it was past noon.

"Will this affect the pageant?" Tom asked.

Suddenly his interest made sense. I'd forgotten that he was one of the village trustees. A little concern for my well-being might have been nice, but instead of *Sorry you had to endure such an ordeal,* he'd gone straight to what was *really* important to him.

"Honestly, Tom, I don't know what effect this will have in the long run, but I've brought the script home with me to work on." I smiled sweetly at him. "If you'd like to volunteer to give me a hand with it, I wouldn't say no."

He waved off my suggestion, literally holding both hands in front of him, palms out, and moving them side to side. "Sorry, Mikki. I would if I could, but between the shop, and my civic responsibilities, and keeping up with our two teenagers, I don't have time for anything else."

Ah, yes, I thought — *the old "my job is more important than yours" ploy.* Why did I

84

have the feeling that I was going to hear that "too busy" excuse from just about everyone I approached for help with the manuscript?

All at once I was too tired to care if the project succeeded or not. I leaned my head against the curved portion of the back of my chair and closed my eyes. They popped open again at the sound of Tom getting to his feet.

He's taller than I am even when we're both standing. Just then, he seemed to tower over me. He wasn't looming. I wouldn't have put up with that. But between his height and the breadth of his shoulders, the sight of him was rather daunting.

"The board of trustees needs to know if you're still willing to produce the pageant."

It took a moment for the question to register, but when it did, I sat bolt upright. "Whoa! Produce? Who said anything about producing? I agreed to edit a manuscript. Full stop."

"Which puts you in the best position to assist in casting, supervise the collection of props, and acquire costumes."

I felt my jaw sag in astonishment. "Are you out of your mind?"

When I shot to my feet, he backed up, inching closer to the porch steps, but he

85

was far from being in full retreat. "You're a very organized person. Exactly what we need to rein in expenses and handle the details the director won't have time for."

"The director will have to find himself another flunky. I have more than enough on my plate trying to doctor the script."

I closed my mouth with a snap, realizing that I'd just made a verbal commitment to go with the one implicit in bringing the binder home with me. It looked as if I was going to do that rewrite, after all. Irritated as much at myself as with Tom, and feeling more than a bit overwhelmed by the task ahead of me, I brushed rudely past my next-door neighbor and unlocked my front door. I had my hand on the knob, about to bolt inside, when I thought of something else that needed saying. I turned my head to glare at him over my shoulder. My tone of voice was decidedly frosty.

"If you expect this pageant to go from page to reality in under a month, then you'd better start recruiting more people to work on it. A whole lot of people. You can start by finding a good costume rental company."

Without giving him time to respond, I let myself in and closed the door firmly behind me. For good measure I locked it, knowing full well that the click of the dead bolt

86

would be audible on the other side. Then, before I could forget again and with only seconds to spare, I punched my code into the security system keypad to stop it from deciding I was an intruder.

"Way to get along with the neighbors, Mik," I muttered to myself as I listened to the thump of Tom's footfalls going down the porch steps.

The familiar feel of feline fur rubbing against my ankles had its usual soothing effect. Unfortunately, it didn't last. Once I'd reset the alarm system and abandoned my keys and laptop case on the hall table, Calpurnia did her best to trip me as I headed for the kitchen, winding herself between my ankles at every step.

I didn't want to think about the pageant until later. Much later. Lunch first. Then my own work. Then a long soak in a bathtub full of bubbles followed by a hot meal. Although I'm not much of a drinker, I considered adding something tall, cold, and alcoholic to my dinner plans.

This agenda went out the window the moment my landline rang and Ronnie North's name came up on the caller ID. I should have let the call go to my answering machine, but I picked up because I wanted to give her a piece of my mind. Since she was not only a member of the historical society's board of directors but also, like Tom, one of the board of trustees for Lenape Hollow, I had her pegged as the source of his misconception about my role in the pageant. I intended to make it crystal clear to her that I would *only* deal with the script, not any additional responsibilities involved in putting on a show.

She launched into a diatribe of her own before I could utter a single word. I held the receiver away from my ear, staring at it in disbelief. How had this morning's horrific discovery become *my* fault? I wasn't the one who'd put that body in the wall. I wasn't the one who found it, and I hadn't been involved in the decision to authorize repairs on the historical society's headquarters.

Having removed my right hearing aid — it squeals if I leave it in when I'm on the phone — I dropped it into a small bowl on the kitchen counter and struggled to comprehend what Ronnie was blathering about. Since her volume was set to screech, I could hear her perfectly well, but she wasn't making much sense.

A one-sided dialogue ensued. I didn't manage much more than the occasional *But, Ronnie* — or *Ronnie, you* —. Frustrated, I

88

was tempted to hang up on her, but since I felt certain she'd run out of steam eventually, I forced myself to wait until she wound down.

Big mistake! I'd underestimated my old nemesis. She concluded her rant by snapping out a command: "We've scheduled an emergency meeting of the board of directors for eight o'clock tonight at my house. Be there."

Then she hung up on me.

I cradled the receiver, shaking my head and envisioning a corporate boardroom with everyone except Ronnie seated around a long conference table. She floated above them, holding the strings attached to their arms.

Smiling at the image, I reached for my hearing aid. My expression turned into a puzzled frown when my fingers found only the smooth ceramic interior of the bowl. With a sense of resignation, I dropped my gaze to the floor, unsurprised to discover Calpurnia having a grand old time batting something small and oddly shaped across the kitchen floor.

At least she hadn't tried to eat it.

CHAPTER 8

Ann Ellerby, Ronnie's housekeeper, answered the door when I arrived at the mansion on Chestnut Drive for the board meeting. She isn't anyone's stereotype of the longtime faithful servant. Her uniform consists of jeans and a sweatshirt in winter and jeans and a tee in summer. The T-shirt she wore on this occasion was so faded that I couldn't make out the slogan written on the front. That was probably just as well.

"Ah, the sacrificial lamb," she said by way of greeting. Ann has always been something of a wiseacre.

"Thanks so much for that image. Where are we meeting?"

"They're in the formal dining room and everyone else is already here. I'll show you the way."

I appreciated the offer of a guide. Ronnie owns a good-sized house and I'd only visited it a couple of times before. I'd never been invited for a formal, sit-down meal.

I didn't pay much attention to the décor as we went, although it was probably well worth admiring. Ronnie has been married three times and each successive husband was wealthier than the last. She'd spared no expense when it came to decorating her house or, for that matter, her person. Although I think her attempts to disguise her age are misguided, I can't fault her taste in other areas.

Ann flung open an ornately carved wooden door to reveal a large, brightly lit room containing a mahogany dining table with seating for twelve. Eight of the chairs were occupied. A sideboard and a drinks cabinet completed the furnishings. Open French doors let the mild evening air drift inside and drew my eyes to the artfully landscaped garden beyond. Given the season, there was still plenty of sunlight left to admire the view.

"It's about time you got here," Ronnie said.

"Always the gracious hostess." I advanced into the room just as a clock elsewhere in the house started to strike the hour. "You said eight. It's eight."

I had a sneaking suspicion that she'd told everyone else to come at seven-thirty. A

91

quick glance at Darlene's face confirmed my theory. She hid a smile behind her hand.

I recognized only two of the others gathered in Ronnie's dining room, and one of them was not a member of the board. I sent Greg Onslow a curt nod of greeting. Despite the fact that he's only in his mid- to late-thirties, he has streaks of white in his hair. They may be natural, but it's just as likely that he had them added to give him gravitas. There are certainly other things about him that are phony, starting with his claim that he only wants what is best for Lenape Hollow. Making a profit for Mongaup Valley Ventures always comes first with Onslow. The perpetually cold, calculating look in his otherwise attractive green eyes is a dead giveaway.

Gilbert Baxter, the historical society's director, sat next to Onslow, looking much as he had earlier in the day. He hadn't been in the building when we made our grisly discovery, but I felt certain the police had contacted him shortly thereafter. Had he called this meeting, I wondered, or was it all Ronnie's idea?

With a preemptory gesture, she waved me into the vacant chair between Darlene and an attractive, dark-haired woman who was by far the youngest person in the room. She was also the rudest, ignoring everyone else while she texted. I caught a glimpse of the screen as I settled into my seat, enough to tell me that the message she was typing had nothing to do with the pageant or the historical society.

"This is Stacy Javits," Ronnie said, indicating the twenty-something beside me. "The town supervisor appointed her as town historian, which automatically makes her a member of our board." If Ronnie's pursed lips were anything to go by, she did not approve of the appointment.

Stacy spared me a nanosecond's worth of sideways glance. "Hey."

"Hey yourself."

"And I'm Sunny Feldman."

The woman sitting to Ronnie's right had a husky voice that would have been described as sexy in someone half her age. If Stacy was the youngest member of the board, Sunny was clearly the oldest. Since I could remember her as a mature adult when I was a child, that placed her somewhere upward of eighty. If memory served, I'd still been in grade school when her picture appeared in the local paper at the opening of a new building at Feldman's.

"Nice to meet you," I said.

Since she was seated, I couldn't tell how

tall she was. My best guess was short. She was plump, with a round, cherubic face, but the intensity in her dark brown eyes as she studied me dispelled any notion that she might fall into the sweet little old lady category. I could tell right away that an energetic individual with an intelligent, active mind lurked behind that fluffy façade.

"This is our mayor." Ronnie indicated the gentleman to her left. "Anthony Welby."

"Call me Tony." The mayor stood to reach across the table and shake my hand. "Call me Tony," he said a second time, as if I'd objected to the informality.

His grip was firm and he placed his free hand on top of mine as he grasped it. The contact was brief and practiced, lasting just long enough to assure that we had time to lock eyes. Coffee-colored and fringed with long lashes, his radiated sincerity. When my gaze dropped a bit lower to his wide smile, I found myself staring at four very large, very white front teeth. I couldn't help noticing that the one on the far left was slightly crooked.

The mayor certainly knew how to make an impression. Only when he was sure he had my full attention and had held it for the length of time necessary to fix his image in my mind, did he settle back into his chair.

"And this is Diego Goldberg," Ronnie said. "He'll be directing the pageant."

I couldn't help but blink at the unique combination of first and last names.

"Jewish father. Puerto Rican mother," Goldberg said with a rueful grimace. He appeared to be in his early thirties, with close-cropped black hair and dark brown eyes that were alight with interest. "It's the first thing everybody asks."

"Good to meet you," I responded, and meant it. His genial manner was an antidote for Ronnie's ill-disguised hostility. Besides, if not for the fact that he'd volunteered, the board would be trying to rope me into directing the pageant.

"I hear you taught language arts," Diego said.

"I did. Junior high. You?"

"Eleventh grade. I don't envy you having to deal with kids just hitting puberty. They're hard enough to handle at sixteen and seventeen."

"This is all very interesting, I'm sure," Ronnie interrupted, "but we're here to discuss the fate of our pageant, not compare lesson plans."

"I still think it was a mistake to schedule our celebration for mid-August," the mayor said. "A mistake. How can we hope to draw

95

people away from the casino *and* compete with Monticello's annual Bagel Festival?"

"Not to mention the festivities at Bethel Woods for the anniversary of Woodstock," Darlene said, sotto voce.

This remark led, inevitably, to a fast round of "where were you then?" among those old enough to have been at Woodstock. The now iconic music festival had not been held in the village of Woodstock. It had taken place just down the road from Lenape Hollow in the town of Bethel. Back in 1969, I'd already moved out of the area. I'd watched events unfold on the nightly news, along with the rest of the country, hardly able to believe that they were happening less than a dozen miles from the place where I'd grown up. Only much later did I learn that most of the locals hadn't been all that thrilled to have history made in their backyards. The music and the mud may have been memorable, but so was the massive cleanup.

"The quasquibicentennial is not in competition with any of those things." Ronnie sounded impatient, making me suspect they'd had this particular discussion many times before. "Our celebration will provide an alternative form of entertainment for people already in the area and draw in others."

The words *pipe dream* floated into my mind. I let them drift out again.

Mayor Welby's gaze swept around the table, pausing briefly on each person before he zeroed in on Gilbert Baxter. "Mr. Director, I'd like to make a motion." He stood. "I move that we abandon the pageant."

"Will someone second that?" Baxter asked.

If I'd been a member of the board, I'd have supported the mayor's proposal, but no one with a right to speak uttered so much as a peep, and it died without ever going to a vote. Eyebrows knit together in irritation, Welby resumed his seat.

Darlene cleared her throat. "Before we discuss this further, don't you think we should ask Mikki if she's willing to continue with the project?"

"She already agreed to take it on." Ronnie snapped out the words.

"I didn't exactly sign a contract," I reminded her, "and all you asked me to do was edit. Not rewrite. Not produce. Now, I'm not saying I won't help out where I can, but if the pageant is to be a success, other people need to pitch in."

"I'm already donating the venue," Onslow said.

"Yes, we all know how generous you are,"

Ronnie said. "Do you have staff you can loan us?"

Although she doesn't care much for me, she despises Greg Onslow. She'd seated him as far away from her own chair as was humanly possible.

"I'll ask for volunteers."

He didn't sound enthusiastic. Neither was I. I'd met a few of the employees of Mongaup Valley Ventures and had not been impressed.

"What is it you need help with, Mikki?" Tony Welby asked. "The writing? The casting? Where do you need help?"

"The casting is Diego's province," I said with a nod in his direction, "but I'm sure he'd be happy to have someone take on costuming, props, scenery, and lighting. I'm not certain what else is involved in an outdoor production."

"That pretty much covers it," Diego said. "As to the writing, I could definitely use some help with the script. Frankly, the pageant that was presented twenty-five years ago is not only boring, it's riddled with historical errors. It also runs way too long for a modern audience to tolerate."

"How long should it be?" Sunny asked.

"Sixty minutes or less," Ronnie proclaimed.

No one disagreed with her.

I didn't care for her authoritarian attitude, but that length seemed about right to me, too. I turned to Stacy. "You're the logical person to work with me on the rewrite."

A bemused look on her face, she glanced up from her nonstop texting. "Me? Naw. I don't know anything about stuff *that* old."

"You're the town historian. You must have some background in the field."

"Well, yeah, but my thesis was on the era of the big hotels. You know — from the 1920s through the 1960s, when people called this area the Borscht Belt and all the big names from vaudeville and Hollywood came here to party and perform."

"But you majored in history, right?" Surely she'd learned a little about life before the twentieth century.

"*Theater* history," she corrected me.

Rather than pound my head on the table, I forced a smile. "Then perhaps you can help Diego mount the production."

"Theater *history*. I'm not into acting or directing." Her eyes were once again fixed on the tiny screen and keyboard. Her thumbs flew, but I had a feeling that her brain was fast approaching a state of atrophy. Exasperation made me short with her.

"If you aren't interested in history, why

on earth did you take on the job of town historian?"

"Uncle Harold said it would look good on my résumé."

"Uncle Harold?"

"Local judge," Darlene supplied in a stage whisper.

I glanced around the table. "Helpful suggestions? Anyone?"

"I plan to use some of my students as actors," Diego said. "Summer jobs are hard to come by and a lot of them are at loose ends. Maybe one or two of them could help you with the script, too."

The idea didn't thrill me.

"What about music?" Onslow asked. "That might liven things up."

I seized the opportunity. "Thank you for volunteering. You're in charge of finding out what's available."

Before he could come up with an excuse to get out of the job, the mayor interrupted us. One eye on his watch, he stood. "I apologize for leaving in mid-discussion, but I have another meeting to go to. I do apologize."

Nine at night struck me as an odd time to conduct business. Eight o'clock had been pushing it.

"Any other ideas for help with the writing?" I asked when he'd gone.

"Shirley can pitch in," Baxter said. "As long as there are police in the building, she can't resume her normal duties anyway."

"*If* she's willing, I'd welcome her assistance. It's a pity she wasn't invited to this meeting, since she has a vested interest in the historical society. What about Grace Yarrow?"

"Who?" Darlene's blank look told me she didn't recognize the name.

"She's the woman who wrote the original pageant twenty-five years ago. Does anyone know where she is now?"

Ronnie gave a derisive snort. "I remember her. She was a twit, and unreliable, too."

"I think she got a job offer in New York City," Baxter said. "She had big dreams about becoming a successful playwright."

"So much for that idea." I took a deep breath. "All right, I have another suggestion to make. What if the revised pageant isn't *just* about the founding of Lenape Hollow? In the 1790s, people moved here, built homes, farmed, and raised families. All that's important, but it's not exactly edge-of-your-seat drama. What if, instead, the pageant showed Lenape Hollow's history throughout its entire two hundred and twenty-five years?"

Darlene perked up and a semblance of interest appeared on other faces. Greg Onslow went so far as to remark that the longer time span would make it easier to add music to the program.

"Maybe we can get the high school band to play," Diego suggested.

"Or that group that plays for dances at the Elks Club?" Sunny countered. I suspected she was being facetious, but maybe not.

"There are a couple of barbershop quartets in the area," Baxter mused. "Maybe one of them would be interested. It would all have to be on a volunteer basis, of course. Don't forget we have a very limited budget."

This was the first I'd heard of any budget at all, but I left contemplation of what that meant for another day.

"We can cover the 1790s and early 1800s fairly quickly." Especially since I'd leave out fictional conflicts with so-called savages and plagiarized stories about apple seeds. "No more than ten minutes. That's enough to show the original settlers choosing the location for their village."

"On Chestnut Mountain, where the pageant will actually be performed."

Onslow's smug tone annoyed me, but I had to give him points for authenticity.

"Many soldiers from Lenape Hollow fought in the Civil War," I continued. "That should be included. And, all along, there was a steady growth in population, with many of the newcomers in the late nineteenth and early twentieth century coming here from New York City."

"The air was healthier in the mountains," Darlene said. "This area drew patients suffering from tuberculosis."

Baxter grimaced. "Let's not emphasize *that* part of our history."

His attitude was right in keeping with the way local residents felt when the first sanitarium opened its doors. Plugging the healthful benefits of fresh air to attract tourists was one thing. Connecting those benefits to the fight against a deadly disease was quite another.

"What we should emphasize is the diversity of the people who settled here," I said. "Many of the new arrivals had distinctly different backgrounds from the founders, most of whom were descended from Dutch ancestors living in the Hudson River Valley or English settlers from various New England states."

"You need to include the founding of the Feldman," Sunny said.

Stacy put down her cell phone. "I know

all about that." She began to tell us, in detail, how small, family-run boarding-houses evolved into internationally known resort hotels. The withering look Sunny sent her way went right over her head.

"While all that's true," I said, interrupting Stacy in mid-sentence, "the Feldman isn't in Lenape Hollow. Feldman is a separate hamlet in the *town* of Lenape Hollow. I hate to split hairs, but this pageant is supposed to be about the history of the *village.*"

Stacy looked put out, but Sunny didn't take offense. Instead she pointed out that, in spite of the fact that her family's hotel was outside the village limits, it had exerted a tremendous influence on downtown businesses. I had to concede her point. During the heyday of the Feldman, the influx of seasonal employees and tourists caused our population to more than double every summer. As a kid, I hadn't been attuned to statistics, but I'd certainly noticed that a second movie theater opened every Memorial Day weekend and that there were a lot more people around. In the winter months, lines at the grocery store and post office were almost unheard of. In the summer, they were the norm.

By the time I went home that night, I was actually looking forward to working on the

104

pageant. Yes, I'd committed myself to a bigger job than I originally wanted to take on, but I'd also been assured of help with the project. Darlene and I, with Shirley as backup, would tackle the first half of the pageant. Sunny and Stacy would write the part about more recent events. I'd edit the whole. Onslow would recruit musical talent to augment various sections with appropriate tunes. Diego Goldberg, in addition to directing, would contrive to beg, borrow, or rent all the necessary costumes and props.

It wasn't until I was ready for bed that I remembered why an emergency meeting of the board had been held at Ronnie's house in the first place. I could be forgiven for the oversight. No one had so much as mentioned the reason the historical society's headquarters was currently swathed in yellow crime scene tape.

Once recalled, what had happened only that morning refused to leave my thoughts. Every time I closed my eyes, vivid images of plastic-wrapped bodies danced in my head.

CHAPTER 9

The next day was a busy one. After I completed my obligations to my paying clients, I worked on the script for the pageant. It wasn't all drudgery, and there were even bursts of inspiration, but I found myself wishing the board hadn't opted for an outdoor venue. It would have been nice to have a slideshow running in the background. Only excluding the earliest history of the village, there were plenty of photographs to show what things looked like in the good old days.

Darlene had volunteered to concentrate on the Civil War era. We planned to meet at her house at four to compare notes, but in the middle of the afternoon she called me on my cell phone to ask a favor.

"I've found an intriguing bit about recruitment," she said. "Would you mind stopping at the library on your way here to verify it?"

"Verify how?" I had my phone wedged

between shoulder and ear as I fumbled in the cabinet for a fresh can of cat food. From the look Calpurnia was giving me, she wasn't prepared to wait patiently for me to feed her. "You aren't starving," I mouthed at her.

My hearing aid chose that moment to squeal and momentarily cut out. It does that when I press it too hard against something solid.

"Sheesh, Mikki, Will you take that darned thing out?"

"I can only do three things at once!"

Prioritizing, I set the phone aside while I dished up an early supper for the cat. That done, I removed the offending hearing aid and carried it, my cell, and my third cup of coffee of the day to the dinette table. I took a long swallow before I resumed my interrupted conversation with Darlene.

"What is it I'm supposed to be looking for?"

"When I was head librarian, I oversaw a project to digitize all our local newspapers. They were already on microfilm, but the idea was to make everything available online. Unfortunately, it didn't quite work out that way. There was simply too much information and not enough staff or money to finish what we started. All I can call up from home on the year I want is the index on the library's web page. Here's the citation." She rattled off information in what sounded like an elaborate code.

"Hold on." I fished pen and paper out of a drawer and sat down again. I managed two swallows of coffee before asking her to repeat what she'd said.

"Just give that call number to the librarian and she'll show you how to find the right issue of the newspaper on microfilm. Scroll down looking for any article or advertisement related to joining the Union army. It shouldn't take you more than fifteen minutes."

"Uh-huh."

She was assuming I wouldn't go off on a tangent while I searched for the item she wanted. Whether I'm Googling online or thumbing through musty old volumes of history, it's all too easy for me to be drawn into following one thread after another. If I'm not strict with myself, I can end up losing hours at a time.

After promising Darlene I'd do my best, I hung up, fished an apple out of the refrigerator, and caught up on the news of the present day while I ate it. An editorial in the nearest thing we have to a local rag lambasted the police department for their failure to provide sufficient information about the remains found at the historical society.

I wasn't surprised Detective Hazlett didn't have details to share. If no one had reported a missing person at about the same time that wall went up, he didn't have much to go on. DNA from the corpse wouldn't help unless he had someone else's DNA to compare it to. Without a name, how could he hope to find a relative? The same caveat applied to dental records. The police needed a starting point before they could get anywhere, and they didn't appear to have one.

I frowned, considering the situation. I've read enough detective fiction to understand that even bare bones can provide some information. By now, the police knew whether the victim was male or female. I wondered why that nugget, at least, hadn't been given to the press.

Calpurnia butted her head against my leg, reminding me that I'd better get a move on. Self-employed people don't get to play whenever they want to. We don't even get to take weekends off. If I was to have any hope of accomplishing everything on my to-do list, I couldn't afford to waste any more time.

Working for myself, at least in my case, translates into "always working." There is an upside, of course. Although I can't always choose how many hours I work in a week, I do get to pick which ones. I could wait until after supper to finish the editing job I'd started that morning. Plus, if I wanted to, I could work on it in my nightgown, sitting up in bed.

At Lenape Hollow Memorial Library, a fairly new structure built right next door to my old elementary school on North Main Street, the head librarian who had replaced Darlene knew exactly what I was looking for. She set me up at a workstation in the basement and left me happily scrolling through a newspaper from the 1860s. It didn't me take long to find the issue in question. As Darlene had predicted, the confirmation she hoped for was right on the front page in the form of a recruitment notice.

I made a copy and then, since I still had more than an hour before I was due at Darlene's, I conducted a small search of my own. My grandfather once told me that his father enlisted to fight in the Civil War as soon as he was old enough, but that the war ended while he was still in boot camp. Personally, I was glad he never had to fight.

I might not exist if he'd gone to war. On the maternal side of my family, one of my great-grandmothers lost her first husband at the Battle of Fair Oaks. If not for that tragedy, she'd never have married my great-grandfather as her second husband. No second marriage. No me. Funny how things work out.

I was frustrated in my search for information about the boot camp Grampa had mentioned. I thought I remembered him saying it was in Bloomingburg, but nothing turned up for 1864 or 1865. Disappointed, I exited the newspaper files from the 1860s. I was about to head for Darlene's house when my gaze fell on the row of icons on the newspaper's index page. They were broken down by decade and covered not only the nineteenth century but also the twentieth.

It's valid research, I told myself as I clicked on the link for the 1990s. I might find it inspiring to read about the performance of the original pageant. To be perfectly honest, I was also curious to see if the newspaper had reported on the construction going on at the historical society just prior to the bicentennial.

This search yielded pay dirt almost at once. There was a nice article, complete

111

with a photo, announcing that Grace Yarrow, a local playwright, had agreed to provide the script for the pageant. Grace looked very young, although I couldn't make out much of her face. She'd turned away from the camera, as if reluctant to pose for the photographer. I read, not without envy, that she'd had almost a year to work on the project. I printed a copy of the piece and then scrolled through succeeding issues of the newspaper to see what else I could find.

The next item of interest was an advertisement announcing the upcoming bicentennial. It listed all the events, including the pageant. A glance at the date told me that the ad had been published a little more than a week before the big day. I started to scroll down to the next issue — the paper was biweekly back then — when a headline on page four caught my eye: HISTORICAL SOCIETY RENOVATIONS NEARLY COMPLETE.

Naturally, I stopped and read the article.

There had been a great deal more work done on the building than I'd realized. At that point, it had only been owned by the historical society for a couple of years and the organization had grandiose plans for the future. The board of directors envisioned permanent exhibits on the ground floor, which just happened to be the performance venue for the pageant, and climate-controlled archives at the top of the building. That didn't quite jibe with what Shirley had told me about cut-rate paneling, but then newspaper accounts aren't always accurate, especially if their source is trying to make himself, or his institution, sound good.

To start with, the board had concentrated on the basics. They'd hired a contractor, John Chen, to replace all the old windows with new, energy-efficient ones and blow insulation into the walls. Apparently, there was considerable controversy over the decision to close off and wall up an old fireplace. Fred Gorton, a local historical preservation diehard on the board of directors, thought it should be left as it was for its historical significance.

A photograph of the hearth showed some attractive tiles and an elaborate mantel with a mirror above it. To my untrained eye, there was nothing special about it. In fact, it looked vaguely familiar, which probably meant I'd seen other old fireplaces of a similar design. The name John Chen rang a bell, too. Chen and Sons was one of the contractors who'd given me a bid on repairs for my house. I was suddenly very glad I'd gone with another firm. Chen couldn't have been too bright if he'd walled up that opening without ever noticing there was a plastic-wrapped body stuck up the chimney.

CHAPTER 10

That evening, I was in my living room going over some notes I'd made — a change of location sometimes stimulates the brain cells — when an odd tapping noise caught my attention. Only Calpurnia's tail stuck out from behind a chair, but it swung back and forth in a way that indicated she was intensely interested in something. I abandoned my work and got up to investigate.

My first thought was that there was a mouse in the baseboard, even though I'd seen no sign of mouse droppings anywhere in the house. I have nothing against mice, but I'd just as soon not have them deposited on my bed while I'm asleep. That happened far too often when I lived out in the country, and with cats other than just Calpurnia. James and I always had at least one furry housemate.

I shoved the chair to one side and looked down. Calpurnia paid no attention to me, but now I could see that the sound I'd been hearing came from her sharp little claws striking wood.

"If you catch it, you eat it." I started to shove the chair back into place when a stray memory surfaced.

I turned back, frowning, to stare at the wall. Had it looked like that years ago? I seemed to remember an upright piano positioned in front of it when I was a teenager. My father, who played rather well, bought it in the belief that I must have inherited some of his musical talent. Wrong. I lasted through two years of lessons and one recital before we both threw in the towel.

What about before that? When I was very small, could there have been a fireplace? I closed my eyes, trying to call up elusive memories, and what popped into my mind was a Christmas card, one of the picture-postcard variety. The photograph was of me at age five or six, sitting on a stool in front of a hearth and holding a doll. A stocking with my name on it hung from the mantel, a mantel that had been painted white and which my mother used, at other times of the year, to display her collection of Hummels and other small knickknacks.

I concentrated harder and another detail

emerged from hiding. Behind this mini-me I saw that tiles decorated the fireplace. They were very like the ones in that newspaper photo taken at the historical society. No wonder they'd looked familiar!

My parents were not the ones who'd closed it in. They'd needed a place for the piano and hadn't been using the fireplace, but they'd simply placed the instrument on the hearth. It had been just the right size to hide everything behind it. Someone who'd owned this house in the years between then and now had been responsible. They'd hired someone to wall up the fireplace, just as the board of directors at the historical society had paid John Chen to conceal the one in their exhibit room.

Well, not *just* as they had.

Calpurnia continued to worry the baseboard.

"Please let it be a mouse," I whispered.

Hearing my own words, I shook myself. What were the odds that someone had gone around stuffing bodies up chimneys all over Lenape Hollow? I was letting my imagination run away with me.

Unfortunately, now that I'd recalled the existence of our old fireplace, I couldn't stop thinking about it. I went upstairs to my office and dug out the file folder in which

I'd put miscellaneous paperwork left behind by previous owners.

The last time I'd opened it, I'd been hunting for dates when the roof had been repaired. It had been obvious that it needed replacing, either that or use all the saucepans I owned, and then some, to catch the drips every time it rained. Once I'd found the receipt I was looking for, I hadn't bothered going through the rest of the documents.

This time around, I did a better job of evaluating the contents of the folder. I skimmed each page and did a little sorting while I was at it. At the very back, I found a bill for walling in a fireplace.

I was still staring at it when Calpurnia wandered in to see what I was doing. I scooped her up and cuddled her, feeling a sudden need for warm and fuzzy. I knew perfectly well I was reacting foolishly, but it creeped me out to discover that John Chen had been the contractor hired to cover up the hearth. Even more unnerving was the date. The work in my house had been done twenty-four years earlier, within a year of the similar job Chen did at the headquarters of the historical society.

"I am not going to tear that wall down to find out what's behind it," I said aloud.

Calpurnia nuzzled my hand.

"I am not going to start imagining things."

Unfortunately for my peace of mind, that ship had already sailed.

As I shoved papers back into the file, I continued to give myself a stern lecture. Chen and Sons had a reputation for good work and honest dealing. I'd hired a different contractor for the necessary upgrades and repairs on my house only because his estimate of the total cost had been lower.

If I'd had such a thing in the house, I might have made myself a soothing cup of herbal tea when I went back downstairs. The thought made me grimace. Bad enough to be a woman of a certain age who talked to her cat. I didn't need to make myself into any more of a stereotype. I pulled a Sam Adams out of the refrigerator instead. I'm not a big beer drinker, but I do like the occasional cold one, especially on a sultry summer night.

Bottle in hand, I returned to the living room and the notes I'd been working on before Calpurnia started scratching the baseboard. They concerned possible additions to the pageant. I'd made a chronological list of significant events. Darlene and I had already made decisions about most of them.

"Time frame," I muttered, and took another sip of the beer.

Of its own volition, my gaze returned to the wall.

"Time frame," I said again, but I was no longer thinking about plans for the village's 225th anniversary.

Twenty-five years ago, John Chen must have been rushing to complete the renovations at the historical society in time for the pageant to be performed there. Since it had been presented on schedule, he must have met his deadline. I winced at my poor choice of words before returning to my mental list-making.

The author had left town for bigger things.

I paused on that item, realizing that I didn't know exactly *when* she'd departed.

Ronnie had called her unreliable.

I thought about that while I finished my beer, a vague suspicion beginning to grow in my mind. Setting the empty bottle aside, I reached for the phone. It was late, but not that late, and I knew Ronnie was a night owl. She answered on the third ring.

"Why did you characterize Grace Yarrow as unreliable?" I asked without preamble.

"Hello to you, too. Do you know what time it is?"

"If you didn't want to take my call, you

didn't have to pick up." Ronnie checks the caller ID on her landline every time her phone rings, just as I always do. We have something else in common too — we habitually ignore calls from anyone we don't know or with whom we don't wish to speak.

"I barely remember the woman." She sounded peeved, but then she almost always does.

"You called her unreliable," I repeated. "You must have had a reason."

"Of course I did. She had no sense of responsibility. She took off for the bright lights of Broadway a few days before the pageant. It caused last-minute headaches for everyone involved."

Before the pageant? A hard knot settled in the pit of my stomach. That meant before the renovations at the historical society were complete and quite possibly before the fireplace was completely closed off.

"Ronnie, are you *sure* she went to the City?" In this part of the state, "the City" only and always refers to New York.

"Well, of course I am. She never stopped yammering about her big plans, her big break, her big future. Now if you don't mind, I have better things to do than answer foolish questions."

For Ronnie, "if you don't mind" is on a

par with the Southern "bless her heart." She punctuated the rebuke by slamming down the receiver.

I stroked Calpurnia, who had fallen asleep curled up beside me on the loveseat. Ronnie was probably right. I remembered now that Gilbert Baxter had said Grace left Lenape Hollow to pursue a career as a playwright. A writer could work anywhere, but it made sense that she'd want to hone her craft at the center of the theatrical world.

In the photo I'd seen in the newspaper story, Grace struck me as being very young. Everyone had big dreams at that age. More power to her if she'd gone off to pursue them.

If she had.

CHAPTER 11

First thing Wednesday morning, I paid a
visit to Detective Jonathan Hazlett at the
Lenape Hollow Police Station. I'd made a
point of learning a little about him after
meeting him the previous September. He's
in his mid-thirties and has been with our
local police department since about a week
after he earned his degree in criminal
justice. When it comes to investigating serious crimes committed within the village,
he's the one who takes charge of the case.

Although I had to look up the facts, I'd
seen with my own eyes that he had all the
physical and mental attributes one expects
to find in a good law enforcement officer.
He's in excellent shape, just over six feet
tall with thick rust-colored hair, dark brown
eyes that don't miss much, and a craggy,
sun-darkened face that features a beak of a
nose and — I kid you not — a cleft in the
chin. If he had to chase down one of the

bad guys, he'd have no difficulty overtaking him and slapping on the cuffs. He's equally skilled at gathering evidence and marshalling facts during an investigation and he excels at public relations. He has a deep voice and a calm demeanor. Victims of crimes find these qualities reassuring and they work equally well when he has to deal with the media.

That's not to say that Detective Hazlett can't be brusque, especially when he thinks someone is interfering in his investigation. I thought long and hard about whether or not it was a good idea to share my theory about the victim's identity. In the end, I decided I didn't have a choice. On the off chance that he hadn't already unearthed the same information I had, he needed to hear what I suspected about Grace Yarrow.

As it had been the last time I visited it, his office was almost painfully neat. I didn't find any record of military service in his background, but Hazlett is a spit-and-polish kind of guy.

As a detective, he didn't wear the usual police uniform, but he customarily dressed in clothing that varied little from day to day — wrinkle-free slacks, dress shirt, jacket, and tie. His only concession to the warm weather was to wear the tie loosely knotted.

On occasion, he removed the jacket, but since this was an unseasonably cool July morning, he had, as yet, done neither.

He did not seem surprised to see me and there was just a hint of sarcasm in his greeting. "Ms. Lincoln. To what do I owe the honor, and so bright and early, too?"

"I won't take up much of your time, but I came across something in researching the pageant that might be helpful to you."

He waved me into the chair in front of his desk and settled himself behind it, reaching for a notepad and a pen. "Go ahead."

"A young woman named Grace Yarrow wrote the script for the pageant that was performed twenty-five years ago. She left town shortly before it was performed . . . at about the same time workers were finishing up construction at the historical society."

"And you think?" Both his expression and his tone of voice were noncommittal.

I drew in a breath and then spoke in a rush. "I think she may be the person who was walled up in that chimney. I haven't been able to find any mention of her online."

"There could be a great many reasons for that," Hazlett said, but he wrote down Grace Yarrow's name.

"That's true, but from what I've been

told, she left here intending to make her name as a playwright. She was headed for Broadway. If she made even a small impression in her field, there should have been a reference to it somewhere. I tried every search string I could think of and nothing surfaced. I even went into an obituary archive to try to find out if she'd died. That was a dead end, too."

I winced at the inadvertent pun, but Hazlett didn't seem to notice. He scribbled a few more notes to himself and then tapped the end of the pen against the surface of the desk while he considered what I'd told him. The silence between us stretched unbearably. I had dozens of questions I wanted to ask, but I doubted he'd answer any of them.

Finally I cleared my throat and blurted, "Were there any clues to the victim's identity with the body?" My voice shook just a little.

"Ms. Lincoln, you know I can't talk to you about the case."

"Can't you at least tell me if the victim was a man or a woman?"

He chewed that over for a full minute before coming to the conclusion that I might be useful to him. "A woman. That's just about the only fact we *have* been able

126

to establish. How old was this Grace Yarrow?"

"Early twenties, I think." I rummaged in the tote bag I'd brought with me and came up with the copy I'd made of the article with her photo. "I found this in an old newspaper at the public library."

He studied it intently, brow furrowed. "Was she married?"

"Not that I know of."

"Ever have a child?"

I felt my eyes widen. "Can they tell that from an autopsy?"

Not surprisingly, Hazlett avoided giving a direct answer to my question. Instead, he said, "We may have to rely on DNA for identification of the remains."

And a child, I thought, would share part of his or her mother's DNA. I was a little fuzzy on the science, but I knew that much. Aloud, I said, "I don't know if she ever gave birth. No one has mentioned any children. My impression is that she was . . . unencumbered."

"Well, Grace Yarrow is certainly a possibility. I appreciate your bringing her name to my attention."

I couldn't keep the smile off my face. I was sorry for the circumstances, but pleased to think that I might have helped solve a

127

mystery.

"Don't get cocky," Hazlett warned. "I admit it's unusual these days for someone not to have an online presence, but just because you couldn't find her doesn't mean she never left Lenape Hollow. You said yourself that she was planning to go to the City. It's possible that, once there, she failed miserably as a playwright. Lots of hopefuls end up sinking into obscurity. For all we know, she gave up on her dream, got married, and moved to Idaho."

"Idaho? Why Idaho?"

"Why not Idaho? The point is, she could have gone anywhere. Or nowhere. Maybe she ended up addicted to drugs or alcohol and disappeared into Manhattan's homeless population. That said, I may be able to find out. I have resources you don't."

"I hope you *are* able to locate her. I'd much prefer that she be alive and well. But the more I think about it, the more certain I am that we already know where she is."

"You're taking this very personally."

"How can I not? I didn't get much more than a glimpse of the remains, but what I did see is indelibly printed on my mind. To be killed is bad enough, but to be treated in such a manner after death only magnifies the horror of the crime. Whether the victim was Grace Yarrow or some other unfortunate soul, I want her murderer caught and punished."

"Believe me, Ms. Lincoln," Hazlett said, "I share your desire for justice, but until we have a positive ID, there isn't much I can do about figuring out who killed her."

CHAPTER 12

As soon as I left the police station, I headed home. The arborist Dave Hernandez was coming at ten to start taking down trees in my backyard. I wasn't certain what to expect, either during the process or after he was done. Even though he'd assured me that the job wouldn't take long, I anticipated that the rest of my week would be disrupted.

The first hurdle was getting the equipment in. My lot has a narrow frontage. Paths on each side of the house are only wide enough to walk single file. Thank goodness I have a sympathetic neighbor on the side with no fence. Cindy agreed to let a couple of trucks come up her driveway and cut across her backyard to get into mine.

"Just keep clear and let us work," Dave advised while his crew was setting up a chipper and unloading what he informed me was a stump grinder.

I went up to the attic, taking Calpurnia with me.

The top floor of the house has changed a good deal since I was a child. I remembered open space with bare beams overhead and no insulation. Since I had no siblings, one side of the attic became my personal, private playroom. I kept all my dolls and toys there, along with the little rocking chair my mother had been given as a girl and the child-size wooden table and chairs made for me by a great-uncle who was a carpenter. I loved that space, especially on rainy days. I'd climb the narrow stairs and spend hours in splendid solitude. I never had any trouble amusing myself. All my dolls had extensive life stories, and just in case any of them had missed the details, I produced semi-regular issues of the *Doll Land Times,* a gossip-oriented newspaper that reported on their doings.

My parents used the other side of the attic for storage, and as an emergency guest room. Back in the day, there was an old-fashioned double bed there, one with an ornate headboard and footboard. I don't ever remember anyone sleeping in it, but I suppose my mother liked to be prepared.

At some point during the past fifty years, one of the house's owners had made significant changes. Instead of open space at the top of the stairs, there were now doors on either side. Each led into a room with low ceilings that slanted down into painted walls. There were proper light fixtures instead of the bare bulbs I remembered turning on and off by means of a sharp tug on a long string. The hardwood floors of my youth were covered with ugly wall-to-wall carpeting.

Water stains showed on the ceilings where the old roof had leaked. When I could find the time, I planned to repaint. I'd also rip out all that carpeting, but both of those jobs were near the bottom of my to-do list.

At present, these two rooms were empty of furniture. In one, I'd stacked a half dozen boxes I'd brought with me from Maine but hadn't yet unpacked. The window in that bedroom overlooked the backyard and the trees slated to be cut down. The tops of quite a few of them were at eye level.

Still carrying Calpurnia, I took up a post at that vantage point to watch the work begin. I admit to being nervous. If one of those trees crashed into the house on its way down, the damage would be extensive.

Calpurnia squirmed in my arms, but I kept hold of her until the sound of a chain-saw revving up sent her into panic mode.

The feel of claws slashing across my arms and her back legs thrusting forcefully into my abdomen convinced me to release her. She sent me a haughty look before stalking away, but she didn't go far. Since I ordinarily kept the door from the second-floor hallway closed, this was the first time she'd been in the attic. While I turned my attention back to the window, she set about exploring the rest of the room.

The men below looked like they knew what they were doing, and the equipment they'd brought in was certainly impressive. So was the noise level. I watched in fascination as Dave's crew started to take down the first tree. They dismantled it in chunks, using ropes to make sure the pieces landed where they wanted them to. In short order, they had the whole thing down to a stump. Although this particular tall pine had been growing quite close to the house, no part of it so much as brushed the siding.

I watched a while longer, but eventually grew bored. Considering the number of trees they were planning to remove, the same process would be repeated many times. Besides, I had work to do.

One advantage to wearing hearing aids is that I can take them out when I need quiet. Even though my office is at the back of the house and the chainsaws, chipper, and stump grinder were operating at full throttle just outside my window, all I heard was a steady hum and the occasional thump as something large and heavy hit the ground.

When I broke for a late lunch, I was amazed at the progress the arborist and his crew had made. Thanks to the stump grinder, each of the trees they'd removed had been taken down below ground level, after which the hole had been backfilled.

"All you'll need to do to reclaim your yard is plant grass seed," Dave said when I opened the back door to compliment him on his progress. He had to shout to be heard above the racket.

While he took a long swig of water to re-hydrate, I considered the nearest mound. I was struck by the fact that it looked like a little round grave.

"You okay?" Dave asked.

"Fine. I just . . . have you ever accidentally covered over something without realizing it?"

He reached beneath his hard hat to scratch his head. "Like what?"

"Oh, I don't know. A tool, maybe." *A small animal. A child. A body.*

He chuckled. "We keep pretty good track of our tools, and most of them are too big

134

to overlook."

I forced a smile and went back inside.

After I returned to my office, I tried to focus on the captions for Valentine Veilleux's coffee-table book, but my mind kept wandering. Just as an arborist had to pay attention to what he was doing, so did any craftsman. That brought my thoughts back to John Chen. How on earth could he have closed in a fireplace without noticing that there was a body in the chimney? Not to dwell on unpleasantness, but even if he hadn't seen it, surely he must have smelled something.

There was only one explanation I could think of for such an oversight — he knew the body was there and kept quiet about it. From that conclusion came another. He must have been the one who put it there.

"That's ridiculous," I said aloud.

Calpurnia looked up from where she'd been napping in a half-empty box of paper on the floor next to my desk. She studied me intently for a moment before closing her eyes and going back to sleep.

"Get a grip, Mikki," I muttered under my breath. "Even the cat thinks you're losing it."

Resolutely banishing further wild speculation, I went back to editing. After that was done, I turned my attention to the pageant script. I did not, or so I told myself, have time to play detective.

CHAPTER 13

Try as I might, I couldn't entirely dismiss my suspicions about John Chen. On Saturday, after all the trees were down, I gave up trying to talk myself out of satisfying my curiosity.

There hadn't yet been official confirmation of the victim's identity, but it seemed logical to me that the remains were those of Grace Yarrow. That given, I had to wonder what she'd done to tick someone off badly enough that he, or she, had been driven to murder.

It wasn't at all difficult for me to imagine a conflict between Grace Yarrow and John Chen. He'd been working in the space where her pageant was to be performed. The longer it took for him to finish his job, the less time she'd have had for rehearsals.

Ronnie's comments led me to believe that Grace continued to work on the pageant after her script was complete. Producer?

Director? Even if she'd just been hovering in the background to watch her brainchild brought to life, she'd have chafed at any delay.

Twenty-five years ago, John Chen's business had just been getting off the ground. Part of my work on the script had involved taking a look at the demographics of Lenape Hollow through the years. When the census was taken in 2000, not all that long after John Chen was walling up fireplaces, people of Asian descent made up less than 2 percent of the village's population. No matter how many generations Chen's family might have been in the US, he must have felt like an outsider in Lenape Hollow. Had he been treated like one? Perhaps by Grace Yarrow? Had they quarreled?

Rather than continue to speculate, the logical next step was for me to meet the contractor in person. I needed to put a face with the name and judge for myself what sort of man he was.

As I walked downtown, I was reminded of a recent piece on Lenape Hollow in the Middletown *Times Herald-Record,* the nearest thing we have to a local daily newspaper. "You can almost smell the diversity," the author of the article wrote. That was certainly true. Although a Thai restaurant had closed under less-than-savory circumstances, there are eateries offering Chinese, Indian, Mexican, and Italian food. I inhaled the distinctive aromas of each country's cuisine as I passed by.

That census from 2000 gave the village of Lenape Hollow a population of just under four thousand people. That number hadn't changed much by 2010, when those with Asian heritage were still under 2 percent of the population. The number of individuals who'd listed themselves as "Black or African American" had climbed to nearly 15 percent. Those who'd selected "Hispanic or Latino" origin had doubled in just ten years.

These statistics represented quite a change from fifty years ago. Back then, there had only been two or three black students in our entire school, and we'd had not a single Asian or Native American classmate. There might have been one or two kids with Hispanic-sounding surnames, but they hadn't stood out as a separate group.

What I remembered, but hadn't been able to verify, was a graduating class that was about 50 percent Jewish and maybe 30 percent Catholic. The rest of us were affiliated with various Protestant denominations. Why did I think that? Because school always closed for the Jewish holidays — half the class, we used to say, would have been absent anyway. I also had a vivid memory of big gray marks on every Catholic forehead on Ash Wednesday. Don't get me wrong. Religious differences weren't any big deal in my youth. They were just a fact of life in Sullivan County in the 1960s. Another was that faith was a bigger part of one's identity than race or ethnic origin.

My musings ceased when I reached the premises of Chen and Sons, located above a hardware store. Belatedly, I wondered if they were open on Saturday, but the door was unlocked and there were lights showing. I stepped into a tiny outer office crowded with file cabinets and storage units for house plans.

Two men stood beside a drafting table, deep in conversation over a set of blueprints. They looked up at the sound of the door opening. I had the distinct impression that they didn't get a lot of walk-in business. That made sense. When I'd contacted Chen and Sons the previous year, I'd done so by phone. I recognized the younger man as George Chen. He was the one who'd come to the house to give me an estimate.

"Hey, I remember you," he said. "Ms. Lincoln on Wedemeyer Terrace, right? We bid on a job to put on a new roof for you."

140

"You have a good memory." It didn't seem to bother him that Chen and Sons had not been awarded the contract. "Now I'm thinking of remodeling my attic."

That wasn't entirely a lie. I just didn't plan to hire anyone to help me redecorate those two big upstairs rooms.

I'd tentatively identified the other man even before he stepped forward to introduce himself as John Chen. I put his age at early sixties, but his hair was still as black as his son's and the bright-eyed, intelligent, friendly look in his dark eyes mirrored the younger man's expression. He was of medium height and stocky build and the big hand that shook mine was laced with scars. I imagine nicks and scrapes are an occupational hazard for anyone in the building trades.

"I'm Mikki Lincoln. Nice to meet you."

He released my hand and gestured toward the back of the room. "If you'll come with me, I'll check the schedule, but I expect someone will be available to take a look in the early part of next week."

I followed him into a closet-sized space containing more file cabinets, two chairs, and a desk where a computer monitor took up most of the available space. The faint aroma of lemon-scented furniture polish

141

hung in the air.

Still standing, Chen tapped a few keys and studied the screen. I sat down and cleared my throat.

"I believe you were the one who walled up the fireplace in my house."

"Wedemeyer Terrace?" He hesitated, then said, "That was a long time ago."

"Yes. It was well before I bought the house. But I remember that fireplace from when my parents owned the place. I was wondering — would it be possible to open it up again?"

Although I hadn't previously considered the possibility of a working fireplace, it wasn't a bad idea. We'd always had a wood stove for backup heating when I lived in Maine. It would be pleasant to sit before the hearth on cold winter days, and I've always loved the smell of burning applewood.

Again he paused before answering. "I'll have to look it up in my files. See how much we removed."

I expected him to riffle through a file cabinet or call up the information on his computer. Instead, he seated himself behind his desk and stared at me.

His scrutiny wasn't at all frightening, but it did unnerve me a little. It was as if he saw

142

right through my flimsy excuse for asking about fireplaces. Acute embarrassment had me focusing my gaze on my hands where they rested uneasily in my lap. Why on earth had I thought I could barge in here and discover something Detective Hazlett had not?

I felt my face warm to an uncomfortable degree and began to fidget. The silence between us stretched until I could no longer stop myself from blurting out a question.

"Have you been questioned about the fireplace you closed in at the historical society?"

"Talking to the police was unavoidable."

I risked a glance at his face, but his expression was closed and told me nothing.

"I realize you have no reason to extend the same courtesy to me, but I was there when the wall collapsed and shortly afterward I discovered that you were the one who walled up both that hearth and mine."

After another long pause, he responded in a strained voice. "I can assure you, Ms. Lincoln, that your wall is structurally sound. Similar jobs I undertook after the one at the historical society were properly done."

My head snapped up and I stared at him. "Are you telling me *that* wall wasn't sound?"

His grimace was answer enough.

"I think you'd better explain yourself, Mr. Chen."

He shrugged. "There isn't much to tell. The historical society job was the first time I ever closed in a fireplace. It was a rush job, too. I didn't know I was supposed to provide ventilation to the chimney space. As a result, moisture built up and caused damp areas, eventually affecting the entire wall." He cracked a wry, self-conscious smile. "To be honest, I'm surprised there wasn't a serious problem much sooner. You have no need to worry, though. By the time I did the work at your house, I was well aware that I needed to build in what's called an air brick. That's —"

"A serious problem?" I interrupted. "Like finding a body in the chimney?"

Intense emotion flashed in his eyes, but it was gone so quickly that I couldn't tell if it had been anger, frustration, or something else. The temperature in the office seemed to drop a good thirty degrees.

"I can assure you, Ms. Lincoln, that there is nothing similar hidden behind your wall, but if you want it taken down to make certain, Chen and Sons will be happy to oblige."

I stood, prepared to leave. "That won't be necessary." I'd insulted him, but as the say-

144

ing goes, in for a penny, in for a pound. "How could you have worked that close to a dead body and not notice the smell?"

He sighed deeply, his expression bleak. "Don't you think I've been wondering about that myself? The only answer I can come up with is that the poor soul must have been pushed well up into the chimney and secured there right before I bricked in the opening. I plastered over the face of the bricks, then put up Sheetrock. The final step was paneling and skirting board. The very next night they performed the bicentennial pageant in that room. No one noticed any foul odors then, either."

And afterward, I thought, there was probably a lengthy delay before they started to erect displays in that space, time enough for the stench to dissipate.

"I'm sorry to have troubled you," I said. "I hope that someday we will all know what really happened."

"On that we can agree." He rose to walk me out. On the threshold, he paused, a frown creasing his forehead. "You say you were there when that wall collapsed?"

"I was."

"May I impose upon you to tell me what you observed?"

"There was debris everywhere. Chunks of

wallboard. Sheetrock?"

He nodded.

"Some bricks. A lot of dust. I think the paneling may already have been removed. At first the remains looked like a person, as if someone had been knocked unconscious when the wall came down."

He looked puzzled. "Not bones?"

I shook my head. "No. Some parts were mummified. You see, the entire body was wrapped in heavy-duty plastic held together with duct tape."

He gave a bark of laughter, although there was no humor in it. "There's your answer, then. The plastic kept the smell from reaching me. No wonder I never knew the body was there."

CHAPTER 14

The building that housed Chen and Sons was only a block away from O'Day Antiques. Since I was so close, and since I'd been meaning to stop by ever since I realized Tom and Marie owned the place, I turned my steps in that direction. Besides, I wanted to know what they thought of my newly cleared backyard. The arborist had finished the job late the previous afternoon.

The front windows contained a display of dolls and teddy bears. Most of them looked very old indeed. Some were in excellent condition. Others appeared, for lack of a better description, to have been well loved by their previous owners.

Marie caught sight of me while I was still on the sidewalk and beckoned to me from the other side of the glass. "Tom," she called as soon as I set foot inside. "Mikki Lincoln is here."

"Be right out," came his booming voice

from somewhere in the back.

The shop was crowded with treasures and when I inhaled I caught a whiff of the distinctive smells I always associate with old wood, old cloth, and old books. I read somewhere, quite possibly in an online meme, that the aroma given off by old books — what most people identify as a combination of grass, vanilla, and almonds — is actually the smell of the chemicals released when paper, ink, and glue degrade. Of course, some old books just stink, especially if they're been exposed to dampness or once belonged to a heavy smoker.

A primitive painting of a girl with a cat caught my eye. How could it not? The cat was a calico. I stepped closer to examine it and beat a hasty retreat when I caught a glimpse of the price tag.

Tom appeared, beaming, behind the sales counter. "Good job on the trees," he said.

"Yes, it does look much better," Marie agreed.

I smiled back at them, but I was thinking that they'd better be pleased. Ever since I moved in next door to them, they'd been nagging me to do something about the virtual forest behind my house.

"I love the selection you have here," I said, offering a compliment in return.

"Feel free to browse," Marie said.

"Thanks. I'll just poke around a bit. I'm not really looking to buy anything today." *And,* I added silently, *I probably can't afford your prices.*

Despite my good intentions, I soon spotted something in a back corner of the shop that intrigued me. Suspecting what the large, plain case contained, I reached out and opened it. My guess was confirmed. Inside was an antique — I use the term lightly — typewriter.

"That's one serious machine," I murmured.

Tom laughed. "An Olympia. They don't make them like this anymore."

"On the other hand, back in the day, every office had dozens of them."

"And most of them went on the scrap heap when something better came along. I never learned to use one myself."

Of course not, I thought. Tom was considerably my junior, but I was willing to bet that the personal typing class when he was in high school had been almost exclusively a girls' club. It certainly had been in my day.

"I had an old Smith Corona portable that I took to college with me back in the 1960s," I said. "I earned extra money by

149

typing other people's papers."

"You must have been good at it."

I waggled one hand back and forth. "Not fast and not even terribly accurate, but I knew how to use correction fluid to fix my mistakes."

"I understand," Tom said, "that there are typing clubs in some of the bigger cities. Apparently, people who don't much care for computers go there to meet other like-minded souls."

"How interesting."

I was only being polite. I have many fond memories of life a half century ago, but composing on a typewriter is not one of them. I can't speak for anyone else, but I know my own writing has been greatly improved by technology. In the old days, if I realized there was a better way to express something I'd written on page one of a long document, I would resist changing it because, if I did, I'd have to retype the whole darned thing. These days it's much easier to add text and move things around, and it's blessedly simple to correct spelling and grammar mistakes. To be perfectly honest, if we were still using typewriters, I wouldn't be a freelance editor.

"We've had this item for a long time," Tom said. "If you're interested, I can give you a good price."

I started to decline the offer, but he was still talking.

"The only thing wrong with it is one key that strikes a little above the line." He indicated the *A*.

I stared at the machine. "Upper or lower case? Or both?"

"Upper."

Although I felt certain this had to be a coincidence, it did seem odd that Tom's typewriter had the same wonky key as the one on which Grace Yarrow had typed her manuscript. I was intrigued enough to ask where the machine had come from.

Tom hesitated.

"Don't worry," I said after an awkward moment. "I won't care if you tell me you got it at a yard sale for a pittance. I'm just curious."

"If I remember correctly, it came from an estate auction, although not everything in those sales always originates in the same place. It was quite a few years ago. I could look it up if it's important, but our records won't have much beyond the date of the transaction and how much we paid for it."

"So there's no way to trace its original owner?"

"Why would you want to?" He looked

151

genuinely puzzled. "It's critical to know the provenance of a Ming vase or a painting by one of the old masters, but this is just an old typewriter."

"A typewriter you're selling as an antique," I reminded him. I hadn't dared look at the price tag attached to the handle of the case.

"The word is *vintage,* and this isn't one of the cheap models everybody and his brother used to own. You can find those for twenty dollars or less, but this is a precision instrument."

"With a wonky key. Do you have a piece of paper?"

After a bit of hunting, he came up with a sheet of white, twenty-weight, all-purpose paper plucked out of the tray of the printer in his office. I rolled it into place and typed "The quick brown fox jumps over the lazy dog." That sentence supposedly uses all the letters of the alphabet — I've never actually checked to see if it does — and is universally used to test how well the keys on a typewriter work. I typed the words a second time with all caps. The effort reminded me, once again, of how much easier it is to work on a computer keyboard.

It also convinced me that this typewriter *was* the one Grace Yarrow used to write the script for the bicentennial pageant. Whether it had belonged to the historical society or to Grace herself, it suddenly seemed important to gain possession of it.

"How much?"

Tom took off his glasses and made a production out of cleaning them with a pristine white handkerchief while he considered how to answer me. He held the spectacles up to the light, frowned, breathed on the right lens, and swiped at it a second time with the cloth. Finally satisfied, he returned the spectacles to the bridge of his nose, looked down at me through them, and smiled.

"For you, a hundred and fifty dollars."

I couldn't hold back a grimace. "Too rich for my blood, but I'll go as high as seventy-five."

We settled on a hundred if he'd deliver it. No way could I carry something that heavy home with me. I'd collapse under the weight before I was halfway up the first hill.

The triumphant grin splitting my face when I walked out of the shop faded fast. What on earth had come over me? I needed an old manual typewriter like I needed a hole in the head. So what if it might have been used by Grace Yarrow? It wasn't as if the thing could talk.

By the time I reached home, I was overheated, out of breath, and out of patience with myself. I had accomplished exactly nothing and taken way too much time away from my work. If John Chen was a murderer, I'd eat my hat. And when the typewriter arrived, it was going straight into storage in the attic.

CHAPTER 15

"Do you mind carrying it upstairs for me?" I asked Tom when he and Marie brought the typewriter that evening.

"No problem." He hoisted it as if it weighed nothing at all.

I went up first, pausing in the upstairs hall when Marie, who'd been in the house when the previous owners lived in it, remarked on the changes I'd made. Tom, taking it for granted that I wanted the typewriter in my office, went ahead and deposited it on my desk while I was distracted. I didn't bother to correct him, in part because Marie had gone to look out the window, her body language all but shouting that there was something she didn't like about my backyard.

"The forest has been felled." If I sounded a trifle defensive, it was understandable. They were the ones who'd been after me for months to get rid of those trees.

"It *is* an improvement."

Hearing a *but* coming, I rushed into speech. "I asked the arborist to leave the big maple to provide a bit of shade late in the day."

My house faces east and I often work in my west-facing office in the afternoon. Keeping that tree meant there would be only a few times of year when I'd have to pull my shades against the glare.

Tom removed his glasses and went through his polishing routine while Marie continued to stare at the scene beyond my window. Clearly, something was bothering them, but I had no clue what it could be. I wished they'd just spit it out. I hate waiting for the other shoe to drop. I was barely able to stop myself from responding to Tom's delaying tactic with a visual display of my own, signaling "impatience" by crossing my arms, tapping one foot, and glaring at the two of them.

"We never realized before that the houses up there on the hill were so close to us." With a jerk of his head, he directed my attention to the far side of my property line.

What will eventually be green lawn is far from level. There's a flat area right outside my back door, but then the terrain rises steadily. A steep bit sweeps past the other tree I'd insisted upon saving, a tall spruce that might have been around when I was a child. Still climbing, but more gradually, my backyard stretches up to a sort of no-man's land where a thicket of saplings and under-brush marks the edge of my lot. Before the arborist did his bit, the houses on Champlain Street hadn't been visible and their view of my property and the O'Day lot had been blocked.

"It was open like this when I was a girl," I said with a reminiscent smile. "I don't remember climbing all the way to Champlain Street, but we definitely played hide-and-seek in that strip between the back-yards."

Unconcerned about bugs, snakes, or scratches, my friends and I had mounted expeditions that skirted Tom and Marie's land to sneak into the backyard of their neighbors on the far side, property that belonged to a standoffish couple who'd erected a high brick wall on three sides of their lot. The fourth side, at the back, had remained open, the only barrier to access a row of trees. Hidden there, we'd spied on them as they frolicked in their outdoor swimming pool. One time, when they were in Florida on vacation, we'd been bold enough to take a clandestine swim. Our

157

parents would have grounded us for a week if they'd ever found out.

Seeing my smile, Marie's scowl deepened. "This is no laughing matter, Mikki. When I was working in my garden yesterday afternoon, I had the distinct impression that someone was watching me. And I worry about our children. They shouldn't have to fear they're being observed every time they step outside."

Tom and Marie have two teenagers, although I rarely see either of them. During the school year, when they aren't working in the family business, they always seem to be busy with extracurricular activities. This summer, they both had jobs at a local hamburger joint.

"Why do you think our neighbors on Champlain Street are any more interested in us than we are in them?" I asked.

"Well, you hear stories, don't you? And those windows look like eyes."

Her gesture drew my gaze back to the houses on the ridge above us. She was right. The windows were a little creepy, but I still thought her concerns were groundless. The people on the hill would have to use binoculars in order to invade our privacy.

"If you want something to worry about," I said, "consider this. I can see right into your house from my windows, just as you can look back into mine."

"I would never —"

"Marie, you can't help it. Our houses are too close together. If your kids yell at each other, I can hear them. If you don't close the curtains in your bedroom . . ." I let the implication sink in.

"See, Marie," Tom said, conveniently forgetting that he'd been in agreement with her only moments earlier. "I told you you were fussing over nothing. We'll see ourselves out," he added. Taking his wife's arm, he led her away, still sputtering in indignation.

I stayed where I was, my eyes glued to the scene beyond the window. I hoped I hadn't just permanently wrecked my relationship with my neighbors, but facts were facts. For myself, I was tremendously pleased with the new look of my backyard. This was much closer to what it had been when I was growing up.

One of my earliest memories of my father was when he dismantled the old barn that used to stand just short of our back property line. He used the boards to build the garage. That wasn't the only building on the property back then. The previous owners had kept chickens. So did we, for a little while.

Then Daddy converted the chicken coop into a perfect little playhouse for me and furnished it, during the summer months, with the child-size table and chairs that lived in my attic playroom the rest of the year.

Facing the entrance to the playhouse there had been a swing set with two swings and a slide. Had I also had a sandbox? I rather thought I had. My memory placed it just beyond the swings.

"Enough with the nostalgia," I murmured, and turned away from the window. It was the present day that demanded my attention. In the course of the next week, I would have to find time to plant grass seed in all those brown patches where trees had once stood. My backyard wouldn't look like much this year, but by next summer it would be lovely and green . . . and I'd have three times more lawn to mow than I did now.

There's always a downside.

The typewriter Tom had delivered looked incongruous in the midst of all my modern technology. It was significantly bigger than my laptop. Heck, it was bigger than the average personal computer and a lot more unwieldy. Before I could properly examine my impulsive purchase, I had to move the laptop, a set of speakers, and the larger keyboard I sometimes use when I work in my office.

I was still uncertain why I'd paid good money for this behemoth. I certainly wasn't going to type on it, and it was way too big to display as a knickknack. Eventually, I'd lug it up to the attic, but in the meantime I felt free to indulge my curiosity. I opened the case.

Metal catches held the typewriter in place. When I peeked beneath it to see how to open them, I spotted a scrap of paper. It was torn and yellowed and felt brittle when I extracted it. On it were typed the words *meet, usual,* and *bring,* and a time, *9:30.*

I was instantly intrigued. If I was right about the wonky *A,* this machine had once been used by Grace Yarrow. Had she typed this note to arrange a meeting? Or had someone sent the message to her? Had it, perhaps, lured her to her death?

None of the words contained a capital *A* to prove they had been typed on this typewriter, but I couldn't think of any other reason for the torn-off bit of paper to have ended up caught in the case.

I slid a fresh sheet of printer paper into the carriage and typed a test line. Then I took the original pageant script out of my desk drawer and compared them. I may not be qualified to testify on the matter in a court of law, but I was more convinced than ever that this was the same machine Grace had used twenty-five years ago.

And what if she had? Did that mean anything? The typewriter had probably belonged to the historical society, and they'd undoubtedly sold it when they up-graded to something more modern.

I wondered, suddenly, if Tom had been a member twenty-five years ago. If so, he'd have known where the machine came from. Surely he'd have said . . . unless he didn't want me to know. He'd implied that trying to trace its provenance would be futile.

Was I really considering the possibility that Tom O'Day was a murderer?

I looked again at the scrap of paper, try-ing to apply common sense. The odds that it had anything to do with Grace Yarrow had to be a hundred to one against. I was wasting my time theorizing this way.

Closing the typewriter case, I heaved it off my desk and set it on the floor to be dealt with later. I balanced the script atop the pile of papers stacked on a nearby bookshelf while I restored my desk to order, all the while thinking that I'd have to return the binder to Archives soon. In the meantime, I should probably continue to take good care of it.

I opened the drawer where I'd been keeping it, swiveled my chair to pluck it off the shelf, and swung around again just in time to see Calpurnia squeeze herself inside the drawer. There was just room enough for her to turn around and settle in. She looked up at me with big, bright eyes, as if wondering what my problem was.

"Do you mind?"

She is also prone to appropriating empty cartons and shopping bags. She once tried to stuff herself into an empty tissue box I'd set aside to recycle. Since my desk drawer was the spot she'd apparently chosen for today's nap, she *did* mind. Ignoring me, she closed her eyes.

"Fine. Stay there."

I considered the binder in my hand. It would be perfectly safe on the shelf, and I needed to focus on more important things, like checking my email and working on client manuscripts until it was time for supper.

Instead, I opened the script. I told myself it wouldn't hurt to do one last quick read-through. I'd skim the highlights, just in case there was something else in the original version that deserved to be incorporated into the new pageant.

When I got to the apple seed story, I read with a heightened awareness. The first time through, I'd been fixated on trying to remember where I'd heard the details before. I hadn't paid proper attention to the surname Grace substituted for the real one.

It was Baxter, as in Gilbert Baxter, current director of the historical society. Coincidence? I doubted it. Baxter might not have been director twenty-five years ago, but he had been involved with the historical society and with the pageant. He'd known Grace well enough to suggest that she'd gone to the City to pursue a career as a playwright.

She couldn't have chosen the name Baxter by accident.

I thought again of the words on the scrap of paper. *Had* the typist been setting up an assignation? Could it have been between Grace and Gilbert Baxter?

"But which one of them wrote it?" I asked aloud.

Calpurnia opened one eye.

Was Baxter in a position to coerce Grace into using his family name? She certainly gave his ancestor a more prominent role in the pageant than he deserved. Maybe she balked at the last minute and was going to remove the plagiarized scene.

Calpurnia climbed out of the drawer and nudged my elbow.

"You're right. I'm letting my imagination run away with me. Again. That would be a pretty stupid reason to kill somebody."

I placed the manuscript in the drawer and shoved it closed, but I didn't find it quite as easy to put away my suspicions.

CHAPTER 16

Monday dawned bright and sunny with a warm breeze. For variety, I was working on my front porch when a car pulled into my driveway. I recognized it as Detective Hazlett's unmarked vehicle even before he got out. I winced when I heard the alarming thumps the engine gave as it cooled.

"You ought to get that fixed," I said when he'd taken a seat in one of my cushioned wicker chairs. "Your car has a worse cough than mine does."

One corner of his mouth quirked up in a rueful smile. "You should have heard it *before* it was in the shop."

"That can't be good when you're trying to sneak up on the bad guys."

"I'm not usually called upon to do a lot of sneaking."

I closed my laptop and gave him my full attention. This was the friendliest and most relaxed I'd ever seen him . . . and I was instantly wary. "To what do I owe the honor of your company?" I asked, echoing his question to me when I'd last visited his office. "And would you like a cup of coffee?"

"I'm good, thanks. I'm here to thank you for your help."

"That's a switch."

His dark brown eyes never revealed much, and he'd mastered the art of keeping his craggy, suntanned face impassive, but there was a hint of a smile playing around his lips. "Your tip was right on the money. The victim has been positively identified as Grace Yarrow. The press release will go out this afternoon."

Is it inappropriate that I did a little happy dance inside my head? Let's face it. It's gratifying to be proven correct.

"Thank you for the heads-up," I said. "She did seem to be a likely candidate."

He started to rise.

"Wait a minute! You must know a little bit more than that. Do you have any suspects?"

"Just about *everyone* is a suspect at this point, Ms. Lincoln. The only reason you aren't on the list yourself is that you weren't living in Lenape Hollow back then." He resumed his seat, his steady gaze fixed on my face. "Do *you* have someone in mind?"

"Well, I *did* wonder about a couple of

people. The murderer had to have had access to the historical society building." I gave a short, self-deprecating laugh. "And I had a bad moment when Calpurnia heard a mouse in the wall." She'd presented it to me a few days afterward, well chewed and quite dead.

"What wall?" I could hear the bafflement in his voice, and it wasn't over Calpurnia's identity. He'd met my cat.

"The one, as it turns out, that John Chen put up over my living room fireplace less than a year after he did the same job for the historical society. When I realized that, I had a few qualms about what might be hidden in my chimney, especially when Calpurnia started showing such an interest in the baseboard."

"You don't need to worry on that account. Chen was one of the first people we talked to, even before we got an ID on the victim. He's in the clear."

I waited for him to tell me why the contractor had been ruled out, but whatever alibi Chen had provided, Hazlett wasn't inclined to share it. I decided to take the detective's word for it. After talking to John Chen myself, that wasn't hard to do. I'd already written him off as a suspect and moved on to other, more likely candidates.

Even if Hazlett wouldn't share their names with me, I felt certain he had the same individuals on his list of suspects. How could he not, now that the victim's identity had been established?

I shifted in my chair. "What I don't understand is the total lack of concern about Grace Yarrow when she supposedly left town. Didn't anyone find her abrupt disappearance suspicious?"

"Apparently not. None of her acquaintances reported her missing and she was estranged from her family. No one was concerned when they didn't hear from her."

"But what about her belongings? She must have had an apartment or a house in the village and —"

Hazlett held up one hand, palm out, to stop my questions. "You know I can't give you details of an ongoing police investigation, even if the crime did take place a long time ago. I've only told you as much as I have out of courtesy. Without your hunch, we'd likely still be dealing with a Jane Doe."

"So the murderer not only hid Grace's body," I mused aloud, "but also disposed of all of her worldly goods."

Hazlett stood, neither confirming nor denying my supposition.

I came to my feet as well. "I have something to show you. It's the typewriter Grace Yarrow used to write the pageant script."

"How the devil — ?"

"Chance. A fluke. Dumb luck." I led him inside, up the stairs, and into my office, and pointed to the heavy carrying case sitting on the floor next to my desk. "I bought it at O'Day Antiques. Tom O'Day says it came from an estate sale, but at some point it was in Grace Yarrow's possession because she typed the script for the bicentennial pageant on it." I explained about the wonky, uppercase *A*.

"Okay. I admit it's a curious coincidence that you ended up with a typewriter that may have belonged to her, but I don't see —"

"There was a scrap of paper in the case, caught beneath the machine." I produced it. "I can't swear it's been there for twenty-five years, but it might have been, and it could be a clue, especially if the entire message was intended to set up a meeting between Grace and someone else, maybe the same someone who killed her."

I didn't name any names. I didn't think I needed to. Along with everyone else who'd worked with Grace a quarter of a century ago, Gilbert Baxter must already be near the top of Hazlett's list of suspects, and if

170

Tom O'Day had any connection to the bicentennial, he'd be there, too.

The detective continued to look skeptical and refused to speculate further about the typewriter's provenance, but with clues scarce to the ground, he wasn't about to risk losing one. After scolding me for my careless handling of the scrap of paper, which had undoubtedly smudged any older fingerprints, he put it in an evidence envelope. Then he gave me a receipt for it, and for the typewriter, and took both away with him.

CHAPTER 17

Patience is not one of my virtues. I know full well that crimes aren't solved overnight, but two days after that conversation with Detective Hazlett, I was still thinking about Grace Yarrow's murder and wondering if there wasn't more I could do to help bring her killer to justice. Since I'd taken over her old job, so to speak, I knew all the major players. I might even have met the person who murdered her.

I decided to start by talking to Darlene, the only long-time historical society member I was certain was innocent of any crime. I found her in her side yard, relaxing in a lawn chair with a book. Her walker sat to one side. Simon, his collar attached to a long line that ended at a divot, sat on the other, close enough that Darlene could reach out and pet him but far enough away from her chair that he couldn't knock her ass over teakettle if he got too rambunctious.

He started to bark the moment he spotted me. His tail wagged furiously as I walked toward them across a carpet of green, inhaling that wonderful new-mown-grass smell and the fainter scent drifting toward me from the rosebushes on either side of Darlene's kitchen door. A low-voiced command from Darlene held the puppy in place. I was impressed.

"Did you hear the news about Grace Yarrow?" I asked.

"Who hasn't? Since there haven't been any hurricanes, earthquakes, or other natural disasters this week, it was the lead story on last night's local news." Darlene inserted a bookmark in the paperback mystery she'd been reading and placed it carefully on the table beside her, giving me her full attention. "What do you know that I don't?"

I stopped to stroke Simon's silky fur and tell him what a good dog he was. Then I pulled over a second lawn chair and plunked myself down facing my friend. I hadn't shared my theory about the identity of the body with anyone except Detective Hazlett, and Darlene didn't know about my visit to him, or the one to John Chen, or about my acquisition of the typewriter, either. I filled

173

her in on everything I'd been up to and on my suspicions, too. By the time I finished relating my most recent conversation with Hazlett, she was shaking her head.

"I *knew* you had something on your mind."

"I've been trying to put it *out* of my mind. I have enough on my plate as it is."

"But?"

"But maybe there's more I can do to help the police. I know they have all kinds of resources to investigate crimes, even crimes that took place a long time ago, but there could be some things they don't spot because they don't have an insider's perspective."

"And you do?"

"I know most of the people involved, then and now, and you know even more of them."

"Mikki, I'm not sure —"

"Don't you want Grace Yarrow's killer to be caught and punished?"

"Of course I do, but I just don't see how —"

"I'm not going to do anything outrageous, but I thought I'd compile a list of everyone who was active in the historical society twenty-five years ago. I already have the darkest suspicions about Gilbert Baxter, but I'm certain there are other possibilities."

174

"Why Baxter? No. Never mind. I don't want to know."

"Yes, you do."

She looked away, then back. "Okay. Yes, I do."

I reminded her of the apple seed story. "What if Grace chose the name Baxter for a reason? Either Gilbert Baxter pressured her into showcasing his ancestor, or she was trying to win points with him by inventing a phony history for his family."

"That would hardly give him a motive to kill her."

"People kill for all kinds of stupid reasons."

"Sure. In fiction." Darlene gestured toward her discarded paperback.

I couldn't make out the title or author from where I sat, but I knew her preference was for cozy mysteries where humor and the character arc of the amateur detective were often more important than giving the villain a sensible motive.

"Real life can be just as random as the plot of one of your novels," I insisted. "Besides, what harm can it do to consider the possibilities?"

She reached out with one hand to ruffle the fur on Simon's head. As if the contact comforted her, she left it there. "Fine. I

175

wasn't active in the historical society back then, but I think I remember who was on the board at the time of the pageant. You should get Shirley to look it up for you, in case I miss someone."

"Great. So — Baxter?"

"He wasn't on the board, but he was a member, and he was *in* the pageant. Didn't you notice his name in the program? He played his own ancestor."

"Either I didn't notice or I'd forgotten." At the time, I hadn't been suspicious of him. I hoped I didn't wind up having to have to track down all the actors, but for now I'd concentrate on the folks who'd worked most closely with Grace. "Who *was* on the board of directors?"

Darlene shifted uncomfortably in her chair and used her free hand to rub her ankle, one of the many joints afflicted with arthritis. "Ronnie."

"No surprise there."

"Bud Graham. I think he lives in Florida now."

"That name doesn't ring a bell. Can you think of any personal connection he might have had with Grace Yarrow?"

"I don't remember anything, but it *was* a quarter of a century ago. I doubt I'd be able to recall any names at all if we hadn't just been working on the new pageant."

I fished a pen and a small notebook out of my bag and wrote down the two names. "Who else? Was Sunny on the board back then?"

"I'm not sure. Maybe." She grinned. "Stacy certainly wasn't. Or Diego. They'd still have been in school."

"The mayor?"

She frowned, trying to remember. "Tony Welby wasn't on the board but he could have been a member of the historical society. He used to be a teacher before he went into politics, and I'm pretty sure he's always had an interest in the past."

"Who else?" Her grimace gave me a clue. "Your sister?"

Darlene nodded. She and Judy might be on the outs, but she didn't like having to include her only sibling on my list of suspects.

"Don't you think the police have already questioned everyone who was around back then? That would have been a logical step when they were still trying to figure out who the victim was."

"Probably," I agreed, "and they'll definitely have to question them again, now that they know it was Grace who was killed."

"So you'll just be duplicating their efforts

if you contact these folks."

"Maybe, but I still think I might notice something the detectives don't. Besides, no one questioned you, did they?"

She had to cede my point, but that concession just put more worry lines in her brow. "You could get yourself in trouble."

"With the police?"

"With the killer. If you start snooping around, you're going to tick people off, and if one of them *is* guilty, making him or her nervous about how much you know isn't exactly a smart move."

"I've thought about that, but the risk is minimal. No one's going to take me all that seriously. They'll chalk up my nosy questions to curiosity and write me off as a harmless old lady."

"Hah!"

"Think of it this way. If I learn everything I can about the situation back then, I should be able to rule out a lot of people as suspects, starting with your sister."

"Or not."

"You don't seriously think — ?"

"What I think is that you should leave this whole thing alone." Under her floppy sun-hat, Darlene's face was grim. Her hand clenched in Simon's fur, making the puppy yelp in protest.

In for a penny, I thought, and went for the pound.

"I might drive over to Monticello to pay Judy a visit. Since she was on the board back then, she must have memories of the bicentennial. If I tell her we're still working on the new script, I can ask her if she has suggestions for making it better and lead into my other questions that way."

"You don't need to go pestering Judy. I can tell you what you need to know to exonerate her."

Pen poised, I waited.

Darlene sighed. "Twenty-five years ago, when she was on the board of directors, she was married to her first husband. Max Kenner was a first-class louse if there ever was one. It was a rough time for her. She was too busy trying to straighten out her personal life to have much to do with the bicentennial."

"I'm sorry to hear that. So, were you and she close back then?"

Darlene avoided meeting my eyes. "Not especially, but I knew what was going on."

I reached out and placed one hand on her forearm. "What aren't you telling me? What happened between you two?"

She gave a short, humorless laugh. "A lot of things, none of which are relevant to what

179

you're looking into. Judy and Max divorced a couple of years later."

"And?"

"Fine! There is more. About twelve years ago, she met a married guy named Brohaugh. It took him another two years to split with his wife and marry her, after which they moved to Monticello. The first Mrs. Brohaugh was a friend of mine. She was devastated by the divorce. She's practically a hermit these days, and since she blames me for introducing Judy to her husband, I am *not* one of the few people she still talks to."

"I'm sorry," I said again. "That must have been awful for everyone, but what happened after the bicentennial doesn't guarantee there was no conflict between your sister and Grace Yarrow before it took place."

"I'd have heard about it if there was," Darlene insisted, "and until you mentioned her at the meeting at Ronnie's house, I didn't even remember Grace's name. I suppose I must have heard who was writing the script at the time, but the pageant wasn't really on my radar. Running the public library took all my energy. When Frank and I had free time, we took a lot of trips. Even that long ago, it was clear that there would come a day when I wouldn't be mobile enough to enjoy traveling on trains, planes, or busses. We were determined to make the most of every moment."

"Did you attend the pageant?" I knew Frank had, since he was the one who'd remembered it and suggested a revival.

She shook her head. "After all this time, I don't remember why I didn't go. Maybe I was sick, or had to work." Her mouth curved into a crooked smile. "Or maybe I've been lying all along and actually knew Grace Yarrow well enough to hate her guts."

The maniacal laugh that accompanied this "confession" would have done Snidely Whiplash proud. Simon whined and backed away from her. Twirling the ends of an imaginary moustache, Darlene smiled with her eyes, but her tone of voice was deadly serious.

"If you think Judy might be guilty, then you'd better add me to your list of suspects, as well. I'm just as likely."

Sending her a withering look, I put away my notebook. Clearly, she'd said all she intended to about the bicentennial *and* about her sister.

CHAPTER 18

That afternoon, I drove to historical society headquarters to return the pageant manuscript and the *Gazetteer and Business Directory of Sullivan County.* Darlene had been right. Shirley easily accessed a list of the board members from twenty-five years ago. She didn't ask why I was interested. Along with the rest of the inhabitants of Lenape Hollow, she now knew the identity of the remains.

As Darlene had already told me, Ronnie's name was on the list. So was Sunny Feldman's. A quarter of a century ago, Ronnie had been Veronica Henniker, still married to, or maybe the widow of, her second husband. Sunny was listed as Roberta Feldman and Darlene's sister as Judith Kenner. Bud (actually Lester) Graham turned out to have been the director back then. The other board members were Elise Sanders, Melvin Osterhout, and Fred Gorton.

"Do you know anything about these people?" I indicated the last three names.

We were in Shirley's office, surrounded by her well-organized clutter. An open window let in the stench of hot tarmac. The day had turned into a real scorcher. The hum of a passing vehicle was the only sound that reached us. Inside the building was equally quiet. I was the only visitor.

"I know they're all dead," Shirley said.

"From natural causes, I hope."

Shirley gave a snort of laughter. "So far as I know."

"But you were acquainted with them?"

"Oh, yes. They were still here when I took this job, although Mr. Gorton was already in his nineties by then."

"And this Lester Graham? He was in charge?"

"He had the title. He was the one who hired me. But director wasn't a paid position until quite a few years later. Bud Graham was a go-getter. He was in public relations at the phone company and he knew how to write grants. He did some fancy fund-raising before he retired and moved to Florida. Gilbert Baxter isn't making enough to live the high life, but these days the director gets a salary. As for me, when I started I was paid minimum wage for twenty hours a

183

week. Thanks to Bud, the board upped my pay and increased my hours."

"Are you a full-time employee now?"

She nodded. "With benefits. Even though the building is only open thirty hours a week, I put in forty. Sometimes more. I'm librarian, secretary, and docent."

I was impressed. Many, maybe even most, small historical and genealogical societies are wholly staffed by volunteers. Having a professional on the premises meant visitors could actually find the records they were looking for.

"How long has Baxter been director?" Since Shirley and I stood side by side behind her desk, with the list on the flat surface in front of us, I turned my head slightly to catch her expression when she answered.

"Ever since Bud retired — thirteen years now. Before that Baxter sold real estate full-time. He still keeps his hand in. That's why he takes off so often instead of sticking around to play Mr. Big Shot."

Nothing showed on her face, but I heard the disapproval in her voice. I wondered if it was merited. I tend to sympathize with those who need to work more than one job to make ends meet. My kindly feelings toward Gilbert Baxter, however, remained tempered with suspicion.

"I gather that he was a member of the historical society long before he became director."

"That's right, and he was on the board for several years while Bud was still here. He was elected in . . . let me think. It must have been when Mr. Osterhout died. That's a good fifteen years ago."

"Baxter knew Grace Yarrow. I wonder how well."

"I wasn't here then, so I can't say for certain, but it seems to me that everyone involved with the bicentennial pageant must have worked closely with her. The first time I came across her name was when I went looking for a copy of this." Shirley tapped her knuckles on the manuscript I'd returned to her.

"Don't you think that's odd? That no one mentioned her to you, I mean."

Shirley shrugged. "A few years had passed by the time I got here. Since she doesn't seem to have been particularly well liked, maybe everyone preferred to forget all about her. As I understand it, they thought she jumped ship just before the big day, leaving it to others to pick up the slack. That's no way to make yourself popular."

"Only she didn't leave. She was murdered.

And one of the people who knew her back then must have killed her. Tell me more about Gilbert Baxter."

"Now, look, Mikki, you know I'm not crazy about my boss, but if he stuffed Grace Yarrow's body up the chimney, why on earth would he authorize someone to do repair work on that wall?"

"I don't imagine he expected it to collapse."

"He couldn't be certain it wouldn't. Besides, since Charlie was looking for the source of a leak, Baxter had to realize that might involve taking down part of the wall and replacing it. To someone who knew what has hidden there, the potential for discovery must have been obvious. Baxter may be many things, but stupid isn't one of them. If he was afraid the body would be found, he'd have thought of a way to stop the renovations."

"The board as a whole voted to make those repairs, right? Maybe Baxter didn't have any choice in the matter. He had to cross his fingers and hope for the best."

"Still —"

Shirley broke off at a faint sound from the doorway. My heart sank to my toes when I looked up and saw Gilbert Baxter standing in the vestibule just outside the office. I couldn't tell how much of our conversation he'd overheard, but it had obviously been enough to turn his face livid with rage.

"In my office," he said through gritted teeth. "Both of you. Now."

CHAPTER 19

Flashback!

I was sent to the principal's office only once when I was a student at Lenape Hollow High School. It was for the relatively minor infraction of talking during a fire drill, but I still remember the awful feeling of doom that hung over me as I walked through that door. I felt something akin to that same sensation as I crossed the vestibule between Shirley's office and Gilbert Baxter's. When beads of perspiration popped out on my forehead, I'd have liked to blame the building's lack of air conditioning, but the truth was much simpler. I was scared.

Get a grip, I told myself. *Gilbert Baxter is no Principal Wannamaker.*

Come to think of it, Principal Wannamaker wasn't all that scary, either.

Of course, I'd never suspected Oscar Wannamaker of being a cold-blooded killer.

188

My capricious mind promptly produced another memory from my teen years, the lyrics of a little ditty we used to sing to the tune of the Notre Dame fight song: *"Cheers, Cheers, for Lenape High. You bring the whiskey. I'll bring the rye. Send old Wannamaker out for gin, and don't let a sober sophomore in."*

Oh, yes — politically incorrect both then and now. Don't I know it! In the present circumstances, recalling them was also completely inappropriate, but the memory made me smile and at the same time banished the worst of my fear.

"Do you think this is funny?" Baxter demanded.

Since that's exactly what Principal Wannamaker had wanted to know, I came very close to laughing out loud. Instead, I shrugged and settled into one of the two chairs facing Baxter's enormous antique desk.

Shirley slid into the other. "You're taking this much too seriously, Gilbert," she chided him. "We were merely speculating. Considering possibilities. After all, *someone* murdered that poor woman."

He deflated like a popped balloon. The fury drained from his face, leaving behind only a grim scowl and a glower. "It wasn't me."

Gray eyes moved from Shirley to me and back again. He tugged at the end of his little goatee, as if that would help him decide how to deal with our suspicions. I studied him in return, wondering what I'd been so worried about. Even if he *had* killed Grace Yarrow twenty-five years ago, he did not pose an immediate threat. He lacked the physical strength to overcome the two of us. I doubted he'd be stupid enough to try. Unless he had a gun hidden in his desk drawer, the worst he was likely to do was fire Shirley and order both of us out of the building.

I leaned toward him, pasting an encouraging look on my face — the one I once used on students needing to be coaxed into revealing the *real* reason they didn't turn in their homework.

"Why don't you tell us about Grace?" I suggested. "Help us understand what she was like and why someone hated her enough to kill her."

"I've already answered questions for the police. Surely this is a matter best left to them." His words were clipped, his voice cold, and I couldn't help but notice that the lisp I'd heard the first time we met was considerably less pronounced.

190

"Do you really want them to keep poking into everyone's past? The cops always uncover *other* secrets, you know. Things that have no connection at all to the case pop up in the course of an investigation, things people innocent of the crime in question would just as soon not have exposed to the light of day."

Baxter gave a low moan and buried his head in his hands. Long, elegant fingers that had recently been treated to a good manicure burrowed into his salt-and-pepper hair. Shirley and I glanced at each other with what I'm sure were identical expressions of confusion.

"Gilbert," she said in a bracing voice, "unless you *did* kill her, there's no sense in making a mountain out of a molehill. What *do* you know about her?"

"She was . . . difficult," he said in a muffled voice.

"Yes," she said with a trace of impatience, "that much is obvious."

"I didn't know her very well," he insisted. "I wasn't on the board back then."

"We know that, too, but you were involved in the pageant," I said. "You took on the role of one of your ancestors, a role Grace augmented by appropriating a story from the history of Fallsburgh. Why did she attach your family's name to it? Did she owe you a favor?"

His head jerked up, a look of surprise on his face. He started to sputter a denial, until he got a good look at my implacable expression. "How did you find out?"

"It was someone way back in *my* family who promiscuously scattered those apple seeds."

"She said it made good theater. And you can't deny that Joshua Baxter *was* one of the founders of Lenape Hollow. I didn't see the harm in embellishing the story a little."

"This is the *historical* society, Gilbert." Although Shirley's lips were pursed in a stock expression of disapproval, her eyes glittered with barely suppressed amusement. "We're supposed to be able to separate fact from fiction. How would it look if this perversion of the truth became public knowledge? That the director of this institution colluded to spread fake history would create a terrible scandal."

"Now just a minute! You can't tell anyone. It wouldn't just ruin my reputation, it would damage the entire organization. The organization that pays your salary," he added, in case she'd missed his point.

"No one wants to discredit either you or the society," I said, "but you see the problem. The longer the police investigation drags on, the more irrelevant information will come to light. What else can you tell us about Grace?"

"I didn't kill her. You have to believe that. I had nothing against Grace. I had no reason to wish her ill."

"Who did?"

He hesitated, but only for a moment. "Ronnie North for one. She couldn't stand Grace. And there was a woman on the board back then who accused Grace of trying to seduce her husband."

Taken aback, I stared at him. "Which board member?"

He lifted his thin shoulders in a shrug. "Who remembers after all this time?"

"Sunny Feldman?" I asked. "Elise Sanders? Judy Brohaugh? No. Sorry. Twenty-five years ago she was Judy Kenner."

"I don't remember." He spoke firmly but the way he avoided meeting my eyes made me suspect he remembered perfectly well. For some reason, he didn't want to share the name.

I tried asking for the same information in a different way. "Do you know if Grace was involved with anyone?"

"I don't *know* anything, but it wouldn't surprise me. She was . . . free with her

193

favors. The way I heard it, the board had serious doubts about approving her to work on the project. Her . . . reputation had preceded her."

Sure, blame the victim. Baxter's claim made me question everything he'd told us so far. Ronnie had called Grace a twit, not a tramp, and my old nemesis was not one to mince words. Then again, if Baxter was telling the truth, he'd just put a woman near the top of my list of suspects. Could Ronnie have been the one who accused Grace of trying to steal her man? I didn't know if she'd still been married to husband number two at that point, or if she'd been a widow already working on acquiring husband number three. Either way, she'd certainly have taken exception to another woman's attempt at poaching.

"Do you remember any of the names of men who . . . associated with her?" Shirley asked.

"It was a long time ago. I barely remember *her.*" Abruptly, face brightening, he sat up a little straighter. "Wait a minute. Think about it. There's no reason her killer had to be someone connected to the historical society at all. Some discarded lover probably murdered her."

"You say you barely remember her, and

yet you were the one who told me she left Lenape Hollow because she had a job offer. Why did you think so?"

A new storm brewed in his gray eyes. I began to see a pattern. The more direct the question, the more irritated he became. And every time he offered information, it was to deflect our attention from the specific to the general.

"It was just an impression I had," he said through clenched teeth. "She was always talking about how she was sure her big break was just around the corner. Look, I don't know what more you think I can tell you. I'm not the one who killed her. I had no reason to."

"Who were her friends? What about her family?" I asked.

"She was a local girl," Baxter said, "but as far as I know, she didn't have any family left in the area. I suppose she had friends from high school, but I don't know any of their names. Tony Welby might recall. He was one of her teachers and worked part-time as a guidance counselor back then. When we needed someone to write the pageant script and she applied for the job, he wrote her a recommendation."

"Was his honor the mayor a member of the historical society back then?" I asked.

"Oh, yes." Baxter's lips twisted into a sneer. "That was shortly before he ran for state office the first time. He joined every civic, fraternal, and charitable group in the area — anything to make a good impression on potential voters."

"Do you have any idea where Grace lived? Maybe one of her neighbors still remembers her." *And who visited her,* I added to myself.

"I think she rented one of the small upstairs apartments on South Main Street. Above where the Woolworths used to be."

"Across from Ivy's Beauty Shop?"

Baxter looked uncertain, but I had a clear picture in my mind of a nondescript door located between the five-and-dime and a store that sold ladies' dresses. At the top of the steep flight of stairs behind it, off a landing, were two more doors that faced each other. One opened into an apartment. The other was Ivy's.

I spent a lot of time in that beauty parlor as a child. Customers entering found themselves in a hallway. A tiny kitchen was straight ahead. Turning left took them past the bathroom and on into the two rooms devoted to doing hair and nails. To the right of the entrance was Ivy's bedroom, and on its far side there was a living room. Its big front windows overlooked Main Street. On the days when Ivy did my mother's hair, a once-a-week ritual, she used to stash me in there, out of the way. I'd play quietly with my dolls until Mom was ready to go home.

That Baxter was able to recall where Grace lived seemed suspicious to me, and I was about to ask him if he had ever visited her at home when the sound of the front door opening and closing reached us. A moment later, someone rapped on the frosted glass that bore the director's name.

"Just a minute," Baxter called. Lowering his voice to a warning whisper, he glared at the two of us. "It would not be good for the society's reputation, or for the forthcoming festivities, if you were to speculate about any of this in public. Are we agreed on that point?"

"Certainly." Shirley's reply was brisk and unequivocal, if not necessarily truthful.

My answer came out sounding more than a little sarcastic. "I wasn't planning on talking to the media," I drawled.

Let him make of that statement what he would! It was as much of a promise as he was going to get. In just a few hours, when the pageant-writing committee met at my house for a previously scheduled final work session, the murder of Grace Yarrow would inevitably come up in conversation. I intended to take full advantage of the opportunity to speculate about who might have killed her, while at the same time picking the brains of the two women who had been on the board of directors twenty-five years ago. A good old-fashioned gossip session might go a long way toward revealing who had known what back in the day.

As soon as Shirley admitted Baxter's visitor, we left the room. I nodded to Detective Jonathan Hazlett on my way out, not at all surprised that he wanted another word with the director. My only regret was that I had no excuse to linger and eavesdrop on their conversation.

CHAPTER 20

The meeting at my house that evening was our last chance to work out problems with the script before we handed it over to Diego. I'd invited Darlene, Sunny, and Stacy. Ronnie had simply announced that she intended to show up, too. Her excuse was that she'd appointed herself head of publicity for the pageant.

Initially I wasn't happy about the prospect of having her there. Who needs unsolicited input at such a late date? As things turned out, though, I was glad she was coming. It would save me the trouble of seeking her out to ask questions about Grace Yarrow.

"I always admired your mother's flair for decorating," Ronnie said when she walked into the dining room.

"A compliment, Ronnie?"

If it was, it was a backhanded dig at the clutter currently surrounding us. I'd had to put the extra leaves in the table to make room for all our notes and reference books, not to mention the various versions of the script.

"What I remember is that she put plastic runners over the carpet in the hall so we wouldn't get it dirty by walking on it." Darlene's comment proved she had known Mom a lot better than Ronnie had.

"She had her quirks," I agreed. At least she hadn't also covered the chairs and sofa in plastic as some housewives did in the 1950s.

Darlene stopped what she was doing to look around. "We all slept in here, on the floor, rolled up in blankets, at those pajama parties you used to throw."

"So childish."

Ronnie's remark stung, the more so because I'd invited her to all those parties and she'd never once returned the favor. Of course, her parties tended to be a bit wilder than mine when we were in high school. Since she was a cheerleader, all the jocks showed up, usually bringing their own supply of enjoyment enhancer.

Where was I on those weekends? Usually at the movies with a group of dateless girls who hung out together throughout our teenage years.

"Your mom must have baked for days

beforehand to produce all the goodies she served," Darlene said, still reminiscing.

"I hate to shatter your illusions, but she picked up the cold cuts at the deli, the one that used to be just down the street from where O'Day Antiques is now, and she drove to Liberty to buy all those wonderful cookies, cakes, hard rolls, and bagels."

"From Katz's," said Sunny, and heaved a longing sigh.

"Best bakery ever." For once, Ronnie, Darlene, and I were in complete agreement.

Although glimpses of our high school days weren't what I'd hoped to encounter in a stroll down memory lane, I went with the flow. At some point, I'd find an opportunity to fast-forward this nostalgia-fest and focus on the period just before the bicentennial.

"Remember how we all got charm bracelets for our sixteenth birthdays?" Darlene asked. "Do you still have yours?"

"Of course," Ronnie said. "I treasure it."

I shrugged. "Mine is around somewhere, probably in one of the boxes in the attic."

"Excuse me," Stacy interrupted, "but aren't we supposed to be putting the finishing touches on the pageant?"

The puzzled and slightly bored expression on her face suggested she'd spent the last few minutes trying to translate a conversation carried on in Klingon. For once, there was no sign of her cell phone. She was serious about getting some work done.

"Quite right," Ronnie agreed. "Can someone bring me up to speed? If you'll synopsize what you've written, scene by scene, I should be able to pick out what will be most effective in the promotions."

"Maybe you could just listen in on our discussion and take notes," Darlene suggested.

"I have too much else to do to spend all evening on this."

I thought fast. "Darlene, why don't you and Stacy sit Ronnie down and take her through highlights of the script while Sunny and I go get the snacks and drinks from the kitchen?"

Obligingly, Sunny eased out of her chair and fumbled for her cane. She was eighty-five years old, a fact emphasized by the bulging veins and creased skin on the backs of her hands. It would have been more reasonable to ask her to work with Ronnie and recruit twenty-four-year-old Stacy to give me a hand, but Stacy wasn't around twenty-five years ago.

I'd prepared one platter of cheese and crackers and another with raw veggies — thin carrot and celery sticks, cherry tomatoes, broccoli florets, and zucchini spears. I took them out of the refrigerator along with a container of dip and followed that up by hauling out pitchers of lemonade and iced tea. Everything went onto a wheeled serving cart for the short trip into the adjoining room.

Sunny watched me without comment until the last of the items had been loaded aboard. "What am I supposed to do? Push it?"

"You're supposed to help me with something else entirely."

I cocked my head to better hear the murmur of conversation in the dining room. I couldn't make out words, but all three women were talking. Sunny and I should have a few minutes before anyone wondered what was keeping us.

"Grace Yarrow," I said bluntly. "You've heard they identified her as our Jane Doe?"

"Who hasn't?" Her tone of voice and her facial expression gave nothing away.

I leaned back against the kitchen counter and folded my arms. "You knew her."

"Slightly."

"You were on the board back then. You must have voted to approve choosing her to write the bicentennial pageant."

"Well, I certainly didn't want to do it

myself. Get to the point, Mikki. I'm old. I could croak waiting for you to stop beating around the bush."

"You'll probably outlive us all. But my point, and I do have one, is that it was probably someone connected with the historical society who murdered Grace and hid her body in the chimney. Suspicion will haunt everyone in the organization and cling to our celebration of the founding of Lenape Hollow until that person is identified."

I didn't think it was possible for someone so much shorter than I am to look down her nose at me. Sunny managed it. "What, exactly, do you think I'll remember after a quarter of a century?"

"How about the name of the person on the board of directors who accused Grace of seducing her husband."

A faint smile hovered around Sunny's mouth. "I trust you don't suspect me. I've never been married, and contrary to popular belief, I don't eat my lovers after we have sex."

I was searching in vain for a clever comeback to that remark when Calpurnia rescued me. She appeared out of nowhere to glide over to the cart, go up on her hind legs, and snag a piece of cheese.

Sunny's smile blossomed into a grin.

"What's his name?"

"Her. It's Calpurnia."

"After Caesar's wife?"

"Because she's a calico and she purrs."

When Cal rubbed her head against Sunny's legs, the Feldman heir chuckled and reached down to stroke the cat's soft fur. Then she plucked another small slice of cheese off the serving cart and fed it to her.

"Don't encourage the little beggar."

"Why not? We girls have to stick together."

That sounded promising. "About the board members —"

"All right, already. Ronnie was one of them, as was Darlene's sister, Judy, and Elise Sanders. Elise died several years ago. She was five-foot-nothing and skinny as a rail. There's no way she could have stuffed anybody up a chimney, let alone a woman of Grace's full-bodied proportions. I doubt I would have been able to heft her either, especially if she was *dead* weight."

Ronnie and Judy on the other hand, were both sturdily built. Twenty-five years ago they'd been in their early forties, older than Grace but still capable of bashing her over the head. That either one of them could have disposed of the body without help was harder to imagine, but not impossible.

Tucking her cane under her arm, Sunny

grabbed hold of the serving cart with both hands and used it like a walker. Pushing it ahead of her, she headed for the dining room. "Food's ready!" she called out as she went.

Calpurnia was right on her heels.

I was about to follow them when the landline rang and my sister-in-law's name popped up on the caller ID on the kitchen extension. Since Allie usually preferred email to talking on the telephone, I picked up, worried there might be some sort of family emergency.

"Allie? Is everything okay?"

"I just wanted to hear your voice. It's been too long."

"I'm sorry. I know I haven't been good about keeping in touch. Things have just been a little hectic around here. I've been helping out with a pageant to celebrate the founding of Lenape Hollow."

I didn't tell her I'd discovered a body. My sister-in-law is a worrier. There was no sense in giving her any more cause than she already had to fuss about my moving so far away from the rest of the family. After a few more minutes of back and forth, I told her I had people in the house, working on the pageant script, and needed to get back to them.

206

I'd just said good-bye when Ronnie poked her head into the kitchen from the hall. I took one look at her face and braced myself for trouble. Just the fact that she'd taken the long way around, through the living room and hall instead of the door that went directly from the dining room into the kitchen, told me she wanted to ream me out in private.

"Do you really think I could have killed that Yarrow woman?" Ronnie demanded.

"I don't know. Did you?"

"If I had, I'd have found a much more efficient way to dispose of her body."

"Now, that I do believe. I take it Sunny shared the gist of my conversation with you. Did she also tell you I was asking about husband-poaching? According to Gilbert Baxter, someone on the board at the time of the bicentennial made that accusation against Grace Yarrow. Was it you?"

"Certainly not. Twenty-five years ago, I was in my second widowhood and hadn't yet met my third husband. I had no interest in what Grace got up to."

"Did you know she had a reputation for being fast?"

Ronnie shrugged. "It was none of my business who she slept with."

"What about Elise and Judy? Did they care?"

Looking thoughtful, she came down off her high horse. "To tell you the truth, I don't even remember hearing that Grace was involved with any married man. Then again, since I didn't think much of her, we had very little direct contact. I wasn't close to Elise or Judy, either. Neither of them would have chosen me as a confidante."

"Would they have confided in Gilbert Baxter?"

The look Ronnie sent my way suggested I'd lost my mind.

"He *is* the one who told me the story. He made it sound as if this woman wasn't making any secret of her suspicions. Since he wasn't on the board himself, how else would he have heard about her claims?"

"Obviously, you misunderstood what he told you."

"The only thing that's obvious to me is that you don't know diddly-squat about Grace's personal life." *Or aren't willing to admit it!*

Before she could make another snarky remark and draw me into a pointless sniping match, I turned my back on her and took the direct route to the dining room. Ronnie was always able to rattle me when we were in high school. I was better at dealing with her now that we were both in our late sixties, but she still has the power to upset my equilibrium. A childish squabble was the last thing I needed.

I paused to glance back over my shoulder when I reached the door. "We should get back to the others. I'd like to finish up at a reasonable hour. Diego is expecting delivery of the final script sometime tomorrow."

Ronnie stayed put and glanced at her watch. "It's later than I realized. How fortunate that I already have all the information I need for the press release."

Without so much as a thank-you for my hospitality or a word of farewell to the other women, she spun around and headed down the hallway toward the front door. I winced at the sound of the screen slamming shut behind her.

After that, it took us less than an hour to finish making the final tweaks to the script and polish off all the food I'd prepared. Grace Yarrow's name did not come up again until Darlene and I stood on the porch watching Sunny and Stacy get into their respective cars and drive away.

Balancing on her walker, Darlene heaved a deep sigh. "I guess you're going through with your plan to talk to Judy."

"I think I need to, don't you? Did Sunny tell you about the claim Gilbert Baxter made?"

"That Grace was trying to steal someone's husband? Yes, she did. If the husband in question was Max Kenner, Grace probably succeeded. I've already told you what he was like. Judy divorced him because he catted around."

"I don't suppose Judy confided anything else to you?" I'd had the strongest feeling, during our earlier conversations about Judy, that Darlene was holding something back.

"She was never big on sharing secrets, but I don't remember her ever mentioning Grace's name. Then again, when Judy went off on a tangent, complaining about one thing or another, I tended to tune her out. She never wanted advice. She just needed to vent."

"So the real rift between you two didn't come until later, after she took up with her current husband?"

"We were never close."

There was that evasiveness again. Darlene's response wasn't really an answer. I would have pressed the point, but she was making her slow, cautious way down the porch steps, heading for the van parked in my driveway.

I can take a hint. For the moment, I let the subject drop.

CHAPTER 21

I sent the script to Diego as an email attachment as soon as I'd incorporated the final tweaks made at Wednesday evening's meeting. He emailed back to acknowledge its receipt and invite me to meet him at Harriet's the next day for lunch. I accepted, but not without some misgivings.

Directors have been known to ask for changes.

The place was busy when I arrived. It isn't all that big and almost every table was occupied. I gave myself points for recognizing all but one of Ada's customers. The exception was a young man sitting alone at a table in the center of the restaurant. He looked to be somewhere in his late twenties and was casually dressed in jeans and a Red Sox T-shirt. I approved of the latter. How could I not when I'd spent some fifty years living in New England?

Diego was waiting for me at a table for

two and had chosen the chair with a view of the door so he could keep an eye out for me. "Over here, Ms. Lincoln."

"Call me Mikki."

I sat down across from him, my back to the rest of the patrons. I was just as well pleased to be spared distractions. I tend to be a people watcher. I could still hear bits and pieces of the conversations going on around us, but I was able to ignore them and focus on what Diego thought of the pageant script.

"I think it's great," he said. "Lively. Lots of interesting characters. Given how little information you had to go on about the early settlers, you did a remarkable job of fleshing them out."

"It helped that one of them was an ancestor of mine," I confided. "I just thought about my grandfather when I was writing dialogue for John Greenleigh."

He chuckled. "I imagine Ms. Feldman drew on memories of her relatives as well. Of course, she actually knew the characters she was writing about."

We chatted in this vein for a quarter of an hour. Or, to be honest, I babbled on about stories we'd uncovered in our research while he polished off his soup and sandwich. I'd barely touched my BLT when Diego announced he had to leave.

"I need to get the scripts printed for the casting call tomorrow and handle a few other details. You should come to tryouts."

"To try out? I don't think so."

"To advise. Who knows better than you do what to look for in our aspiring actors?"

He signaled Ada for the check and refused to let me pay for my own food. I didn't argue. Neither did I commit myself to anything. Although I admired his enthusiasm, I didn't believe for one minute that Diego was going to coax Oscarworthy performances out of our local talent. I'd be happy if he ended up with warm bodies who could get their lines out without mumbling.

Once he left, I concentrated on finishing my sandwich. I had a full afternoon ahead of me. I hadn't precisely neglected my clients while working on the pageant, but between that and my preoccupation with Grace's murder, they'd received less of my attention than they deserved.

I started and gave a little squeak of alarm when a hand touched my shoulder.

"Sorry," said a deep male voice. "I didn't mean to scare you."

I turned to find the young man I'd noticed earlier standing behind me. The well-worn athletic shoes he wore explained how he'd been able to approach me unheard. They used to be called sneakers for a reason.

My gaze returned to his face, although it gave me a crick in the neck to look up at him. He was tall and slender with brown hair, blue eyes, and a friendly smile. I felt my eyes narrow as I noticed his nose. It had a familiar shape, the same one I saw in my mirror every morning.

"Who are you?" I asked in a sharp voice that came out much louder than I'd intended.

Every head in Harriet's turned our way, sending us curious looks.

"Sorry," he said again. "It's just that it's so great to finally meet you." He pulled out the chair Diego had vacated and sat down. "My name is Luke Darbee and I'm your second cousin twice removed."

CHAPTER 22

I studied Luke while, at his urging, I finished my lunch. That certainly did look like the infamous Greenleigh nose. It's just a little too big for most faces and has a tendency to give some of the less fortunate members of the family a ratlike profile.

"How did you know who I was?" I asked when I'd consumed the last crumb.

"Oh, that's easy. I heard that guy call out your last name and then you told him to use Mikki instead. I already knew Michelle Greenleigh Lincoln was the last of the Greenleighs left in Lenape Hollow. I was planning to stop by your house after lunch. I really wanted to meet you while I was in town."

"And just why *are* you in town?"

"I'm on an ancestor hunt. I was hoping you'd know where some of our Greenleigh ancestors are buried." His enthusiasm was unusual for such a young man, but he exuded sincerity.

"There are quite a few generations in the Lenape Hollow cemetery, all the way back to the first Greenleigh to settle here."

"Will you show me?"

How could I resist the eager light in his eyes? We left Harriet's together.

"It isn't far, but it is uphill. Do you want to drive us there or shall I?"

"Depends." He grinned at me as he pointed to an ancient Vespa parked in front of the police station. "That's my transportation."

"I'll drive."

The trip was short, but long enough for me to learn that Luke had spent the last few months traveling around the country. He'd stayed at campgrounds while he climbed various branches of his family tree. It seemed like an odd hobby, especially for one so young, but the excitement with which he spoke about it convinced me his interest was genuine.

"Are you thinking of writing a book about your adventures?" I asked when I parked by the side of the road that ran through the cemetery.

He shrugged and hopped out of the car without answering. "So where's the final

resting place of the original John Greenleigh?"

I showed him, and gave him a recap of
what I knew about Lenape Hollow's first
fence viewer, including the fact that he was
to have a significant role in the upcoming
pageant. Luke stared at the weathered stone
for a few seconds before glancing my way
with a puzzled expression on his face.

"Didn't he have a wife?"

"Ah, well, there you have a small family
mystery. He did, yes. Her name was Sarah
Thorndike and they married while they
were still living in Connecticut. According
to the date that's come down to us, she died
a few years after her husband, but there's
no record of where she died or where she
was buried."

"Maybe she went back to Connecticut."

"That's one possibility. Another is that she
went to live with one of their children in
another town. She might even have remarried. After all this time, it's unlikely we'll
ever know for certain."

We moved on to the graves of John's son,
the second John Greenleigh, and his wife,
and then crossed the road to where my
grandfather's parents, Nathaniel and Lucy,
were buried. Their children had erected a
large stone with the name Greenleigh on it

in huge letters and their given names and life dates, in much smaller print, below.

"Nathaniel purchased one of the larger plots from the Lenape Hollow Cemetery Association," I said, "the entity that provides maintenance in perpetuity for everyone buried here. My grandfather held the deed, but since he had his own plot, he passed it on to my father. My parents moved to Florida when they retired, and originally planned to be buried there, but in the end they came home again. These two small stones mark their graves. They didn't want anything fancy."

Since, until recently, I'd lived so far away, I'd never gotten into the habit of putting flowers on their graves. Fortunately, the Cemetery Association takes care of keeping everything tidy. They planted flowering trees throughout, giving the whole place a peaceful, pretty, well-kept air, and the view is spectacular. The cemetery is located on a hill overlooking the village. From where we stood, I could pick out church steeples, the tree-lined street where I live, and even the historical society building.

"My mother is the one who started researching my family tree," Luke said, "and she used to rope me into helping her. It's kind of addictive."

I smiled at that comment. I'd avoided most of the temptations of genealogy myself, but I certainly knew what it was like to become so fascinated by a subject that no detail seemed too small or obscure to pursue.

"It was my paternal great-grandmother who was a Greenleigh," he continued. "Her father was Lawrence Greenleigh, Nathaniel and Lucy's youngest son. That's how you and I are related. Second cousins twice removed, like I said."

"Lawrence Greenleigh," I repeated, frowning. I'd heard that name before, and there was a story connected with it, something — "Oh, dear."

Luke sent a questioning look my way.

I put a hand on his forearm. "I don't know how to tell you this, but you aren't who you think you are."

My grandfather had been a great one for telling family stories to anyone who would listen, but as far as I knew, he only confided the truth about Lawrence to a few of his closest relatives. I was one of them.

"What do you mean?" Luke asked.

"Lawrence wasn't really Nathaniel and Lucy's son."

"Do you mean he was adopted?"

"Not exactly." I guided him toward a

solitary gravestone at the edge of my great-grandparents' plot.

"Joan Greenleigh," Luke read. "1871 to 1910."

"Joan was Nathaniel and Lucy's oldest daughter. She never married, but she did have a child. That's according to my grandfather, who was Joan's younger brother and a witness to her son's birth. Lawrence was that son. Joan's parents passed him off as their own to preserve their daughter's reputation. You aren't my second cousin twice removed, Luke. You're my second cousin *thrice* removed."

From the stunned look on his face, he was having trouble taking in what I'd just told him. I sympathized. It isn't easy to give up preconceived notions about who we are.

"Well, at least I'm still a Greenleigh," he said after a moment.

I patted his arm. "Why don't you come back to the house with me? Stay for supper?"

He shook his head. "Thanks, Mikki, but I've got some thinking to do. That's quite a bombshell you just dropped on me."

"Where are you staying?" I asked when I'd driven him back to where he'd parked the Vespa.

"I'm set up at a campground on the other

side of Monticello. I've been tracking down some relatives over that way, too."

He thanked me for my help, and we exchanged cell phone numbers, but he didn't say anything about returning to Lenape Hollow. As he put-putted out of sight, I wondered if I'd ever see my new-found cousin again.

CHAPTER 23

Right up until the moment I got into my car and started the engine, I was of two minds about attending tryouts. Despite my resolution to let the chips fall where they may, I felt a need to know early on if Diego would be able to find actors capable of portraying the characters I'd envisioned. If he couldn't, it would probably take me the entire two weeks until the performance to brace myself for disappointment. No matter how the pageant turned out, I'd have to present a brave face, smile, give compliments, and generally behave as if I was pleased with the result.

Civic duty, right?

Diego had spoken of recruiting students, so I wasn't surprised to see a great many young faces as I entered the auditorium at the high school. It hadn't changed much in fifty-plus years, except for looking shabbier than I remembered. It also had a faintly sour smell.

The "new" school had opened when I was a junior. It was showing its age. To tell the truth, the "old" school, still used for grades one to six, had withstood the effects of time much better than this building. I wasn't sure when that structure had gone up, but it was obviously back when construction was meant to last several lifetimes.

I took a seat near the back, trying to remain unobtrusive. My location gave me a good view of new arrivals. I was some startled, as folks say in Maine, when I saw my newfound cousin, Luke Darbee, saunter in. For a moment, I thought he might have come looking for me, but instead of glancing around, he headed straight for the front row, where a couple of dozen wannabe actors were waiting for the director to begin his spiel.

I'm not sure why I was so surprised. I didn't know Luke well. We'd only just met and most of our conversation had been about our mutual ancestors. I remembered mentioning the pageant to him, but not that he'd shown any particular interest in it. It puzzled me that he was here, obviously planning to try out for a part. How had he even heard about the tryouts?

I didn't have to look far for an answer to

that question. He must have seen the write-up Ronnie sent to the local newspapers. The press release had gone out not only to our little bi-weekly rag, but also to the daily published in Middletown.

There was no reason Luke shouldn't involve himself in the project. John Greenleigh was his ancestor, too. Still, it struck me as odd. If he won a part in the pageant, he'd be obliged to stick around for another two weeks.

Diego handed out pages and had everyone pair up and read the same bit of dialogue, a funny scene Sunny had written based on a real encounter between a local woman with an attitude and a comic who'd made frequent appearances onstage at the Feldman.

Originally, I didn't plan to stay until the bitter end, but the casting process proved more interesting than I'd anticipated. There were, thank goodness, some talented youngsters in Lenape Hollow.

Although we hadn't written in any singing parts — the music was to be background only — Diego also had everyone vocalize. I assumed he wanted to get an idea of their range. Luke had a pleasant baritone. He was also one of the better performers, so I wasn't surprised when he was cast as both

John Greenleigh and the Feldman comic. Almost everyone would be playing more than one role, with quick changes between scenes as the centuries rolled by onstage.

Luke was being offered congratulations all around when I stood up to leave. Spotting me, he called out my name and bounded toward me like an oversize puppy. "Hey, I didn't know you were here. You should have said something."

Caught up in an enthusiastic hug, I didn't have enough breath left to reply. That was probably just as well, since I wasn't sure how to react to this sudden familiarity.

"Did you know I was coming?" he asked when he finally released me.

"How could I? I wasn't even aware that you knew about the casting call."

"You're the one who told me about the pageant."

We stood in semi-darkness halfway near the exit. I couldn't see his face clearly, but I had a feeling I knew what was coming. I tried making a preemptive strike.

"How are you going to manage to get to all the rehearsals? It's a bit of a commute to the other side of Monticello." I tried to keep the suspicion out of my voice when I asked the question, but I was certain the next words out of his mouth would be an attempt to cage an invitation to stay at my house.

"I'm moving to another campground closer to Lenape Hollow," Luke said, surprising me yet again. "There are sites available over at a place called Mountain View Acres."

A little silence fell between us as we left the building and started across the parking lot to the place where I'd left my car. It took me a moment to make the necessary mental adjustments. It appeared I'd misjudged Luke, and that fact disturbed me.

I cleared my throat. "Congratulations on being cast in two of the meatier parts in the pageant."

He chuckled. "No small parts, only small actors, right? Congratulations to you, too. From what I heard this evening, the old bicentennial script was a mess. You and your team pulled off a small miracle."

Flattery. You've got to love it.

"And that business at the historical society," he added as I unlocked my car door. "Wow. I didn't realize until someone told me just now that you were right there when they found the body."

"It's not the first thing I'd tell a stranger." And because he *was* a stranger, distant relative or not, I was once again beginning to feel a little nervous about his intentions. He

227

was as stoked as the Energizer Bunny, which made him unpredictable.

"I saw in the paper that they identified her. Grace Yarrow? Funny name. Did you ever meet her?"

"I wasn't living here when she was killed."

I had to maneuver around him to slide into the driver's seat. When I tried to close the door, he caught the top of the window with one hand to keep it open.

"Since I'm going to be around for the next two weeks, we ought to get together for coffee or something."

"What a good idea," I said with patently false enthusiasm. "I have your cell number. I'll call you."

With that, I tugged hard enough on the door to close it and immediately hit the button to lock it. I smiled at him through the window as I started the engine and gave a little wave after I backed out of my parking space. He waved back and headed off toward the far end of the lot at a trot. I could just make out the Vespa in the shadows.

I told myself I was overreacting, but I kept checking my rearview mirror as I drove home. I was safely inside my house with the security system armed before I breathed easily again.

I turned to find Calpurnia watching me. "What?"

She didn't answer.

"Don't you think it's odd that a young man who claims to be traveling around the country should decide to get involved in a local history pageant?"

And why, I wondered, had he made a point of bringing up Grace Yarrow's name? He couldn't have been more than a year or two old when she died.

I was halfway to the kitchen when I stopped in my tracks. Calpurnia, who had been trailing after me, sent me an exasperated look, one that said more clearly than words that her food bowl needed replenishing. I shook my head, bemused by my own flight of fancy.

"I just had the craziest thought," I told her. "Being obsessed with finding out what happened all those years ago can result in making weird connections. You know that, right?"

She didn't care.

I foraged in the cabinet for a can of cat food while the idea that had just come to me percolated at the back of my mind. Those who had known Grace, at least the ones I'd spoken to so far, all appeared to agree she was sexually active. No one had mentioned a child, and yet, way back at the beginning of the case, Detective Hazlett had asked me if she'd had one. I'd taken his question to mean that the autopsy had found indications that Grace had given birth.

Not all young, single women who have children out of wedlock keep them, especially if they don't have family to help out. That was even more true in the past than it is today. Any child born to Grace Yarrow would be over twenty-five years old, but perhaps not by much . . . right around Luke's age.

Talk about jumping to conclusions!

I fed the cat before opening the refrigerator to find a snack for myself, all the while shaking my head at my own foolishness. Of course, Luke was who he said he was. He had the Greenleigh nose. But there *was* something off about him. Something he wasn't being open about. At my first opportunity, I resolved to do a little digging into his background.

That went on my mental to-do list right after "talk to Judy Brohaugh." I'd already made arrangements to meet with Darlene's sister the next day. Using the excuse, feeble as it was, that I wanted to ask her about her memories of the bicentennial, especially the pageant, I'd finagled an invitation to have lunch with her at her condo in Monticello.

I closed the refrigerator without removing anything to eat. If I expected to get any work done before I left for Judy's place, it was time to pack it in for the night.

I was hoping for a solid eight hours of sleep. Instead I fell into a nightmare in which shadowy figures chased me around my backyard armed with sheets of heavy-duty plastic and rolls of duct tape. Flashes of lightning revealed their faces to me one by one: Gilbert Baxter; Ronnie; Judy as she'd been when I last saw her years ago; Tom O'Day; and last but not least, a small child with the Greenleigh nose.

Suddenly, in the manner of dreams, I was inside the house but still being pursued. I fled from room to room, and then out onto the small balcony that adjoins my upstairs office. I climbed over the railing onto the roof of the garage and ran down the gently sloping surface to the low point over the path that runs between my property and Cindy's. It's an easy jump, only a little more than six feet, but just as I was about to fling myself over the edge, a great chasm opened up. The roof turned into a cliff with jagged rocks below. I teetered there, caught be-tween two terrors, and then I went over, a soundless scream issuing from my lips.

The fall woke me.

After I untangled myself from the bed-sheets and used the top one to wipe the sweat from my face, I couldn't get back to sleep. I stared at the ceiling until the first rays of sunlight streaked into the room and the cat came to stand on my chest to insist that I get up and feed her.

CHAPTER 24

Judy's condominium complex wasn't the easiest place to find. I had only the vaguest memories of downtown Monticello and those were mostly from the times my father drove me to a studio somewhere in the vicinity of Broadway for ballet lessons with Miss Bimboni. I did work in Monticello at the telephone company one summer, but I spent most of my time indoors. Back then, the first generation of computers had only just been introduced. I handled long-distance calls at a workstation that looked like the command center for a spaceship. TSP? I think those were the initials it went by, but I no longer have the slightest idea what they stood for. I do remember that I made friends with a coworker — I don't remember her name, either — who had a friend whose family owned a motel not far away from where we worked. We were invited to swim in the motel pool when we worked a split shift. That motel was the one landmark I recognized. I was surprised that it was still there and that it looked much the same as I recalled. Not much else is unchanged.

After driving in circles and then backtracking, I eventually located Judy's address and even snagged a parking space that wasn't too far away. She must have been watching out her window for me, because she buzzed me into the building while I was still reaching for the intercom button.

"Come on up," said a disembodied voice. "Second floor. Second door on your left."

I wouldn't have recognized her. Although she's only a few years older than her sister, she'd let herself go big-time. The loose caftan she wore only emphasized the excess weight, and her face was puffy and unhealthy looking.

I'm not one of those people who preaches about the dangers of being overweight or looks down on those who have trouble taking off the pounds. Svelte would never describe me, either, although I was almost too skinny as a child. But the way Judy moved, ponderously and with exceeding care, hinted that she might have more in common with Darlene than either sister realized. I couldn't help but notice the telltale signs of arthritis in her hands and fingers when she waved me into the kitchen.

The delectable aroma of homemade chicken soup greeted me when I stepped through the door. For a moment, I thought a healthy meal might be in the offing, but once I was seated, Judy added grilled cheese sandwiches to the menu, slathering both sides of the bread with real butter before slapping them into a greased fry pan and putting three slices of cheese on each.

I have to admit, the result was delicious.

A few minutes later, seated at the kitchen table and scarfing down the calories, we studied each other. Judy broke the silence just before it began to feel awkward.

"Hell getting old, ain't it?"

Both the comment and her deliberate misuse of the English language surprised a laugh out of me. "You got that right," I agreed, matching her colloquial manner of speech.

Sometimes even a stickler for proper grammar has to let her hair down.

We exchanged basic renewing-our-acquaintance chitchat, during which I did most of the talking. I answered her questions about why I'd moved back to Lenape Hollow, and told her what I thought of our old hometown in the present day. Inevitably,

Darlene's name came up.

"I hear she was stupid enough to agree to serve on the board of directors at the historical society," Judy said.

"She *is* on the board." Stupid didn't come into the equation.

My careful answer seemed to amuse her. Her lips twitched. "I know you two were close in high school. I guess you've still got each other's backs."

I took a sip of lemonade to give myself time to think. There had been an undercurrent of resentment in that crack about the board of directors, but had it been directed at Darlene, or at the historical society? Judy's move to Monticello had obliged her to give up her own seat on the board. With the exception of whatever person held the post of town historian, every other board member was required to reside within the village limits.

The previous night's bad dream had made me think twice about keeping my lunch date with Judy, but separate from my desire to help right the old wrong of Grace's murder, I wanted to talk to her because, optimist that I am, I hoped to find a way to mend the rift between the two sisters. I was certain Darlene wasn't telling me the whole story behind their estrangement. There was more to it than Judy's marriage to the ex-husband of one of Darlene's friends.

Wary of putting my foot in my mouth and making things worse, I said, "It's been good to renew old acquaintances. I've been surprised by how many of my former class-mates still live in this area. And of course I remember you, a little, from back then."

Judy's smile turned rueful. "I was certainly littler in the good old days. As you can see, I'm now twice the woman I used to be."

I almost choked on my drink. Those were the exact words Darlene used to describe her own weight gain.

Judy chuckled at what she took to be embarrassment on my part. "Never mind. When you called, you said you wanted to ask about my memories from twenty-five years ago, not fifty."

"Right. About the bicentennial." I didn't want to come right out and ask if it had been her husband Grace Yarrow tried to seduce, so I took another bite of my grilled cheese and waited to see if she'd volunteer any information.

After a moment she said, "I'd never have figured you for a member of the historical society, and they sure roped you into taking over a thankless task. I'm surprised they didn't stick Shirley Martin with running the pageant. She's good at grunt work. Or did she wise up and find a better job?"

I wiped grease off my fingers before picking up my soup spoon. "Shirley is still there, and she's been a tremendous help, but I was recruited because I have specific skills." I explained about my editing business. "The powers that be wanted to put on another pageant like the one performed for the bicentennial, and they thought the same script might still be usable."

Judy polished off her soup before she spoke again. "I'd have thought they could do better than that."

"Well, we did end up completely rewriting it."

"Of course you did. The original was a piece of crap."

"It had . . . problems," I conceded.

Judy's face came alive when she grinned at me. "It did have its moments, though. Did you know I played one of the founders' wives? No lines, of course, but we rented costumes from one of those companies that supplies reenactors, so it all felt very authentic." A faraway look came into blue eyes very like her sister's. "The thing I remember best is when the scrim got caught on one of the lights at dress rehearsal and nearly started a fire."

"Scrim?"

"You know — a semitransparent curtain, so the audience gets only an impression of the actors behind it. It was a dumb idea in the first place, but it was supposed to be artsy."

"Some people must have enjoyed the performance. They remembered it all these years later and asked for a reboot."

"Well, no one booed. There was one bad moment, though, when we spotted Mr. and Mrs. Daly in the audience. They weren't supposed to be back in Lenape Hollow for another month."

"And that was bad because . . . ?"

"Because we'd *borrowed* one of the out-buildings from their place to create part of our set." She put air quotes around the word and winked for good measure. "Two of the guys on stage crew took it apart, put the sections on a truck, and cobbled it together again inside the historical society building to represent the sort of humble dwelling the first settlers lived in."

"Did the Dalys recognize it?"

"If they did, they never mentioned it, but I have to say that having them at home made it a whole lot trickier to put the shed back." She popped the last bite of her sandwich into her mouth, watching me

239

closely as she chewed. After a final swallow of lemonade, she added, "From what I've seen lately on the news, swiping a building wasn't the only crime someone committed back then."

"Grace Yarrow was murdered at about the same time," I agreed.

Lips pursed, Judy shook her head from side to side. "Hard to believe."

"Why? As I understand it, she disappeared quite suddenly. Surely someone must have wondered what happened to her."

"No one cared. We weren't exactly heart-broken to see the last of her. Not only was she a pushy broad, but she kept changing her mind. Playwrights should never be allowed to direct their own shows. We may not have had any lines, but she moved us around like puppets, and never to the same place twice. Besides that, she was downright irrational about everything to do with the pageant. She's the one who decided the Dalys' outbuilding would be perfect as part of the set. She ordered those boys to go get it for her. What if they'd been caught? They could have ended up in jail."

"Boys? What boys?"

"The ones on the stage crew. They were seniors in high school that year. Old enough to think Grace was sexy. Too young to worry

240

overmuch about breaking the law when the result would make her happy."

"Stage crew," I repeated, wondering why it had never occurred to me to search for information in that direction. "I don't suppose you remember any of their names?"

"Hardly."

"It doesn't matter." I was speaking more to myself than to Judy. "I can find out. I have a copy of the pageant program."

"More people to tap for their memories?"

A hint of sarcasm had crept into her seemingly innocent question. When I didn't answer right away, she came to her own conclusion.

"You aren't really here to ask me questions about the pageant, are you? It's Grace's murder that interests you. I heard about that business last fall."

I frowned at her reference to the unpleasant events of the previous autumn. The two situations were entirely different. I do not make a habit of poking my nose into murder investigations. On the other hand, I couldn't deny that I wanted answers from Judy about Grace Yarrow.

"Busted." I tried and failed to sound apologetic. "I wasn't sure you'd agree to talk to me if you thought I was trying to find out who her enemies were."

"Why should I mind? If you've learned anything at all about her, you already know that she ticked off just about everyone."

"Even you?"

"Moi? The epitome of cool and collected?" Judy rolled her eyes. "Of course, me. Not only was I on the board, I was the one who had to tell her to rein in her spending. Do you know how much it costs to rent a scrim?"

"Do you remember Gilbert Baxter?" I asked.

She looked surprised by the question. "Gil? Sure. He took over as director when Bud Graham retired."

"Did he quarrel with Grace, too?"

"Probably." She stood and started to clear the table. "Why are you asking me about Gil?"

"Because he's the one who told me that one of the members of the board back then — Elise Somebody, or so he thought — accused Grace of trying to seduce her husband. Did he get that right?"

Actually, Baxter had said he couldn't recall which board member had made that claim, but I wanted to see how Judy would react if I pinned the charge on someone other than her. Although she stood with her back to me, her body language spoke volumes. She tensed, shoulders and neck taut with it, and the plates and bowls she was carrying clattered loudly when she set them down on the counter.

"That would be Elise Sanders," she said without turning. "She died a few years back, but I think her ex is still alive. They got a divorce around the same time I dumped my first husband."

"Was Elise's spouse fooling around with Grace Yarrow?"

"I have no idea."

"Are you sure? You were on the board with her. Baxter wasn't and yet he —"

"He wanted to be. Elise probably let him think she'd recommend him to replace her when she retired, and I suppose she might have unburdened herself to him, but she certainly didn't say anything to me." Judy returned to the table with a plate of cookies and the pitcher of lemonade, refilling my glass without asking if I wanted more.

"Maybe it wasn't Elise's husband Grace took up with."

"If it had been mine, I'd have let her have him, the no-good louse."

"Do you think it's likely Grace made a play for Elise's husband?"

More relaxed now, Judy resumed her place at the table. "Let's just say she liked to be

243

the focus of attention of every male in her vicinity, and she showed a special interest in the ones she thought could help her career."

"As a playwright? I understand she talked about moving to the City."

"It costs money to live in the Big Apple, and I can't see Grace being content to starve in a garret. Maybe what she was really after was a patron, but the pickings were pretty slim in Lenape Hollow. Besides, she wasn't nearly as irresistible as she thought she was." She chuckled. "She tried to vamp Tony Welby at one of the rehearsals. He was still teaching at the high school back then, but he was about to launch his political career, and he was married. He shut her down hard and fast, and before at least a dozen witnesses. She didn't like that experience one little bit."

I added the mayor to my mental list of people to interview. I'd completely forgotten that he was once Grace's guidance counselor, and that he'd written a recommendation for her when she applied for the job of writing the pageant.

"Do you really think Elise could have killed Grace?" Judy's skepticism was obvious.

"After what Gilbert Baxter told me, I thought it was possible, but then Sunny

Feldman described her as a small woman, someone lacking the physical strength to murder a big girl like Grace, let alone stuff her body up a chimney."

"That's true," Judy agreed. "A good puff of wind would have blown Elise away, but I guess I can understand why Gil tried to cast suspicion on her. She isn't around to contradict him, being dead and all."

The suggestive undertone in her voice was impossible to miss. I sat a little farther forward in my chair. "Why would Baxter *want* to steer me toward anyone?"

"Well," she said, "as I remember it, Gilbert Baxter was not one of the ones inclined to resist when Grace batted her eyelashes. They were *dating* while Grace was working on the script." Once again, she resorted to air quotes, just in case I wasn't clever enough to recognize a euphemism when I heard one.

Funny how Gilbert Baxter had left out that trifling detail.

When Judy insisted she knew no more and couldn't, or wouldn't, elaborate on Baxter's relationship with Grace, I shifted my focus to the other purpose behind my meeting with her. Sadly, my attempt to bring about a reconciliation between the two sisters never got off the ground. Every time I mentioned Darlene's name, Judy changed the subject.

CHAPTER 25

Sunday morning, the day after my trip to Monticello to talk to Judy, I got off to a slow start. I toasted a second bagel, topped off my coffee, and returned to the dinette table to contemplate, bleary-eyed, the list I'd made the night before. It was a long one: all the people I hadn't yet asked about their memories of Grace Yarrow.

"Why do I even care?" I asked Calpurnia.

For once, she looked interested, but maybe that was just because there were still a few tiny bits of scrambled egg on my plate. She hopped into my lap, nose twitching.

"The murder of Grace Yarrow took place a long time ago. The police probably consider it a cold case, something to work on when they have extra time, but not a priority. Still, it's their job to solve the crime, not mine."

Calpurnia edged closer to the food. One paw came up to forage. Rather than let her climb onto the table, I put the nearly empty plate on the floor for her. I know. I shouldn't encourage her. So sue me.

While she cleaned up every trace of my breakfast, I continued to ponder what it was that motivated me to poke my nose into something that was really none of my business. True, I'd seen Grace's remains up close and personal and wanted her killer found and punished for what had been done to her, but I'd never met the woman. Given what I'd learned about her, I doubt I'd have liked her. Was I on a quest to right an old wrong or was this just some sort of intellectual exercise?

No one deserved what had happened to Grace, I told myself, and I was in a unique position with regard to those who had known her before her death. No matter why I was pursuing this, the fact that these people would talk to me, more or less willingly, and tell me things the police might not think to ask about, seemed sufficient reason to keep asking questions. With only moderate effort on my part, I had a good chance of stumbling upon something relevant to the investigation.

"Naturally," I said aloud, "if keeping my eyes and ears open and asking a few questions produces tangible results, I will at once share what I learn with Detective Hazlett."

Calpurnia, having polished off my left-overs, responded to this virtuous statement of intent with a yawn.

"Am I boring you?"

As if in answer, she flipped her tail at me and walked away.

Snooping aside, I had plenty to keep me busy that day, activities with no connection to Grace or the historical society. I spent the next six hours working on clients' manuscripts. After those were done, I tackled the boxes stored in the attic. I wouldn't be able to start redecorating until I'd gone through them.

The first carton I opened was labeled "pictures of the kid" and contained old photographs. My father took an extraordinary number of photos of me while I was growing up. Since I have no children of my own to inherit them, I gave serious consideration to tossing the lot. I didn't know why I'd saved them in the first place. I'd just never been able to bring myself to throw them away.

Once I started sorting, I discovered one reason why it was helpful to hang on to such mementos. Quite a few of the photographs showed portions of my house as it had been during my childhood. I even found a copy of the Christmas card I'd remembered, the one that showed me sitting in front of the hearth with my Christmas stocking hanging from the mantel behind me.

I stared at that posed shot for a long while, thinking that maybe I *should* have the fireplace opened up again. It would be nice to sit by a crackling fire on a cold winter's evening. I made a mental note to have another talk with John Chen.

Another picture showed a group of neighborhood children. We stood in the driveway, before the boards from the old barn had been repurposed to build the garage. Behind my head, I could just see the section of trelliswork that covered the gap between the floor of the front porch and the ground. Part of the basement wall showed as well. I frowned, trying to call up another elusive memory. There was something about those lightweight crisscrossed pieces of wood . . .

All at once, I remembered, and the memory brought a smile to my lips. One section of the skirting pulled out to give access to the area beneath the porch. I recalled how dark and dirty it had been under there, smelling of damp earth and infested with bugs and spiders. At age six or so, I'd thought it was the best hiding place in the whole wide world.

The second box I opened contained more recent memorabilia — yearbooks from my teaching career. These, I promised myself, I *would* get rid of. I could do without seeing pictures of myself as I slowly grew older. Avoiding the "teachers" section, I flipped through a few, looking at group photos of former students. I recognized very few faces. Even in the most recent years, it was a struggle to identify anyone.

Once I'd put everything back in the box, I sealed it with strapping tape. If I couldn't recall the names of young people from as little as ten years ago, students I'd seen day in and day out throughout an entire school year, how could I expect members of the historical society to have clear memories of events and people from a quarter of a century in the past? If they remembered anything at all, they were likely to confuse the details. I'd already seen proof of that in the stories I'd heard so far. They hadn't contained too many outright contradictions, but not everyone had remembered events the same way.

An hour later I went back downstairs. For all my doubts, I remained committed to learning all I could about Grace Yarrow's stint as pageant writer and director. The only way to gain a true picture of the past was to continue asking questions of everyone who had been around at the time. The memories were there. They just needed jogging. When I had accumulated enough recollections, I should be able to reconcile the details, weeding out individual biases along the way. Although the effort might ultimately prove to be a waste of time, it could just as easily lead to the discovery of significant information about Grace's murder.

That I'd found some old student newspapers in the boxes in the attic inspired a better excuse to use going forward. I intended to say I was writing an article about the bicentennial. That would give me a logical reason to question people who'd known Grace. With that cover story, I should be able to persuade everyone from the mayor to the boys on the stage crew to talk to me. I might even be able to convince Gilbert Baxter to answer more of my questions.

At best, my subjects would take advantage of the opportunity to reminisce. At worst, they'd humor the annoying old lady with too much time on her hands and cooperate just to get rid of me.

CHAPTER 26

Bright and early the next day, I drove to the municipal building. I didn't think Tony Welby would be too busy to see me. The only question was whether or not he'd be in his office. Lenape Hollow isn't big enough to need a full-time mayor.

The town clerk and other office help have a large work area. The mayor occupies a space not much bigger than my walk-in closet. Granted, I have a large walk-in closet, but I expected the person in charge to have better accommodations.

He smiled at my bemused expression, once again showing off the large, slightly crooked front tooth I'd noticed when we met at Ronnie's house. "I have a reputation to maintain," he joked. "I got this job on the promise I'd pinch pennies. My first act as mayor was to move in here and rent out the original mayor's office to the State Gaming Commission. They turned it into a

Lottery Prize Claim Center. Win-win, as they say. Win-win."

I squeezed myself into the miniscule office and took a seat in the single chair facing his cluttered desk. Although the mayor wasn't a large man, he gave the impression of being the biggest thing in the room. He regarded me with expectant curiosity.

"What can I do for you? Mikki, isn't it? What can I do for you, Mikki?"

I wondered if Welby knew he had a habit of repeating part of what he'd just said. I'd noticed him doing the same thing the first time we met.

Pasting a smile on my face, I lied through my teeth. "I'm writing an article on spec about the quasquibicentennial, a sidebar to coverage of the event. The big day is coming up fast now. Less than two weeks away. I'm hoping you'll be willing to share some of your reminiscences about the first pageant and the other events the historical society sponsored twenty-five years ago. I understand you were a teacher at the high school back then."

He nodded amiably and leaned back in his chair. "Teacher and part-time guidance counselor. Guidance — what a thankless job! I don't know where I found the energy to volunteer for so many worthy causes, too."

I interrupted before he could find a phrase to repeat. "We were all a lot younger a quarter of a century ago."

"Isn't that the truth! Well, I don't know that I remember a great many details. It's all a bit of a blur in hindsight. A bit of a blur."

"You didn't have a role in the pageant, but I gather you went to some of the rehearsals."

"Well, yes. I put in an appearance. I was running for office, and of course I wanted to see how my protégé was doing. You've heard, no doubt, that I supported hiring young Grace Yarrow to write the script. Grace Yarrow." He shook his head, a forlorn look on his face. "Such a shame what happened to her."

"I had heard." I'd been wondering how to broach the subject and was relieved he'd introduced it himself. "Did she show promise as a writer when she was your student?"

He waggled one hand from side to side. "She was only so-so at everything she did. To be honest, I helped her more because I felt sorry for her than because she had any real talent. The poor kid needed someone to give her a break. Her parents divorced and when they both left town, she moved in with an aunt so she could finish school here in Lenape Hollow. The aunt was more interested in her own social life than in looking after her niece. It was no surprise when the girl ran wild. Ran wild," he repeated, shaking his head.

"Is she still living?"

"The aunt? No. She died a few years ago. Years."

Another dead end.

"If you went to bat for her, Grace must have had some ability to string words together." It made no sense that he'd recommend a complete amateur. "Wasn't the pageant intended to be the centerpiece of the bicentennial?"

"The *parade* was the big attraction," he corrected me, "and Grace was adequate for the task. Not that she was there to see it through. Still, the script she wrote was produced and people seemed to enjoy it. My wife and I were in the audience." He nodded as if to himself. "Yes, people seemed to enjoy it."

"Did you believe at the time that Grace had run off to pursue a career on Broadway?"

"To tell you the truth, I didn't give it much thought. I suppose you've already

256

heard there were . . . conflicts toward the end. Frankly, everyone breathed a sigh of relief when she left. Ronnie took over as director and the whole thing came off without a hitch. Without —"

"Ronnie North directed the pageant?" There was *another* little detail no one had bothered to mention to me.

"She was Ronnie Henniker then, but yes, she did. Yes, she did."

I couldn't help myself. For about thirty seconds I seriously considered the possibility that Ronnie had killed Grace so that she could take her place. Then I came to my senses. Ronnie liked to be the center of attention, but she'd been on the board back then, just as she was now. If she'd wanted to replace Grace as director of the pageant, she could easily have done so without the use of violence.

"Ronnie North," Mayor Welby repeated. "Remarkable woman."

"Good thing she never took it into her head to run for your job," I quipped.

His laugh had a hollow sound. "True. True. Now, then, what else can I tell you? I'm afraid I don't recall any particular anecdotes. You're looking for colorful stories, I assume, to capture your readers' interest."

I stared at him in confusion. I'd gotten so caught up in thinking about Ronnie and Grace that I'd momentarily forgotten the excuse I'd given him for asking questions in the first place. There was a little too much enthusiasm in my voice when I blurted, "Exactly. Exactly."

Damn. Now I was repeating myself! The habit was infectious. I hoped he didn't think I was mocking him, but he appeared to be oblivious to his own verbal quirk.

I couldn't help but wonder if his constant repetition of words and phrases had so annoyed his constituents that it eventually cancelled out the force of his personality. Welby had an abundance of charisma, but he'd never been elected to any office higher than state legislator. Then again, maybe he'd decided that being a big fish in a small pond was a better gig. I didn't ask. I was only interested in his life at the time he first threw his hat into the ring.

"If you don't mind," I said hesitantly, "there is one other thing I'm curious about. This isn't for the article."

"Yes?"

His eyelids had dipped to half-mast. A fringe of lashes long enough to make any woman envious prevented me from seeing the expression in his eyes, but I sensed a certain wariness in that one-word question.

"I don't mean to embarrass you, but someone mentioned that you quarreled with Grace a day or two before she disappeared."

"Curious?" he repeated. "No, I think the term you're looking for is out-of-line. Yes. Out-of-line. You've no call to be questioning me about an incident I'd just as soon forget."

"I've heard one version of the exchange. I'd like to hear yours."

He glowered at me for a long moment before abruptly relenting. "I overreacted to something Grace said." He shrugged. "It was an overreaction. That's all it was."

"Was she . . . flirting with you?"

His jaw tensed. "I don't know what she was up to, but her comments were inappropriate and since the entire cast of the pageant was in earshot, I was not about to laugh them off. There must have been at least twenty people present and Grace not only crossed a verbal line, she rubbed herself against me in a suggestive manner. At that, I'm afraid I lost my temper. I told her what I thought of such behavior in no uncertain terms, after which she apologized and said she'd only been teasing. I accepted her apology, and that was that. That was that."

259

"She'd never tried anything similar before that day?"

"With me? Of course not."

"But you'd known her for some time, when she was a student?"

He made a pyramid of his hands and stared at it while he spoke. "My duties as a guidance counselor were limited to helping students choose a college. It would have been inappropriate for me to inquire into Grace's behavior, but I couldn't help but hear the rumors. She had an active sex life, even before she graduated from high school. Even before." He shook his head as if he found that difficult to believe. "I attributed her recklessness to low self-esteem."

"Someone told me she liked older men, especially if she thought they could help advance her career."

"Well, that's blunt!"

"Her . . . habits didn't make you hesitate to recommend her to the board of the historical society?"

"My intent was to assist a former student in achieving her career goal. Her personal life was none of my business. I can't say I was surprised when she left so suddenly, but like everyone else, I assumed a better opportunity had come along. I *was* embarrassed when she left people in the lurch. I apologized profusely at the time. Profusely."

Of course he had. He'd been about to run for office. He'd been worried that he'd be blamed for Grace's actions.

"I wonder sometimes if I could have done more to help her." Regret underscored Welby's words and his shoulders drooped. "Perhaps if I'd referred her to a psychiatrist, or convinced her to enroll in the local community college, things might have turned out differently. She was a difficult youngster, though, likely to do just the opposite of what anyone in authority suggested." On a long, drawn-out sigh, he repeated, "Just the opposite."

"You *tried* to help," I said.

He seemed to appreciate my attempt to console him, but had no further information to offer about Grace's associates or her activities, other than those relating to the pageant, in the days before her death.

After I left the mayor's office, I had much to consider. If Grace had acted inappropriately with Tony Welby, a man who had only wanted what was best for her, then she hadn't been a very good judge of character. It followed that she might have been mistaken about the way someone else in her life would react to her behavior. When provoked, that person had struck back, and Grace Yarrow had ended up dead.

CHAPTER 27

That afternoon, I made a phone call to Florida and talked to Bud Graham. My pretext of writing an article about the bicentennial worked wonders with him. He was happy to reminisce about the good old days when he'd been in charge of the historical society. He sounded as if he missed Lenape Hollow, making me wonder why he didn't come back, at least during the summer months when the weather was warm. I wasn't sure how old he was, but the tremulous quality of his voice confirmed he was getting on in years, and the occasional pause for a phlegmy cough suggested he had health issues, as well.

"Why are you asking me about this again?" he asked after recounting the same story Judy had told me about the scrim getting caught on a stage light.

"We're celebrating the 225th anniversary of the founding of Lenape Hollow." Hadn't

I already told him that? I wondered if his memory was going.

"I got that, but you keep asking about the pageant in particular. Why?"

"Because we're doing it again. Well, a version of it, anyway."

There was nothing wrong with his memory! My explanation set off a rant about the stupidity of repeating something that had been a waste of time and money the first time around.

"Badly conceived, badly written, and badly produced," he declared as he wound down.

"The new version is much better," I assured him, "despite the time constraints and the furor when the wall collapsed."

Dead silence reigned on the other end of the phone line.

I cleared my throat. "I guess you haven't heard about that."

"Guess I haven't. You want to fill me in?"

As succinctly as I could, I gave him the details.

Given his strong feelings about Grace's work, I expected some reaction. He didn't say a word until I prompted him by asking if he had any theories about what might have happened.

"You asking me who killed her?"

"Do you know?"

He gave a strangled laugh that started him coughing again. When he caught his breath, he was short with me. "You don't need to know that for this article you're writing."

"No, but you can't blame me for being curious. Grace was killed at the historical society, Mr. Graham. Odds are good that the person who murdered her was someone you knew from your work there."

This concept seemed to stump him, but not for long. "I'd lay odds on Elise if she wasn't so tiny. Maybe she had help."

My heart began to beat a little faster. Was he onto something? "Who would have helped her back then?"

This time his answer came without hesitation. "That Baxter fellow had the same reason as Elise to be ticked off at Grace. The way I remember it, Grace dumped him to take up with Elise's husband."

Clutching the phone a little tighter, I asked, "Did you ever hear either of them threaten her?"

"Can't say as I did." He chuckled. "Nope. The only one doing any threatening was Judy Kenner. Heard her light into Baxter one day when I was trying to concentrate on some paperwork and they were in the vestibule."

"I'm confused," I admitted. "Why was Judy upset."

"Because Baxter dumped her to take up with Grace, of course. What? You think people with an interest in history are stuffy? Peyton Place had nothing on Lenape Hollow back in the day."

Flummoxed is the word that best describes my reaction to this statement. By the time I figured out what else I wanted to ask him, Bud Graham had hung up on me.

CHAPTER 28

I'd already made plans to have supper at Darlene's house that evening. Frank had a meeting to go to, and she needed a guinea pig for a new recipe she was trying, a delicious Middle Eastern dish with a name I couldn't pronounce. The whole house was redolent with enticing, exotic aromas.

During the meal, I brought her up-to-date on the results of my amateur sleuthing. The only thing I left out was Bud's claim of an affair between her sister and Gilbert Baxter. We were clearing away the dishes and I was working up to broaching that subject when the front doorbell rang.

"It's open," Darlene shouted. "Come on in."

I sent her an amused look. "You'd better hope it isn't our friendly local ax murderer."

It was worse. Ronnie North stormed through the living and dining rooms and into the kitchen, eyes shooting sparks, breathing fire . . . well, you get the idea. All that heat was directed at me.

"There you are! Honest to God, Mikki, you are such a pain in the butt."

"What did I do?"

"You told Bud Graham you're writing an article about the bicentennial. You made it sound as if I authorized it."

"Oh, well —"

Darlene interrupted before I could plead guilty. "Settle down, Ronnie. This has nothing to do with you."

We both turned to look at her. I hadn't come right out and told Bud that Ronnie had suggested I talk to him, but in the process of explaining who I was and what I was doing, I *had* allowed him to leap to that conclusion.

"Mikki's starting a blog," Darlene announced.

As much as I wanted to deny it, I thought better of contradicting her and kept my mouth shut. If Darlene's lie got Ronnie off my case, who was I to object?

"It's going to be called 'Lincoln's Language Log' and it's mostly about writing," Darlene elaborated. "You know — Mikki's pet grammar peeves? But she's also planning to blog about local events and life in Lenape Hollow. Right, Mikki?"

"Uh, right. Although I haven't settled on the name for the blog yet."

Faced with Darlene's earnest enthusiasm and unaware that my friend had been lobbying me unsuccessfully for months to do something on social media to promote my editing business, Ronnie backed off. She didn't apologize, of course. Admitting she was wrong went against her nature.

"You might have been clearer about that when you talked to Bud." Her lips pursed into a thin, disapproving line.

I leaned back in my chair and attempted to appear nonchalant. "I take it he phoned you?"

"He did. He wanted to know if the police have made any progress in finding Grace Yarrow's killer." She paused, her frown deepening. "I must say, he didn't seem too distraught when I told him the investigation appeared to be stalled."

"They haven't discovered anything at all about what happened to her?" Darlene asked.

"Not that I can see, and I asked the mayor himself to monitor their progress for me." Smug satisfaction laced her voice. "It helps to know the right people. Tony Welby has enough influence to get answers the general public can't."

Having impressed us with her importance in the pecking order of the village, Ronnie cut her losses and declared she had a pressing commitment elsewhere. I waited until I heard the front door close behind her before I spoke.

"I am *not* starting a blog."

"You'll have to now. She'll be on the lookout for it."

"Let her look," I muttered.

Darlene ignored me. "If you don't want to call it Lincoln's Language Log, we can go with the other title we discussed."

"The Write Right Wright Writes?"

"That's the one."

"We've been over this before, Darlene. I don't want to blog under any name. Aside from the amount of time it would eat up, I don't have anything to say. Blogging is useless if you don't have followers, and the only way to get them is to post something new and interesting every single day."

"You have lots of pet peeves when it comes to writing."

"Not enough to for three-hundred-sixty-five blogs a year."

"That's okay. As I told Ronnie, you're also going to post pieces about life in Lenape Hollow. Just think of all the wonderful topics you can explore."

270

I sighed and went back to clearing the table, the task we'd left unfinished when Ronnie barged in on us. "Such as?"

"Nostalgia is a gold mine. Stories from our high school days. Bits of trivia. You can start with charm bracelets. After we were reminiscing about pajama parties the other day, I was hunting for something else in my jewelry box and came across mine. It has three horse charms." She grinned. "I was mad about horses in those days."

"Did your bracelet come with a charm that showed the number sixteen with a high-heeled shoe on either side of it?"

"It did." Her grin broadened. "Learning how to walk on stilts was a rite of passage back then."

"Except that our mothers wouldn't let us wear anything but those little ones — what do they call them?"

"Kitten heels."

We both laughed at the memory.

"We wanted so badly to be grown up and sophisticated," I said. "Now I sometimes wish we could regain the innocence of youth."

"No, you don't."

"No, I suppose I don't. Do you think Ronnie's right about the police being sty-mied?"

"Well, if her good friend the mayor said so . . ." There was more than a hint of sarcasm in Darlene's voice.

"I wonder if what I've learned so far can help them? I'm sure the people I spoke with told me more than they revealed to Detective Hazlett, but I'm not sure any of it means anything."

"You should talk to him," Darlene said. "Let him sort the wheat from the chaff. Just be prepared to listen to the standard lecture afterward. He'll remind you you're not Nancy Drew and then warn you not to meddle in police business."

I shook my head, remembering what the mayor had said. "Not Nancy Drew. At our age, the amateur sleuth of choice has to be Miss Marple."

CHAPTER 29

We were both wrong.

The next day, after I'd shared the results of my snooping with the good detective, he informed me that Mrs. Pollifax couldn't have done better. I stared at him, stunned. Not a fictional amateur detective, but a fictional spy?

"Was that a compliment?"

His eyes warmed by a fraction of a degree at hearing the suspicion in my voice. "It was, but don't let it go to your head. I'll be honest with you, Ms. Lincoln. We're getting nowhere on this case. Any insight you have to offer is more than welcome."

"I thought I'd have to defend myself. Say something like, 'I can't help it if people talk to me,' or 'I just hear things' before you suggested that I might want to remove my hearing aids."

"Good one. I had no idea I was so clever."

"Did the autopsy reveal anything helpful?"

He hesitated and then, with a "oh, what the hell" shrug, told me that Grace had been killed by a blow to the head.

"That doesn't help you much, does it? Anyone could have done it."

"Good summary."

I hesitated, remembering my far-fetched, briefly held theory about my young cousin. It was no more likely to be true now than it had been the night of tryouts, not when we shared a physical feature as obvious as the Greenleigh nose, but that didn't rule out a variation on the theme.

"Did the autopsy reveal whether or not Grace had ever had a child?"

His gaze sharpened. "Why do you ask?"

"Humor me."

"It's apparently possible to determine that when dealing with a fresh body, although not with a hundred percent accuracy. Given the condition of the remains, no such determination could be made."

He waited for me to explain why I wanted to know.

"You're the one who asked me if Grace had children. Remember? No one has suggested that she did, and even if there was a child, he or she would hardly be a suspect in her murder. He'd have been what? Two or three years old at the most?"

"She was twenty-four when she died. Given what we've learned of her life, she could have had a child at fifteen or even younger. But you're right. Even a nine- or ten-year-old, presumably given up for adoption and unaware of his real mother's identity, isn't a likely suspect. An adoptive parent would also be a long shot."

So much for that idea.

He looked down at the notes he'd made while we talked. I'm not good at reading upside down, but even I could see that he'd listed five names at the bottom of the page: Gilbert Baxter, Elise Sanders, Ronnie North, Bud Graham, and Judy Brohaugh.

"You should add those boys on the stage crew," I said. "The ones Judy told me about. I looked up their names on the program." I rattled them off and he dutifully wrote them down.

When he looked up, there was a faint smile on his craggy face. "If you were thinking of interviewing these men for your imaginary article, Ms. Lincoln, I can save you the trouble." He tapped the middle name with the eraser end of his pencil. "This gentleman, now a respectable businessman in our little community, came in of his own volition as soon we released the victim's identity. He thought we'd want to know what he remembered about her."

"And?"

The twinkle in his eyes was a good match for his smile. "He offered a detailed account of an encounter between himself and Grace Yarrow that took place in a supply closet at the historical society. It was apparently the most memorable sexual experience of his young life."

"Let me guess — he didn't notice anything beyond her . . . physical attributes."

"Young men are somewhat single-minded at that age. Seventeen, in case you're wondering. She was older, experienced, and she warned him that if he ever bragged about what they'd done, he'd regret it. She threatened him with a very jealous ex-boyfriend."

I sucked in a breath. "Gilbert Baxter?"

"Let's not jump to any conclusions. And, Ms. Lincoln? Although I want to hear about anything further you might happen to learn, it would be best if you stopped asking pointed questions. The person we're looking for cracked open Grace Yarrow's skull. I'd hate to have the same thing happen to you."

"I'll be careful," I promised. "In particular, I'll stay away from Baxter."

It wasn't so much being bashed over the head that worried me. It was that the killer

276

had so successfully hidden his victim's body that it took a freak accident twenty-five years later to reveal his crime.

Stupid murderers make mistakes and get caught.

Smart ones? Maybe not.

CHAPTER 30

I went home resolved to get some editing done, but wouldn't you know it? Everything I read seemed custom designed to send my thoughts straight back to Grace Yarrow's murder. I turned to Valentine Veilleux's coffee-table book, hoping that working on the text to go with cute photographs of kittens and puppies would distract me. It didn't. The first jpeg file I called up showed a droopy-eared mutt staring with abject longing at a white poodle walking away from him.

"Oh, for heaven's sake!"

I shut down the file. Then I closed my laptop. Calpurnia, who was curled up on the windowsill in a sunbeam, opened one eye, gave me a hard stare, and closed it again.

"Obviously, my subconscious is not about to let things be," I muttered.

She had no reaction to that statement.

I'd come home from the police station fully resolved to meddle no more. Anything else I learned about the case would be purely by accident, or so I told myself. Only a few hours later I already knew it wasn't true. I'd thought of several angles I could pursue without coming into direct contact with my prime suspect.

There was no doubt in my mind that Gilbert Baxter had the best motive for killing Grace — jealousy. I could imagine him rationalizing with the old "if I can't have you, no one will" excuse. But there were loose ends, things I might yet discover that tied — you should forgive the pun — into the larger mystery. Those bits and pieces might also exonerate other people, Judy Brohaugh in particular. If Bud Graham was right and she'd been seeing Baxter before he took up with Grace, she had a pretty good motive for wanting the other woman out of the way. For Darlene's sake, if not for her sister's, I wanted to eliminate Judy as a suspect in the murder of Grace Yarrow.

I glanced at my watch. Diego had scheduled a rehearsal for five o'clock. It was the first one to be held outdoors at the site where the pageant was to be performed. Darlene had told me that she and Ronnie planned to be there. As members of the board, they assumed they had a standing invitation to kibitz. I smiled to myself. Diego Goldberg might appreciate having someone there to distract those two from taking too keen an interest in the way he staged the production. Wasn't it lucky that they were also the two people most likely to confirm or deny Bud's salacious memories of the good old days?

Up until now I'd avoided telling Darlene what he'd said about her sister, but it wasn't as if she didn't already know that Judy was capable of indulging in an illicit affair. Once I shared that story, I hoped she'd be able to offer some insight into how serious the relationship might have been, and into how Judy was likely to have reacted when it ended.

The gate at Wonderful World, Greg Onslow's aborted attempt to create a theme park, had undoubtedly been inspired by *Jurassic Park*. Both sides stood open, giving access to a long, winding road that ended in an enormous parking lot. At least twenty cars had arrived ahead of me, but they took up only a fraction of the available space. Onslow dreamed big.

When I got out of my green Ford Taurus, I was uncertain which way to go. I stood beside the car, turning my head this way

and that, hoping for a clue. At first everything was quiet. Almost too quiet. No
birdsong. No traffic noise. Then I heard a
burst of laughter off to my right. As soon as
I headed in that direction, I spotted a paved
walkway winding through the trees.

A few minutes later, I came out into the
open. My jaw literally dropped at the sight
in front of me. It appeared I'd been wrong
about the lack of construction at Wonderful
World. Onslow had built himself an amphitheater. Wide stone steps led down to a
center stage, past stone benches set into the
hillside.

Nothing like this had existed fifty years
ago. When I was growing up in Lenape Hollow, Onslow's land had been two separate
parcels. One had contained what was left of
the grounds of a turn-of-the-nineteenth-
century grand hotel and the rest had belonged to the village. The swimming hole
and picnic area had been reserved for the
use of year-round residents, not that many
summer people would have been aware of
being excluded. The whole setup had been
pretty rustic.

As I descended, I kept a sharp eye out for
Darlene and Ronnie and spotted them
about halfway down and off to my left. I
was just wondering how Darlene had man-

aged the steps when I caught sight of a ramp designed for wheelchairs and scooters. Thinking back on the path I'd followed to get to this point, I realized that although it looked as if it was paved with individual flagstones, it was actually perfectly smooth. Whoever had designed the amphitheater seemed to have thought of everything.

Rehearsal had not yet begun. When I noticed Diego, deep in conversation with my cousin Luke, I continued on down to speak with them first. They greeted me warmly when I joined them.

"I hope you don't mind if I sit in on rehearsal."

"Delighted to have you," Diego said, "and I'm glad to have the chance to thank you for recommending Luke here. He's an excellent actor and an even better assistant director."

I sent my cousin a considering look, wondering exactly what he'd told Diego. There had been no recommendation involved, since I hadn't known he intended to try out. If he'd implied that I *wanted* him to have a role in the pageant, then he'd out and out lied. I didn't bother to hide my disappointment in him, but neither did I make an issue of it. When Diego called "places," I turned quickly away, meaning to

282

climb back up to where Darlene and Ronnie were sitting and deal with Luke later.

Unfortunately, I wasn't watching where I was going. I stumbled over someone's abandoned backpack. Arms wind-milling, I caught my balance but only narrowly avoided a fall. Luke caught me by the shoulders to steady me.

"Are you okay? You could have broken something if you'd hit the stage floor. It's solid rock and old people have brittle bones."

Although I heard genuine concern in his voice, I was still miffed at him, and I didn't much care for his choice of words. "My bone density is excellent, thank you," I snapped, "and you might want to consider referring to people my age as mature. Adjectives like 'old' and 'elderly' should be reserved for folks in their eighties and nineties."

I didn't give him a chance to apologize. Without further incident, I left the stage and began to climb. My back to the rehearsal, I sidled into the row of seats in front of the one where Darlene and Ronnie were sitting.

"Have a nice trip?" Ronnie asked.

Darlene sniggered.

I refused to rise to the bait. Instead I said

brightly, "I had no idea this was here. When did Greg Onslow build it?"

"He didn't," Ronnie said. "Although he probably would have if he'd thought of it. The amphitheater was the brainchild of one of the previous owners. That old fool bankrupted himself in the process. All Onslow had to do was repair what was already here."

"To be fair, he also made it handicap-accessible." Darlene grimaced at the admission. She disliked Onslow almost as much as Ronnie did.

Since I wanted to see their faces when I asked my questions, I kept my back to the activity below. I aimed my opening remark at Ronnie.

"I had lunch with Judy Brohaugh the other day."

"So I heard." She gave Darlene the side eye, obviously hoping for a reaction.

Darlene tensed but said nothing.

"Were you interviewing her for that blog of yours?"

Ronnie's voice was so snide that I felt sure she knew Darlene had taken liberties with the truth. Her attitude alone was almost enough to convince me I *should* start blogging.

I also realized that I was going about this all wrong. My exchange with Luke had

284

thrown me off my game. I'd completely forgotten that I'd intended to talk to Darlene about her sister in private and then question Ronnie. I shot an apologetic look her way, but I wasn't about to lose this chance to get some answers.

"Actually, Ronnie," I said, "I was trying to find out what Judy remembered about Grace. She shared several interesting anecdotes, but she was less forthcoming when it came to her relationship with Gilbert Baxter. I'd never have guessed they were so close if someone else hadn't mentioned it."

Ronnie's eyes narrowed. "Bud Graham, I suppose. And they say women like to gossip!"

"What are you talking about?" Darlene reached out to clutch my sleeve. "What did that old blabbermouth say about my sister?"

"He told me Judy was involved with Baxter during the planning for the bicentennial. Is that true?"

"That's what I remember," Ronnie said.

Darlene looked dumbstruck. Her hand fell away from my arm, limp as a wet noodle. "But . . . but . . . he's *years* younger than Judy. How could she . . . ? How could he . . . ?"

"It didn't last long," Ronnie said in a brusque voice. "He moved on."

"Yes. To Grace Yarrow. A tiny detail no one else thought to mention to me."

"I didn't know," Darlene whispered.

Ronnie ignored her, fixing her attention on me. "Why should you care who Judy was fooling around with?"

"It's Baxter who interests me. Baxter and Grace. Remember Grace? The one who got herself murdered?"

"Oh. I see. You're still playing detective." She frowned. "Do you mean to say you think Gilbert Baxter killed her?"

"I think it's entirely possible."

I'd been so focused on Darlene and Ronnie that I'd blocked out our surroundings. I didn't realize someone had come up behind me until he spoke.

"You've got no call to make such a filthy accusation!"

I nearly jumped out of my skin at the sound of Baxter's angry voice. Heat crept into my cheeks as I turned to face him. He was standing only two rows below me, right next to the mayor of Lenape Hollow.

"Tell her where she went wrong," Ronnie challenged him. "If you've got nothing to hide, prove it."

"I don't have to defend myself to you." Although Baxter was clearly ticked off that we'd been talking about him, he was nowhere near as furious as he'd been the other day, when he caught me speculating about the very same thing with Shirley.

Following Ronnie's lead, I went on the offensive. "Do you deny you had an affair with Grace Yarrow?"

"My relationship with Grace is none of your business."

"What about your relationship with my sister?" Darlene demanded.

"That was a mistake. A fluke. Judy was hurting because she'd just found out her husband was cheating on her. I was handy." He sounded surprisingly bitter. "As for Grace . . . well, Grace Yarrow *dated* a lot." He looked to the mayor for confirmation. "Back me up on this, Tony."

"That was always the rumor. I never had any firsthand information. Never firsthand."

"Well, I did. Right from the horse's mouth. She used to brag about her conquests."

I perked up at that. "Can you remember any of their names? I'm sure the police would like to question all of Grace's lovers. And," I added, "if you are innocent, sharing that information might get you off the hook."

He gave a short bark of laughter. "She never bothered with names, just gave graphic descriptions of what she liked them to do to her."

"Are you sure? Not even a hint?"

"Maybe you'd like me to share the nasty details instead? Maybe you'd enjoy hearing them."

"I'm not into cheap thrills." Truthfully, I was starting to feel a little creeped out. "Was that offer supposed to make me any less suspicious of you? If it was, it backfired badly. You're the lover who had access to the historical society. You're the one who knew the chimney was about to be sealed off."

He should have been red in the face and sputtering in indignation by the time I stopped leveling accusations. He surprised me by keeping his cool.

"If I killed her, would I have stuck around all these years? If I'd known there was a body there and thought there was the slightest chance of it being discovered, why on earth would I have authorized repairs on the building?"

Shirley had raised the same points. I'd dismissed them because I'd been certain Baxter couldn't have expected the entire wall to come down. Nothing I'd heard since had changed my mind, but Ronnie was more easily persuaded.

288

"Makes sense to me," she said. "To tell you the truth, Gilbert, I never doubted your innocence, but we needed to get all this out in the open. Mikki's right about one thing. You should go to the police and tell them everything you can remember about the other men in Grace's life."

I kept my mouth shut.

"I agree," the mayor said, putting one hand on Baxter's forearm. "I'd give the matter some more thought first. Sleep on it, but then go to the police station first thing in the morning. First thing."

Between the two of them, they persuaded Baxter to agree.

"Tomorrow, then, but it'll be a waste of time."

He started to turn away, then paused as if struck by a thought. His lips quirked into an expression of wry amusement.

"I *do* remember one thing Grace told me. One of her lovers had a distinctive birthmark in a very . . . intimate location." He chuckled. "I'd like to see the police try to follow up *that* lead."

CHAPTER 31

The next morning I was still working on my first cup of coffee for the day and thinking that I really should start limiting myself to one if I wanted to keep my blood pressure under control — those of us who are approaching age seventy have to think about such things, even if we're lucky enough to have avoided serious health problems so far — when someone rang my doorbell.

At least I was dressed. If I'm anxious to get to work on an editing project, I grab my initial dose of caffeine and settle in at my desk still wearing my nightgown and bathrobe. Sweatpants and T-shirts aren't the height of fashion, but this set was clean and relatively unrumpled and therefore presentable. Besides, anyone who calls on me at the uncivilized hour of eight in the morning shouldn't expect to be greeted by a fashion plate.

Feeling put-upon and a bit grumpy, I

stalked out of the kitchen, down the hall, and into my tiny foyer. I took the precaution of peeking through the small window in the front door before I deactivated the security system. Once I saw who was standing on my porch, curiosity won out over any inclination I might have had to pretend I wasn't home.

"Detective Hazlett," I greeted him. "What brings you out so bright and early in the morning?" I stood back to let him in. "Coffee?"

"Only if it's already made."

"You get your choice of K-Cups."

He went with French vanilla, black, while I made myself a second cup of the local grocery store's "original" blend, sweetened with two packets of Splenda and a dash of half-and-half. I watched him closely as he took his first sip. His expression was even more unrevealing than usual, but it seemed to me that his face had a grimmer cast than I was accustomed to seeing.

When his eyes shifted from his drink to fix on me with a laser-like stare, I held both hands up in front of me. Shield? Surrender? I have no idea what provoked the reaction, but the next words out of my mouth were, "Whatever it is, I didn't do it."

He winced, plainly not amused. My trepidation increased and I had to swallow hard before I could speak again.

"What's happened?"

"I'll tell you in a minute. First I need to know where you were last evening."

My eyebrows shot up. "I'm suspected of something? Seriously?"

"Just answer the question, please."

I took a sip of coffee to soothe a throat that had abruptly gone dry. "I was at the pageant rehearsal for an hour or so. I wasn't paying much attention to the time." Suddenly I remembered why the police might be interested. "Gilbert Baxter was there, too. He was supposed to contact you this morning, but I suppose it's still too early."

"What about after you left the rehearsal?" His stone-faced expression gave nothing away.

"I came home, had a bite to eat, answered some emails, watched a little television, and went to bed. I suppose it was around ten when I turned in. I wasn't paying close attention."

"Can anyone verify your whereabouts between seven and seven-thirty?"

"Only the cat."

I wondered where Calpurnia was. Ordinarily, she showed up the moment a visitor arrived. She'd certainly been front and center when I stumbled downstairs in search of caffeine. Then again, since the first thing I'd done, even before making coffee, was feed her, she was probably taking a postprandial nap.

"Too bad she can't talk," Hazlett said.

His comment alarmed me. "Do I need an alibi?"

I was beginning to have a bad feeling about this conversation. On the other hand, I took it as a good sign that he hadn't written anything down in his little notebook.

"Let's just say I need to cover all the bases. Were you with someone the entire time you were at the rehearsal?"

"Pretty much." I thought back. "I exchanged a few words with the director, Diego Goldberg, and with my young cousin, Luke Darbee, who's in the cast and serving as Diego's assistant. Then I joined Darlene Uberman and Ronnie North in the audience. Gilbert Baxter and Mayor Welby were there, too, but they left some time before I did."

"When, exactly, did Baxter and Welby leave?"

The hairs at the back of my scalp prickled at the intensity in his softly voiced question. "Did something hap— ?"

"Just answer the question, please, Ms. Lin-coln."

I huffed out an exasperated breath. "They took off right after Ronnie, Darlene, and I talked with them. I don't know what time that was. Early. Probably no later than five-thirty or six."

"And you didn't see Baxter again after that?"

"No, I didn't. What's happened? Has he gone on the lam?"

"He's dead."

I felt myself blanch. "Suicide?"

"He didn't kill himself," Hazlett said. "It's nearly impossible to whack yourself over the head with a blunt object."

Just like Grace.

I opened my mouth, then closed it again when I couldn't think how to ask any of the questions tumbling around in my mind. Detective Hazlett wouldn't have answered them anyway. Judging by his interest in my activities during the remainder of the evening, I was on his suspect list.

"It's a good thing I save all my email correspondence with clients," I said. "I also print out copies of those emails and my replies and tuck them into manila folders for easy reference while I'm editing." At his look of surprise, I felt compelled to defend myself from yet another unspoken accusation. "Go ahead and call me a dinosaur! It's easier for me to deal with paper copies than to hunt through electronic files. Besides, my old-fashioned habits are about to make it much simpler for me to prove I didn't kill Gilbert Baxter."

"I never said you did."

"You were thinking it. Wait right here."

When I went up to my office to collect the evidence, I found Calpurnia curled up on the desk next to my laptop. She followed me back downstairs to the kitchen and watched with intent interest as Detective Hazlett looked over the printouts that confirmed I'd been where I'd said I was at the time Baxter was killed.

It struck me then, with the force of a two-by-four upside the head, that someone had just eliminated the prime suspect in Grace Yarrow's murder. We were back to square one.

Hazlett finished reading the printouts and returned them to me without comment. When Calpurnia put her paws on his thigh, demanding attention, he obliged by stroking her. I could have used some reassurance myself.

"So, am I off the hook as a suspect?"

"Looks like you're in the clear, and you

were never a *serious* suspect, even if you did have words with Baxter at yesterday's rehearsal."

"Words? You make it sound as if we quarreled. He just got a little huffy because the three of us were speculating about motives for Grace Yarrow's murder and he overheard us mention his name."

"You accused him of committing a capital crime. I don't think you can blame him for getting a little hot under the collar."

I scowled at him. "I guess it makes sense that you had to verify my whereabouts at the time of his death, but by the time he left, he wasn't upset with me or Darlene or Ronnie. Ronnie had convinced him we didn't really think he was a killer."

He raised an eyebrow at that.

"I still thought Baxter might have murdered Grace," I admitted. "He *was* one of her lovers. He'd been trying to hide that fact."

"He told you that?"

"Yes, he did, and he added a few smarmy details, too. As I've already said, when he left rehearsal, he was planning to meet with you this morning. He intended to tell you everything he knew about the other men in Grace's life."

"What other men? Who were they?"

"He insisted he didn't know any names."

Hazlett didn't so much as bat an eyelash, but I had a feeling that he was mentally rolling his eyes.

Calpurnia abandoned the detective and hopped into my lap, bunting my hand until I took over cat-stroking duties. As always, this simple action had a calming, soothing effect.

We sat in silence for a few moments. He finished his coffee. I let mine go cold. Finally, he shoved back his chair and stood.

"I've got to go."

"Wait! You can't just drop a bombshell like that and not fill in the details. Are you sure his death wasn't just a mugging or a burglary gone wrong?"

"It does *look* as if someone broke into his house," Hazlett conceded, "but it's too early to say for certain if that's what really happened."

I imagined he was thinking the same thing I was. Although there are occasional break-ins in our otherwise peaceful little village, for Baxter to have been the victim of one at this particular time was a pretty big co-incidence.

"Who found him?" I asked.

He hesitated, still on his feet and poised to escape.

"I know you have no obligation to answer my questions, but if Baxter didn't kill Grace, then it stands to reason that he was probably killed because he knew who did."

He sat down again. "I thought you said he didn't know any names."

"That's what he said, but he did mention that Grace used to boast about her other conquests. In detail. Right before he and the mayor left, Baxter told us about one of those details, a distinctive birthmark one of her lovers had. I don't think he knew who the man was then, but what if he figured it out later? If he was foolish enough to contact that person —"

"You need to stop speculating," Hazlett interrupted. "More than that, you need to stop asking questions. If you're right, and the same person murdered both Grace Yarrow and Gilbert Baxter, then the last thing you want is to make him think you're a threat to him. Neither of us will be happy if you to end up as victim number three."

I swallowed hard. He was right. If the killer feared I was getting too close to the truth, he — or she — might decide to make a preemptive strike.

"Don't you have *any* leads?"

"Not at this point." He stared into his empty coffee cup, a morose expression on his face. "It's only thanks to the mayor that we're been able to pin down the time of Baxter's death with such accuracy." He shifted his gaze to me, looking even more grim. "I expect you to keep what I'm about to tell you to yourself until we issue a press release later today."

"No problem." I mimed zipping my lips and earned myself a formidable glower.

"According to Mayor Welby, Baxter was going straight home after he left the rehearsal. They had plans to meet again later that evening for dinner. They had reservations at Jeremiah's for seven o'clock. It was to be a business meal, something to do with a change in the schedule for the quasquibicentennial."

So much for the mayor's penny-pinching policy, I thought. Jeremiah's is the most expensive restaurant in town.

"When Baxter didn't show up and didn't answer his phone, the mayor drove to his house to check on him. He found the front door open and Baxter dead. That was around quarter to eight."

"Hence the questions about my whereabouts from seven to seven-thirty."

He cracked the tiniest of smiles, no doubt at my use of the word *hence*.

"Why not earlier? I'd have had time to

bop him on the head if I stopped by his place on my way home. You're taking it on faith that I didn't."

"Do you even know where he lived?"

"No, but I could be lying, and that's something it would have been easy enough for me to find out."

This time when Hazlett stood, he kept going. "Don't worry. I'm not ruling anything out, but if the same person murdered both Yarrow and Baxter, then there's no way you can be considered a suspect. You weren't living here a quarter of a century ago."

I walked him to the door, still trying to make sense of this new development. I had been so sure Baxter was guilty.

Hazlett was already on my porch when he turned so abruptly that I almost ran into him. I retreated into the foyer, pulling the screen door closed after me, and faced him from the other side.

"If you're right," he said, "and what got Baxter killed was figuring out what really happened twenty-five years ago, then you need to be extremely careful from now on. Too many people know you've been snooping around, and a good many of them could have seen you talking to Baxter at the rehearsal or heard about it afterward."

"I promise I won't take any chances, and

300

I'll contact you right away if I think of anything, no matter how trivial, that might have a connection to either case."

"Good. I'll wait while you lock the door and reactivate your security system."

I made a face at him but followed orders. I'd have been a fool not to. It's a pain to remember to turn it on, and I tend to hit wrong numbers on the keypad if I'm rushing to punch in the code before the alarm sounds, but a woman of a certain age, especially one living alone, knows the wisdom of taking common-sense precautions.

CHAPTER 32

The historical society was open from twelve-thirty to six on Wednesdays. I arrived about five minutes after Shirley unlocked the front door. One look at her face told me that she'd already heard the bad news.

We adjourned to her office to commiserate over ritual cups of coffee. Apparently, Detective Hazlett had gone straight from my place to Shirley's.

"Gilbert wasn't a bad man," she said. Then she laughed at herself. "Listen to me, always the first to criticize him. He was a royal pain, but he didn't deserve what happened to him. The only blessing is that his wife and the boys weren't the ones who found him."

I choked on my coffee and turned to stare at her. "I didn't even know he was married."

I hadn't, I realized, known much about him at all. That was unforgiveable, especially given how convinced I'd been that he was a murderer. I'd looked at his life twenty-five years ago and jumped to conclusions while completely ignoring anything he'd done between then and the present day.

"Sally," Shirley said. "She's from Albany originally, and that's where her folks still live. She and their sons have been visiting them for the last week. The kids are ten and twelve. Will and Bobby."

Now I really felt like a worm, except that all the negative things I knew about Baxter were still true. Just being dead didn't change his personality, or erase his involvement with Grace Yarrow. I filled Shirley in on the last time I'd seen him and what he'd said about Grace, then recounted that morning's conversation with Jonathan Hazlett. Since he'd already interviewed Shirley, I had no qualms about repeating what he'd told me, even if the information hadn't yet been made public.

"So sad," she murmured. "I don't suppose we'll ever know what really happened."

"Don't say that! Surely the police will figure it out."

"Hah! You and I have better odds than they do. They don't even know where to begin."

"And we do?"

She sent me a keen-eyed look. "Even

Detective Hazlett thinks it's likely Gilbert's murder had something to do with Grace's, and you're the one who's been going around asking questions about that one. You probably know more about the dynamics of the historical society twenty-five years ago than anyone, even the people who were here at the time."

"And I can't think of anything that makes me suspect any one of them of killing Grace. Baxter himself was my prime suspect, so I don't have a clue who murdered him. If he figured out what happened to Grace, he didn't share."

We were interrupted by a low humming sound coming from the vestibule. I recognized it at once as Darlene's scooter. She'd have come in the back way, using the ramp that made the lower floors of the building handicap-accessible. I scooted my chair around to the side of Shirley's desk to make room for her to join us, but it was Ronnie who entered the cramped office first.

"Something terrible has happened," she announced.

"I know," I said, "and now I feel bad for suspecting him of killing Grace Yarrow."

Darlene sent me an incredulous look from the doorway.

Ronnie glared. "What the *hell* are you

talking about?"

"You haven't heard?"

"Heard what?" Impatience made her voice sharp. "Spit it out, Mikki. I haven't got all day."

"Gilbert Baxter was murdered last night."

Her sharp inhalation of breath convinced me that Ronnie hadn't known anything about it. Darlene looked equally shell-shocked.

"Apparently, Detective Hazlett hasn't talked to either of you yet, so what did *you* mean?"

Two terrible things in one day seemed a bit much, but I braced myself for more bad news. Declining the stool that was all Shirley had left to offer as seating, Ronnie just stood there, spine stiff and lips pursed. I was about to tell *her* to spit it out when she finally answered my question.

"Diego Goldberg was in a car accident earlier this morning. He's in the hospital with a concussion and a broken leg. Without him, I don't see how the pageant can go on."

"Don't be ridiculous," I said, impatient with her overdramatic manner. "It's been cast. He blocked the scenes. We have volunteers taking care of props and costumes and lighting. All you need to do is find someone to supervise the rest of the rehearsals."

"I suppose that assistant of his could do it." Ronnie sounded doubtful.

"Luke is also in the pageant," I pointed out. "It might be better to find someone who can focus on direction alone."

"Why are you talking about the pageant?" Shirley interrupted. "Doesn't Gilbert Baxter's death mean anything to you people?"

"It means we'll also have to find a new director for the historical society." Ronnie looked thoughtful. "I suppose, if all else fails, I could step in during the interim."

"That's cold, even for you."

She waved off my criticism with a careless gesture, sending a faint whiff of Emeraude my way. "Don't be such a hypocrite. You didn't like him any more than any of the rest of us did."

Nobody had been all that fond of Grace, either, but dislike didn't excuse murder.

Ronnie pinned Shirley with a glare that dared her to come to Baxter's defense. The librarian kept an enigmatic expression on her face and refused to comment.

"Maybe we *should* cancel the pageant," Darlene said, making her first contribution to the conversation since she'd rolled into Shirley's office.

"What?" I swung around to face her. "Why?"

"Aside from Diego being in the hospital? How about the fact that there are two murders linked to the historical society? That's not the kind of publicity we were after, and it isn't as if we're certain we'll be able to draw much of a crowd in the first place. There's still that business of competing festivals."

Ronnie made an impatient sound. "Not that again! It's *because* mid-August is a popular time to hold outdoor events that we chose the date we did."

"You chose it," Darlene corrected her.

The way I was swiveling my head back and forth between them, I was going to have whiplash before the afternoon was out.

"The board of directors, the village board of trustees, and the town council all agreed."

Ronnie's about-face didn't surprise me, not when she'd all but appointed herself interim director. She'd probably insist on taking over for Diego, too. If I were to learn his accident was a hit-and-run, I'd know just who to suspect of driving the other car.

"Do you really think anyone wants to call more attention to Lenape Hollow just now?" Darlene asked. "Baxter's murder will generate all kinds of negative press, and

307

from what Frank's told me, the board of trustees seriously considered pulling the plug on the whole shebang after Grace's body turned up. This will be the proverbial straw that breaks the camel's back."

"Nonsense. The good publicity surrounding our 225th birthday celebration will mitigate the bad."

"Not everyone sees it that way," Darlene argued. "Some people prefer to keep a low profile in the hope that if no one calls more attention to Lenape Hollow, the notoriety will fade away that much faster."

I did a mental eye roll. Time for a little pep talk. "Darlene Uberman, I'm surprised at you. Since when have you been a quitter? And Ronnie — you're the one who sits on both the historical society's board of directors and Lenape Hollow's board of trustees. You probably have more influence than any other individual in this village. I'll bet all you have to do is tell those doubters that the celebrations are going forward with their support or without it, and that will be the end of the discussion. No one's going to argue with you if you stick to your guns."

A pleased smile played around her thin lips. "I intend to do just that, and to assure both boards that everything is under control, but I need the support of everyone in this room. Do I have it?"

With varying degrees of enthusiasm, all three of us agreed.

"Good. Shirley, you are now acting director of the historical society. And Mikki?"

"Yes?"

That Ronnie wasn't taking over Baxter's job suddenly made me wary. I had the uneasy feeling I wasn't going to like what she said next.

"In the interest of keeping everything running on schedule, I'm sure you have no objection to filling in as pageant director. The next rehearsal is scheduled for six o'clock this evening at the amphitheater."

CHAPTER 33

After I left the historical society, I drove to the hospital to visit Diego. I'd never been inside this facility before. It was two towns over and hadn't been built yet when I last lived in Lenape Hollow. Back then, we'd had two small hospitals of our own. One of them had originally been established to treat patients with tuberculosis, since the Catskills, like the Rocky Mountains, were thought to have healthy air capable of cur-ing that dreadful disease.

Diego's room had an antiseptic feel to it, even though I couldn't detect any of the odors I tend to associate with hospitals. The aroma wafting up from a bouquet of as-sorted flowers overpowered every other scent.

The pageant director had one leg in trac-tion. The bruising on the side of his forehead and the slightly loopy expression on his face told their own story.

He spotted me the moment I appeared in the doorway. "I look worse than I feel," he called out by way of greeting.

A woman was sitting in the chair pulled up to the head of the bed. She smiled and introduced herself. "I'm Audrey, wife of this lead-footed fool."

"Mikki Lincoln. I —"

"Oh, you're the one who wrote the pageant."

"Not on my own, but I plead guilty to putting together parts of it." I shifted my attention back to Diego. "I'm so sorry this happened to you, and I mean that sincerely. Ronnie suckered me into taking over for you in the director's chair."

He winced. I decided to take that as a sympathetic reaction.

"Any tips?" I asked. "The most I've done in the past is stage a few in-classroom skits written by my students."

"My absence will hardly doom the production." He sounded resigned, but none too happy about the situation. "Anyone can be a show runner. It's really just a question of the actors buckling down and learning their lines. They have their blocking. We worked all that out yesterday." He winced again, this time because he'd twisted his head around to scan the room. "There's a black loose-leaf binder in here somewhere. Where did you put it, Aud? It has all my notes in it."

His wife unearthed the object in question from the bottom of a stack of books and magazines. Apparently, Diego was a holdout when it came to reading and scorned electronic devices in favor of paper.

A quick glance inside the binder showed me a heavily annotated copy of the pageant script. Fortunately, Diego had neat handwriting that was easy to read. He'd even used different colors of ink to distinguish between lighting cues, notations about props and scenery, and stage directions.

"This is great. Thank you."

"Just make them keep practicing until they can run through the dialogue in their sleep," he advised. "When they do it in costume, with the music and all, the audience should feel that they've gotten their money's worth."

It took me a moment to translate what he was really telling me. "In other words, you don't have the most talented cast in the world?"

A weak smile confirmed my guess. "We work with what we have. Every teacher knows that, right?" He looked down at his leg and grimaced. "This is going to present a challenge when school starts. If I'm *lucky,* I'll be on crutches by then."

"Scooters can be fun. Just ask Darlene Uberman."

He managed a morose chuckle at my pitiful attempt to lift his spirits.

"I don't suppose you could recommend someone with more experience than I have to take over as director?"

Diego seemed to be fading, but he flashed me a smile. "It's okay. You've got this."

"I'm not so sure about that." Half to myself, I added, "Things didn't go very well for the last pageant writer who tried to direct her own work."

Although he'd started to drift off, Diego shook himself awake long enough to mumble a response. "Trusting you with secret."

Startled, I stared at him. My first thought was that he knew something about Baxter's murder, but that didn't make any sense.

"What secret?"

"Secrets," he corrected me, rallying. "Directing secrets. They're in the notes. Purple ink."

"Ah. For a minute there I thought you were about to confess to a crime."

Confusion slowly gave way to enlightenment on his bruised and battered countenance. "Naw," he said. "I couldn't have

313

killed what's-her-name. Grace. I was only a kid at the time."

I wondered if Diego had heard about Gilbert Baxter's murder. I decided it was unlikely. He'd been otherwise occupied for most of the day.

"Too young to interest her," he murmured sleepily. "Too young to *take* an interest. Not like some people." He sent a groggy leer my way.

"I didn't realize you were old enough to remember the bicentennial at all." I knew he hadn't been one of the boys on the stage crew. His name wasn't in the program.

"Nope." The word slurred as he closed his eyes. "Never looked at kiddie porn, either."

"I beg your pardon?"

When the only answer I got was a snore, I looked to Audrey for an explanation. The fact that she was smiling fondly at her husband relieved my mind.

"He's kind of out of it," she said with the hint of an apology in her voice.

"You think? Dare I ask if you know what he was talking about?"

"In fact, I do. There was an incident at the high school several years ago. All this talk of secrets and crimes must have triggered the memory." Her smile vanished. "It isn't a pretty story."

"I'm afraid I'm too curious to let you off the hook."

"Sadly, what happened isn't all that rare. One of the coaches had a heart attack in his office at the high school. He was on his computer at the time . . . looking at pornography of the worst sort. The pictures were still showing on the monitor when Diego stopped by to talk to him about a student whose grades were about to get him kicked off the basketball team. My husband probably saved the coach's life, but since he also reported what he'd seen to the authorities, the man was not particularly grateful."

"There are a few bad apples in any profession, but it's especially appalling when they're in positions of trust — teachers, police officers, scout leaders, preachers. The worst part is that they're so often able to conceal their true nature for years, using their influence to silence those who know, or have been victimized by them."

"You're preaching to the choir." Audrey glanced at her sleeping husband. "Thanks for stopping by, and for taking over for Diego. He'll have enough to worry about for the next little while without fretting about the pageant."

"I'm sure he'll be back in front of the classroom in no time."

"From your mouth to God's ear."

I was in a much better mood when I left the hospital room, in part because of Audrey's choice of words. I hadn't heard that expression since I was a teenager. It brought back a lot of good memories.

CHAPTER 34

By the time I reached the amphitheater that evening, most of the cast had already assembled. They'd heard about Diego's accident and were understandably upset. As soon as they caught sight of me, they stopped milling aimlessly around and turned as a body to stare in my direction.

"Hey, Ms. Lincoln," one of the girls called out. "What's going to happen with the pageant?"

"Nothing." I speeded up my descent but waited until I reached the performance area at the center of the amphitheater before I explained. "The show must go on, right?" I held up the binder. "I have Mr. Goldberg's notes."

A notable lack of enthusiasm greeted this news. I wasn't surprised. Although some of the cast members knew who I was, most didn't have a clue.

"That'll work," Luke said, earning a grate-

317

ful smile from me. "She wrote most of the pageant. She knows what to do."

From your mouth to God's ear, I thought.

"Places, everyone," I said aloud. "We'll start at the beginning."

While Luke and the other young people playing the founders of Lenape Hollow arranged themselves, I tried to imagine them in period costumes. That was no easy task when they were wearing modern clothing suitable for a hot summer day. Almost everyone had opted for some form of shorts, wearing them with T-shirts, crop tops, and even one halter top. Diego's actors were almost all high-school students, making Luke one of the oldest people there. I hoped makeup could age the rest, but I had a feeling adding a fake beard or two wasn't going to be much help.

Once launched into the rehearsal, things progressed slowly but without any serious setbacks. The actors still carried their scripts, but that was only to be expected. In another week at most, they'd have their lines memorized. Exactly fourteen days remained until our one and only performance.

When he wasn't needed onstage — or our version of one, since there was no proscenium or curtain — Luke joined me at the small table set up for the director's use. He

318

didn't say much, but when he did make a suggestion it was usually a good one.

"Have you done much directing?" I asked him.

He shrugged. "Drama major in college."

"Maybe you should be the one in charge."

"Bad idea. Directors who star in their own movies are like lawyers who defend themselves."

"Or writers who direct their own plays?" I asked, remembering what Judy Brohaugh had said on that subject.

He had the grace to look abashed.

"Never mind. With your help and these notes, I'll muddle along." Diego's binder lay open on the table in front of us.

"You ought to ask Adam for suggestions."

I sent him a questioning look. I'd learned a few of the cast members' names, but I didn't yet have all of them firmly attached to faces. Was there an Adam? I couldn't recall.

"Adam Ziskin," Luke said helpfully. "He's rounding up props for this production, but he talks about the one at the bicentennial all the time. Maybe he'll have some ideas."

My memory having been jogged, I remembered seeing the name Ziskin on the program. He'd been one of the "boys" on Grace's stage crew.

"Is he here?" I asked. "Will you point him out to me?"

Luke obliged, directing my attention to an overweight, middle-aged man standing off to one side to watch the actors run through their lines. When he glanced our way, I beckoned to him.

Adam did one of those classic moves, looking behind himself to see whose attention I wanted. When he realized there was no one there, he pointed to himself and mouthed, "You mean me?" At my nod, he ambled over to join us at the director's table.

"You don't look old enough to have worked on the bicentennial pageant," I said after Luke introduced us.

"Well, I wasn't old enough to vote or to buy beer, but I was a big kid and they needed muscle to move the sets around." He was still hefty, but the critical mass had shifted from upper body to midsection.

"How does this pageant compare?" I asked.

He shrugged. "Your script is better than the last one, but that's not saying much. History's kind of boring, no matter what you do with it." As an afterthought, he added, "Sorry to hear about Diego's accident."

"Yes, I suppose you knew him back then, too."

He grinned. "Sure. Little Diego Goldberg. He must have been nine or ten at the time. He tagged along everywhere we went."

"Even when you were dismantling out-buildings in the middle of the night?"

"You heard about that, huh?"

"I hear a lot of things." I glanced at Luke. "Could you check with the cast and see if they're ready to resume rehearsal?"

"Uh, that would be up to you, Mikki. You're the director."

I sent him a too-sweet smile. "Just ask, okay?" My cousin didn't need to hear the questions I had for Adam, or Adam's answers.

By the time I turned back to the older man, a knowing expression had come over his florid face. "Something else you wanted to know?"

"I'm assuming you're one of the people Detective Hazlett interviewed after Grace Yarrow's body was found."

He nodded. "Want me to repeat what I told him?"

"I'll settle for having you confirm that she was rather free with her favors. I don't need to hear the details."

"Okay. Yeah, she was. That summer was a

real learning experience for some of us, and I'm not talking about history lessons."

Some instinct told me that he meant more than a single encounter in a supply closet, the only incident Hazlett had mentioned. "These days that kind of behavior with underage boys would land Grace in jail."

He shrugged. "She wasn't my teacher or my boss, so it wasn't exactly sexual harassment."

"But you *were* underage, and as pageant director she was in a position of power."

His grin widened. "Sure was." Clearly, Adam didn't feel she'd taken advantage of him, but that didn't make Grace's behavior any less predatory.

"Did you know who else she was, uh, seeing?"

The moment I asked, I realized that no one at the rehearsal had mentioned Gilbert Baxter's murder. I knew the press release had gone out, but it was possible the news hadn't reached them yet. Either that, or their lack of interest stemmed from the fact that the cast and crew didn't connect him with the pageant. Although he'd attended the previous day's rehearsal with Tony Welby, he hadn't, so far as I knew, interacted with anyone else besides Ronnie, Darlene, and me.

"She was probably getting it on with every guy in the pageant," Adam said. "My older brother was in the same class with her in high school. He said she was a wild woman even then."

"Did you go to the police with this information or did they track you down with their questions?"

He sent me an incredulous look. "Why would I borrow trouble? They came to me."

I forced an encouraging smile. That meant he wasn't the one who'd told Detective Hazlett about the ex-boyfriend with a temper.

"Did Grace ever mention another lover, one who might have been jealous of her playing around with high-school boys?"

He shook his head. "I'd have told the cops if she had. Huh! You think he was the one who killed her?"

I thought I heard an undercurrent of relief in his voice. Had he really thought Hazlett suspected him of the crime?

"Is there anything you *didn't* share with the police?" I asked.

His eyes narrowed, and his earlier friendliness was no longer in evidence. His defensive walls had gone up. "What are you getting at? And why do you want to know, anyhow?"

Rather than lose his cooperation, I blurted

323

out the truth. "I was at the historical society when Grace's body was discovered. I want the brute who did that to her caught and punished. Promiscuity isn't a crime, and it certainly doesn't warrant a death sentence."

"Okay. Okay. I get it." He eased into the folding chair Luke had vacated, but he was nowhere near as nonchalant as he'd been a few minutes earlier. His hands clenched where they rested on the table in front of him. "I never heard a name, but there was a rumor going around while she was still in high school that she was carrying on with an older guy. I guess he might have had a reason to be jealous, huh?"

"I guess he might," I agreed, although it seemed doubtful to me. That relationship must have dated from a half dozen years before Grace's murder. Still, I wasn't about to rule out any possibility. The affair might have continued beyond Grace's high school graduation. "Do you have any idea who he was?"

Adam shook his head. "My brother said they used to swap stories about Grace in the locker room. Odds are good at least half of those guys were lying when they bragged about what they'd done with her. Maybe the older boyfriend was something one of them made up, too."

I sighed. I'd like to believe attitudes have evolved, and that young men nowadays are more sensitive to women's feelings, but I suspect the "boys will be boys" mentality hasn't changed much over the years.

"Hey, Mikki!" Luke hollered from the staging area. "We're ready when you are."

"You got any more questions?" Adam asked.

"Only one. Do you have a birthmark?"

He sent me another incredulous look. Then he laughed. "No, and I don't have any kinky tattoos, either."

I hid my flaming face by pretending to hunt for my place in the script.

Diego's notes were thorough, and his instructions were easy to follow. He had already figured out solutions to most of the problems that might arise during rehearsals. As he'd assured me, all the production needed now was someone to keep the show running. The job promised to be time-consuming, but not otherwise onerous, and Luke proved to be a willing and knowledge-able assistant.

Working closely with him, I had the op-portunity to probe a bit more into his past. I had no doubts about our relationship — he did have the Greenleigh nose, after all — but from time to time I still had the feeling he was keeping something from me.

"Where's home?" I asked when he joined me at the director's table during a short break in the rehearsal.

"Ohio. My mom still lives there." He caught sight of my raised eyebrows. "What? Where did you think I lived?"

"From the Red Sox T-shirt you were wearing when we first met, I was guessing somewhere in New England."

"Gift from an old girlfriend," he explained. "She was from Braintree."

With a sideways look, I examined the jeans and tee he was currently wearing. The denim was ratty and sported holes at both knees. The T-shirt was clean, but it, too, had seen better days. He was the very picture of a young man on a limited budget.

A short time later, when a piece of scenery had to be rearranged and the actors sloped off to refresh themselves with drinks from the cooler Ronnie had sent over, Luke took me aside. He had a serious expression on his face.

"I owe you an apology, Mikki," he said. "I didn't tell Diego you said I should be in the pageant, but I should have straightened him out when he made that assumption. I just wanted him to know I had a local connection, y'know?"

"Don't worry about it. I'm sure he cast you for your talent, not because of any misconception about how close we are."

Misconceptions are all too easy to come by, I thought when he took his place on-stage as the comic at the Feldman. I'd begun to feel a little guilty that I hadn't invited my cousin to stay with me for the duration. I hated to think of him living rough in a pup tent and commuting to rehearsals on that battered old Vespa. I doubted he was eating right, either. It wouldn't kill me to ask him to come and share a meal or two at my place.

By the end of rehearsal, I still hadn't decided how much, if anything, I felt comfortable offering. The moment when I might have broached the subject was preempted by Spring Ramirez, one of the girls in the cast.

"Hey, Luke," she called to him. "We're going for pizza. My treat," she added. "Today is my eighteenth birthday."

I wondered if she meant to stand them for beer as well as pizza. Then I remembered that the drinking age in New York State was changed to twenty-one sometime in the 1980s. It was eighteen when I was young. We'd considered ourselves quite grown up by then.

Perceptions do indeed change, I thought as I followed the merry band of laughing youngsters to the parking lot. To a girl of eighteen, my twenty-something cousin probably qualified as an "older guy." That gave me more food for thought as I headed home to spend *my* evening with my cat.

CHAPTER 35

For the next couple of days, I was too busy to do anything but edit, supervise rehearsals, and accede to Calpurnia's demands for food, water, and fresh kitty litter. I hit no major snags in any of those areas, but neither did I have time for snooping. This made it easy for me to follow Detective Hazlett's advice and leave looking into the murders of Grace Yarrow and Gilbert Baxter to the police.

Shirley was a huge help. She marshalled the resources of the historical society and saw to it that the million and one details entailed in mounting a production were taken care of — mostly by delegating authority to people who actually knew what they were doing. Programs were proofed and printed, props and costumes acquired, signs made, and ads placed.

Luke was in his element, picking up on ways to tweak the performances. Here and there he added bits of action to make the scenes more lively. Who'd have thought there could be opportunities for humor in a series of historical vignettes?

I found unexpected pleasure in working with young people again. The teenagers Diego had recruited from the high school were a lively bunch. In some ways, their interests were alien to me, but in others I saw a little of myself when I was their age. Times change. Human nature doesn't. The biggest difference I noticed was that where we'd been reticent to talk about certain subjects, and blissfully ignorant of others, these teens weren't afraid to speak up. I learned a bit more than I wanted to in some areas.

"I don't put up with that crap," said Spring, the young lady who'd just turned eighteen. "That old pervert tried to grope me, so I decked him."

She was talking about a custodian at the high school who'd been assigned to help with the concession stand set up in a cloakroom during basketball games. There was zero tolerance for inappropriate behavior, once it came to light. The man had been fired.

"Good for you," I told her.

Thinking back, I'd been fortunate. Or

perhaps naïve. Except for one fellow student at a frat party, I'd never been grabbed against my will or subjected to any other unwanted sexual advances. Let me amend that. If there were other incidents, let's say a sly suggestion on the part of a male colleague, it went right over my head. I had been bullied by the principal of the first school I taught in, but I more or less ignored him, and after a few years he took another job and moved on.

At my age, I assume I'm past the point where anyone is likely to hit on me. My success or failure in business isn't dependent upon anyone but me. In any case, I don't dwell on such matters. I prefer to take joy from the little daily pleasures. The pageant was coming together. The festival honoring the founding of Lenape Hollow was going to take place. Even if only local residents turned out for the event, I'd personally consider it a success.

Then, a week before the performance, I opened an email and faced a new complication. Valentine Veilleux, my coffee-table book client, wrote to say there might be a glitch in publication plans. The editor who'd bought the project had left the publishing house and her replacement wanted changes to the manuscript. Val requested a meeting with me, in person, in two days' time. She'd be passing close enough to Lenape Hollow on her way to a new photo shoot to manage a side trip.

It was an unusual request, and one I could have turned down, but I found it impossible to ignore her plea for help. Besides, I was curious to meet her. What I knew of her from our correspondence, and from her wonderful photographs, intrigued me. Although squeezing a work session into my already jam-packed schedule wouldn't be easy, I emailed back to suggest when and where we could most easily get together.

CHAPTER 36

Mountain View Acres wasn't even on my radar until Luke came into my life, and I had never visited the campground, but it had two advantages. It was nearby and it had space for Val's custom-designed RV. She arrived late the night before our meeting and I drove out there as soon as I was adequately caffeinated the next morning.

Val's appearance was the first surprise. No more than thirty, she was younger than I thought she'd be and what my late husband would have called "a real looker," with long, strawberry-blond hair, bright green eyes behind a pair of stylish glasses, and a trim figure. A wide smile and a throaty voice didn't hurt when it came to making a good first impression, either.

"I love being able to show off my work-space," she said when I stepped inside the behemoth that also served as her year-round home.

Instead of the standard dinette found in most RVs, Val's had a specially built computer workstation where she edited her photographs. The rest of the vehicle was given over to comfy, if cramped, living quarters. There were, essentially, four rooms. Besides her "office," she had a galley-style kitchen, a bath that squeezed in a shower stall as well as a sink and a toilet, and a bedroom with a queen-size bed. She lacked none of the necessities of modern life. The bedroom had a television and DVD player and the kitchen boasted a microwave as well as a stove and refrigerator.

Nice as it was, I'd have gone stir-crazy if I had to spend very long in such a confined space, but then I've never been a fan of the tiny-house craze, either.

Seated on a small, comfortable sofa located opposite the workstation, we spent more than two hours going over the changes Val's new editor wanted in the text of her book. To my mind, there was nothing wrong with the original version, but most of the quibbles were small, nitpicky things and not worth an argument. The rewrite kept Val's vision intact. All in all, I thought the book was in great shape by the time we'd finished.

To be honest, her photographs of dogs, cats, and other animals could have been successfully published without any captions at all. Each of the shots she'd selected had a whimsical flair that set it apart from run-of-the-mill pet pictures.

I stood up to stretch while she cleared away the coffee and muffins that had fueled our marathon work session. Turning, I found myself staring through the window behind the sofa at an even more enormous RV occupying the adjacent campsite . . . and at the much smaller vehicle parked next to it. I blinked, but the beat-up old Vespa I'd seen every day for the last week was still there.

There wasn't a pup tent in sight.

"How odd," I murmured.

"What is?" Val followed the direction of my gaze and smiled. "Oh, that? The scooter doesn't match the RV, does it? The guy who owns both came put-putting in shortly after I arrived last night. I thought my rig was a big one, but his puts mine to shame. Whoever he is, he spent some serious money on his motor home."

"The Vespa belongs to my cousin, Luke Darbee."

She must have heard the strain in my voice. Her features took on an expression of concern. "Is something wrong?"

"Only that I've been laboring under a seri-

335

ous misapprehension that makes me wonder what else I've been wrong about. A luxury vehicle like that one doesn't fit my image of a young man wandering the country to find himself." Or rather, to find his ancestors . . . if that was really what he'd been up to.

I suddenly wished I'd clung to my earlier doubts about Luke. His story had been a little hard to swallow the first time he told it, but his natural charm and his Greenleigh nose had lulled me into accepting that rather improbable tale. Now I had to wonder what he was really after here in Lenape Hollow, and what he wanted from me.

"Appearances can be deceiving," Val agreed. "Just look around you." She gestured at her living space. "I couldn't have afforded all this if I hadn't been left a legacy by my grandfather. Maybe your cousin Luke is like me, a wanderer who sank all of his cash into an RV because he likes to travel. All he needs to do is stop here and there to earn enough money to keep going."

"In that case, he'd have found a job in Lenape Hollow. As far as I know, he hasn't even looked for one." Instead, he was acting in a pageant for no pay and hanging out with kids years younger than he was.

"Maybe he's one of those tech geniuses who made millions by his early twenties."

"He says he's from Ohio."

She laughed. "They don't all live in California, or in Washington State, either."

I considered that possibility and rejected it. "From time to time, I've had the strongest feeling Luke was holding back about something, but why would he want to hide a successful career?"

"Inherited wealth?" Val suggested.

"Maybe." I gestured at the RV. "I suppose that could be a rich boy's toy. There's nothing wrong with having money. What I don't understand is why he'd keep it secret."

"Just a guess here," Val said, "but perhaps he's gun-shy about letting people in on his financial situation."

"I don't understand."

"Well, I've never been rich —"

"We have that in common," I said with a chuckle.

"But there *are* people out there who look on anyone with money as a target. They try to hit them up for loans . . . or worse. Look what happens to lottery winners when they go public."

"Hmmm," I said, thinking it over. "You may be right."

Val glanced at the clock mounted on one wall of the RV. "I've got to hit the road. It was good meeting you, Mikki, and I owe you big-time for all your help on the book. Can I offer you a bit of unsolicited advice before I go?"

"I'd like to think an old dog can still learn new tricks."

"And you said that with a straight face! I love it. Seriously, though — stay here after I leave. Talk to your cousin. Ask him straight out why he led you to believe he was living hand to mouth."

We said our good-byes and I waved as she drove off. Then I squared my shoulders and marched up to the door of the other RV. Luke opened it with a steaming mug of coffee in one hand and a surprised expression on his face.

"Mikki. What are you doing here?"

"Invite me in and I'll be happy to explain."

He did and I did and when I added that I was astonished to find him living in the lap of luxury, he put down the mug and sat with hands dangling between his knees and head bowed, a true picture in dejection. I reached across the slight space between us to pat his arm.

"I thought you were hurting for cash. I came close to inviting you to stay with me until after the pageant, so you wouldn't have the expense of the campground and the cost of gas to drive back and forth."

"I didn't realize." For a moment, he stared off into space. Then he turned his head and met my eyes. "Here's the thing, Mikki. Usually, when people find out I'm loaded, they look at me differently. The way they act toward me changes. All of a sudden, they think I'm a soft touch. Some of them even think I'm too stupid to know when I'm being conned. One girl, a girl I really liked, called me a miser because I didn't hand over a wad of cash, as if that would magically solve all her problems."

The bitterness in his voice made me wince. Val had been right. He had good reason to be circumspect about his financial situation.

"You're too young to be a miser," I said in a mild voice, "but if you think I would have hit you up for a loan, then that's just plain insulting. Don't you know me better than that?"

"I didn't in the beginning. And later . . . well, it just didn't come up, okay?"

I sighed. "I had a feeling you were hiding something from me. I'm just glad it wasn't anything truly terrible."

"Like what?" He relaxed enough to meet my eyes.

"Oh, I don't know. A warrant out for your arrest? A plot to get me — the senile old lady — to sign over my house and life savings to my destitute young cousin?"

"You're about as senile as . . . as . . . well, I can't think of anybody right off the top of my head, but some really smart, really sharp person, okay?"

"Okay. Thank you. I think."

We looked at each other and started to laugh. When I'd subsided, except for a couple of stray giggles, he invited me to lunch to make up for misjudging me.

"My treat," he said. "After all, I can afford it!"

CHAPTER 37

I suggested Harriet's, not because I still had any worries about Luke's finances, but because it's my favorite spot to have lunch. I enjoy the pleasant, homey atmosphere and the simple delight of eating well-prepared comfort food. The aromas that greeted us the moment we walked in made my mouth water — Ada baked some of her own breads and rolls and today she'd prepared something laced with garlic.

"Why the smile?" Luke asked.

"Just a stray memory. My mother was a plain cook, easy on the seasonings. I'd never tasted anything flavored with garlic until I was invited to have supper at a friend's house. I was probably ten or eleven and not particularly good at hiding my feelings. I don't think I actually said 'yuck' when I tasted the chicken, but I did make a face. Luckily, my friend's mom was sharp enough to understand the reason behind my reaction and didn't take offense."

"My mother isn't big on spices or seasonings, either. She doesn't even use salt when she cooks." He contemplated the condiments tray at the table we chose. "That's probably why I sprinkle way too much of it on my burgers."

"Tell me about her," I urged after we'd given our orders.

Luke shrugged. "You know the basics. She raised me after my dad split. She had a good job. She's a CPA, but she was also into amateur theatrics. She used to take me with her to rehearsals when she was in a play, or directing one. Pretty soon, I was hooked, too, same as with the family tree climbing. Her interests got to be mine."

"Did you ever see your father?"

He shook his head. "It wasn't until after he died that I found out he'd come from money, and that a pretty big chunk of it was earmarked for me. You remember Lawrence Greenleigh? The one who was illegitimate? He invented some widget or other that revolutionized the way cars are manufactured. I'm a little hazy on the details, but the upshot is that he had a bundle to pass down to his heirs and, for a miracle, none of them turned around and lost it."

"Lucky you."

"Lucky me," he agreed. "The whole idea of not having to worry about money took some getting used to, especially when I saw the way some of my so-called friends reacted to my good fortune."

Just as Ada set our plates in front of us — a cheeseburger and fries for Luke and a club sandwich for me — the door opened to admit five people all talking at once. Belatedly, I realized that Ada had already shoved two tables together in preparation for their arrival.

"There must have been a meeting of the village board this morning," I whispered to Luke.

He looked up from his burger with mild curiosity. "Oh, yeah?"

At the same moment, Tom O'Day spotted us. His eyes lit up and he hustled over, but it was my cousin he addressed, not me. "I see you finally connected. Excellent."

"You two have met?"

"This is the young man who was looking for you — when? Must be nearly a month ago. Back before the trees came down. Marie and I *told* you about him."

"So you did. I'd completely forgotten."

Too bad I hadn't made the connection sooner. Knowing Luke had been in town before Grace's body was found, and well

343

before it was identified, might have prevented my overactive imagination from going off on a tangent about secret babies. Then again, maybe not.

When Tom rejoined his party, Luke explained that he'd tracked me down on the internet, even finding my home address there. He'd swung by on his way to check out another branch of his family tree, and it had taken him longer than he'd expected to get back to Lenape Hollow. That our first meeting had ended up being at Harriet's had been pure chance.

We finished our lunch and were about to leave when my hearing aid beeped at me to signal that the battery was about to quit. Luke, who had followed my car into Lenape Hollow on his scooter, went on ahead to rehearsal while I stayed behind to fish a fresh battery out of my purse and replace the nearly dead one. As often happens when I reinsert one of the hearing aids, I accidentally turned up the volume.

The words "fooling around with your sister-in-law" blasted my eardrums.

I whipped my head around to stare at the occupants of the joined tables. The voice had been female and the only woman in the group was Ronnie North, but to whom had she been speaking? I had four choices: Joe

344

Ramirez, Tony Welby, Tom O'Day, and Frank Uberman. It took me only a moment to zero in on Frank. He was glaring at Ronnie with ill-concealed outrage.

In that same moment, I realized that Ronnie, for all she'd sounded so loud to me, was speaking in a whisper too low for the other three men to hear. If I hadn't been fiddling with my hearing aid, I'd never have caught her words.

I wished I hadn't. Frank . . . and Judy?

No wonder Darlene and her sister barely spoke to each other!

I made no effort to turn my volume down. Instead, I eavesdropped shamelessly, stretching my ears to hear Frank's response.

"Never happened," he said through gritted teeth.

"So you say." If Ronnie had used that smug, superior tone with me, I'd have been tempted to slap her face. Frank subsided into brooding silence.

Tom, Joe, and the mayor had been engaged in an intense discussion of their own, a debate over some financial issue or other. Tony Welby broke off, oblivious to the tension between Ronnie and Frank, to ask her if she had any immediate concerns about plans for the quasquibicentennial.

"Everything is progressing smoothly," she

345

assured him.

"Good. Good." Welby picked up the check and everyone but Frank stood up.

A few minutes later, after the others had left the café, he was still sitting there. I signaled to Ada to wait a moment before clearing his table and slid into the chair Ronnie had just vacated.

"I'm sorry," I said, "but I overheard part what Ronnie said to you."

His head shot up. The look of anguish on his face nearly brought tears to my eyes. Whatever had happened all those years ago, he was truly sorry for it now. But what *had* happened? And when? And why would Ronnie bring it up now?

"Do you want to talk about it?" I took a quick look around. Frank and I were the only two customers left in the restaurant and Ada was busy out back in the kitchen.

"Not particularly."

"Look, obviously Darlene forgave you, if not her sister, so —"

Frank glared at me. "Darlene doesn't know anything about it because there was no 'it' in the first place. Max Kenner had a real problem with the truth. He'd lie about his affairs and then try to convince everyone that it was Judy who was fooling around."

346

"But she was."

"Oh, I know she broke up the Brohaughs' marriage, but that was years after the perfectly innocent incident Ronnie was needling me about."

"Frank, Judy was having an affair with Gilbert Baxter around the time of the bicentennial."

The look of shock on his face convinced me he hadn't known anything about that relationship. His reaction didn't really surprise me. The Frank Uberman I knew, a man I'd first met when we were both in diapers, doesn't have a mean-spirited bone in his body. He tends to see the best in people, not the worst.

"Surely you can't believe —"

"Oh no, Frank. Not a chance. You'd no more cheat on Darlene than she would on you."

"You were ready to believe it a couple of minutes ago."

"Only because —" I broke off. Why had I, for even a moment, accepted Ronnie's accusation as the truth? Why had I been so certain Darlene had forgiven her husband?

The answers weren't long in coming.

"Someone must have told Darlene that Judy made a play for you," I said slowly. "Probably the same gossip who told Ron-

347

nie." I'd thought all along that there was more behind the way Darlene reacted to the slightest mention of her sister's name than Judy's affair with the husband of one of Darlene's friends.

"Max," Frank muttered. "I guess Darlene might have believed him. Not that I'd been unfaithful, but that Judy tried something. He could be pretty convincing, and if he was out to hurt Judy, that would be one way to do it. But why wouldn't Darlene just ask me if the story was true? I'd have told her the only reason I met her sister at that motel was to give her advice about finding a divorce lawyer."

"Maybe you should have told Darlene everything without being asked." I tried to make my voice gentle, but I knew he heard the critical undercurrent. "And maybe you should have thought twice about meeting her at a motel."

"Max had given her a shiner. She didn't want anyone to see her until the bruising healed. And she didn't want Darlene to know. I promised her I wouldn't say anything."

"Idiot." I sympathized, but it seemed absurd to me that a simple misunderstanding should have lasted for decades when one short conversation early on could have scotched it.

Frank took the insult with good grace, but he was shaking his head, a confused look on his face. "I'm not saying you're wrong, but the timing makes no sense. That's not when Darlene and Judy stopped speaking to each other. The rift didn't come until much later, after Judy took up with Brohaugh."

My forehead knit in puzzlement as I considered the chronology. "What made Ronnie broach the subject today? Were you talking about the bicentennial?"

"Not exactly. We were discussing the whole village-town/county issue, and if it wasn't a case of cutting off your nose to spite your face to make residence in the village a prerequisite for holding office, not only in government, but in groups like the historical society. That led Ronnie's thoughts around to Judy, because she was forced to resign from the board of directors when she moved to Monticello."

"Was Max Kenner still around at the time Judy remarried?"

"I think . . . yes, he must have been, although he moved away shortly after that." His eyes widened. "You think *that's* when he started spreading rumors about his ex-wife? Why? They'd been divorced for years by then."

349

"Who knows? Jealousy? Mean-spiritedness? Does it matter?" I stood. "Come on. You need to go home and talk to your wife. Straighten her out on a few things. If Darlene had just heard from her good friend, the first Mrs. Brohaugh, that Judy was the one who broke up her marriage, and Kenner chose that moment to reveal that his ex had also had an affair with you, or at least made a hard pass, Darlene might have believed it."

"But why wouldn't she confront me? I'd have told her the truth."

"Maybe she was afraid of what you'd say, especially since you didn't tell her about the incident when it happened."

"Because *nothing* happened!"

"Nothing happened *in a motel room,*" I reminded him. We might have gone around and around on the issue all afternoon, but it was already two o'clock. Ada was waiting for us to leave so she could close up. She flipped over the OPEN sign on the door and followed that none-too-gentle hint by stomping over to our table and making a great clatter as she collected plates and glasses.

Frank sent one last anguished look in my direction and left in a hurry. I could only hope he was going straight home to talk to his wife.

hope he was going straight home to talk to his wife.

CHAPTER 38

Since I was in the neighborhood, as in right across the street from the police station, I decided to drop in there after leaving Harriet's. I wanted to know when I could have my typewriter back. At least, that's the excuse I used to get in to see Detective Hazlett.

"I'd like to hold on to it a bit longer," he said.

"Really? Why?"

He shot an enigmatic look my way and didn't answer.

"Have you learned anything from it, or from the note?"

"You know I can't talk to you about the case."

I smiled sweetly at him, a not-so-subtle reminder that he'd already broken that rule on several occasions.

"I doubt there's anything left to find after all this time, but we are trying to be thor-

352

ough. I sent the typewriter and the scrap of paper out to be tested."

"You'd be surprised what could show up. Have you ever seen that meme about the smell of an old book? For the most part, it's the smell of its death — the glue, ink, and paper, all organic compounds, break down over time and release chemicals that give off a distinctive scent. But the meme also points out that paper hangs on to odors. You can often tell something of its history if you just take a good whiff."

He choked back a chuckle. "For instance?"

"Well, smoke, if the book survived a fire or was owned by a someone with a pack a day habit, or the scent of a flower that was once pressed between its pages."

"This paper had no lingering smell of anything, and there was no water damage. No burn marks, either."

"Were there fingerprints?"

"Aside from yours?"

I winced.

After a brief staring match, he literally threw his hands in the air and told me what I wanted to know. "We found a few partials. One may have belonged to Grace Yarrow."

"That's wonderful."

"It would have been, if there had been enough for a positive ID."

"Do you think you'll be able to match any of the other partials?"

"Even if we can, what do you think that would tell us?"

"The identity of Grace's murderer," I said promptly.

He shook his head. "All it would establish for certain is that another person touched that surface at some point in the last twenty-five years. Suggestive, perhaps, but hardly grounds for an arrest."

CHAPTER 39

Rehearsal that afternoon went well. By the time it ended, I was cautiously optimistic about the success of the pageant. I doubted it would come off without a hitch, but all the actors had learned their lines, props had been acquired and were in use, and construction on our minimal set was complete. The only element as yet untested was the music, but I'd been assured that everything in that department was under control.

I had to take that promise on faith. I'm not exactly tone deaf, and I can certainly tell if a singer is seriously off-key, but beyond that I'm no judge of whether something is "good" or not. I listen to audiobooks on long car trips rather than a playlist, but if I were to make one it would probably consist of folk music from the '60s.

It belatedly occurred to me that some of the songs sung by Peter, Paul and Mary or the Kingston Trio back in the day might work very well as the score for our vignettes from the history of Lenape Hollow. I did not suggest we use them. The task of picking the tunes we'd use had been delegated to Greg Onslow and I felt compelled to let that stand. With luck, I wouldn't be in for any unpleasant surprises tomorrow, when the musicians showed up for their first run-through.

That would be Tuesday. The pageant would be performed on Saturday. How many catastrophes, I wondered, could occur in the course of the next five days?

In just one, I'd been hit by one curve ball after another. That those successive surprises had enabled me to solve a couple of minor mysteries was gratifying, but the larger one remained. I found it frustrating that there was nothing I could do to help the police with their inquiries. I was carrying on what Grace Yarrow had set in motion a quarter of a century earlier, but I wasn't any closer to discovering who'd killed her than I had been at the beginning.

Preparatory to leaving, Luke handed me the loose-leaf binder containing the script. He sent an inquiring look in my direction. "Penny for them."

"It's almost as if the pageant is going too well. I keep waiting for disaster to strike."

356

His eyes danced with ill-concealed amusement, but he kept a straight face. "Don't worry. I think I can guarantee we'll have a terrible dress rehearsal, but the good news is that, if we do, it will guarantee a great performance. That's the way it works."

"Uh-huh."

I don't ordinarily think of myself as superstitious, but his teasing reference to this well-known theatrical tradition reassured me. Feeling considerably more cheerful, I checked for anything I might have left behind and then walked beside him toward the parking lot.

"If you're willing to take potluck, I'd be happy to have you come to my place for supper."

"Can I have a rain check?" Gallantly, Luke relieved me of my car keys, unlocked the driver's-side door, and held it open for me.

I tossed the oversize tote containing the binder and a much smaller purse onto the seat on top of the sweater I'd left there earlier. "Hot date?" I asked as I slid in behind the wheel.

"Yeah, right. Who did you have in mind?" Bracing one hand on the top of the car door, he looked genuinely puzzled.

"You and Spring seem to be hitting it off, and you did go out for pizza with her on her birthday."

"Along with almost everyone else in the cast. Hey — gotta eat. But she's ten years younger than I am."

"You're twenty-eight?" I'd had him pegged at twenty-five at the most.

"As of March. Way too old for Spring or any of those other girls. They're nice and all, but they're still in high school."

His grimace made me smile. Way back in history, a man who was ten or more years older than the woman he was courting wasn't problematic. Even now, a man of thirty-five who married a woman of twenty-five didn't raise any eyebrows. But twenty-eight and eighteen? Even if Luke had been the age I'd thought he was, his interest in Spring might have raised some eyebrows. I was relieved to hear him say they were just pals.

"So what are you up to? Not that it's any of my business."

"I'm meeting a guy for drinks to talk about a job. I'll tell you about it if it pans out."

Another surprise! I wished him luck and started the engine.

The drive home didn't take long, but it gave me time to wonder what kind of position Luke had applied for. He certainly

358

didn't have to work, and neither of his interests — genealogy and the theater — were likely to be in great demand in Lenape Hollow. Even at the advanced age of twenty-eight, he was probably too young to be considered for Gilbert Baxter's post at the historical society. The only theatrical endeavors I knew of were in the schools, where teachers took on directing duties in addition to their regular jobs.

I tried to picture Luke at the front of a classroom, attempting to drum information into teenage heads. Nope. It didn't compute, but the image did jar loose a memory. When I was in high school, several of our teachers had been fresh out of college and younger than Luke by a couple of years. There had been one in particular who'd created a minor scandal when he turned up as a senior girl's graduation-night date. There was nothing wrong with that, of course. She was already eighteen and he waited until she was no longer a student before he asked her out.

I was shaking my head as I pulled into my garage. That teacher had probably been no more than four or five years older than my classmate, but no matter how close in age they were, teachers weren't, and aren't, supposed to think of their female students in a romantic, let alone sexual, way.

My late husband was a whole six months my senior. My father had been exactly one month older than my mother. That seems about right to me, but I may be biased.

CHAPTER 40

It took a while for the frantic banging on my front door, accompanied by the steady buzz of my doorbell, to pull me out of my absorption in the manuscript I was editing. I'd removed my hearing aids earlier that day, the Tuesday before the pageant, when it seemed as if every lawn mower in the neighborhood was in use at the same time.

I stuck them back in. Yes, indeed. Someone really wanted to come in. I saved my edits, closed my laptop, and headed downstairs to see what was so all-fired important that it required an in-person visit. Most people know better than to disturb me when I'm working, even if I do work at home. They leave a message on my answering machine or send me an email, knowing I'll check both locations as soon as I wrap up for the day.

I took a cautious peek through the small window in the door and found myself staring at Judy Brohaugh's infuriated face. It was no good pretending I wasn't home. She was staring right back at me. She charged inside as soon as I undid the locks and turned off the security system.

"I suppose I should be grateful *you* have the courtesy to answer your door," she said in a snippy voice. "Unlike my sister."

Since I hadn't spoken to Darlene since yesterday's conversation with Frank, I couldn't be certain what was going on, but I could make an educated guess. "Why don't you come on through to the kitchen and let me make you a nice cup of —"

"Whiskey would be good." Judy stomped down the hall in the right direction. I couldn't recall that she'd ever been in my house before, but the layout was pretty simple. She plunked herself down at the dinette table and looked up expectantly.

"No whiskey. Sorry. Would you like a rum and cola? Or a beer?"

She wrinkled her nose. "Never mind. I suppose it's too early in the day for a drink anyway."

"The sun's over the yardarm somewhere in the world. At least that's what my father-in-law used to say." I took the seat opposite her. "What's going on, Judy? Why are you here?"

362

"I'm here because I want to know what's up with Darlene, and you're the one most likely to be able to tell me."

"Why do you think anything's up?" I countered.

"Because she called me, apologizing all over herself, except that she never explained what she was so sorry about. When I tried to get a sensible answer out of her, she burst into tears and hung up on me." Judy's anger had faded to mild irritation. "I went to all the trouble of driving over here to talk to her face-to-face, and she wouldn't let me in. She wouldn't even talk to me through the door."

"Are you sure she was home?"

"I'm sure. Her van was in the garage."

"Maybe she went somewhere with Frank. He has his own car, you know."

Judy's jaw was set in stubborn lines. "She was home. She's avoiding me. I want to know why."

I hate being thrust into the middle of a family drama, but I couldn't see any help for it. I knew Darlene well. She felt things deeply. If Frank had convinced her she'd been conned by Max Kenner all those years ago, she'd be dealing with big-time guilt. She'd believed a lie and deepened the rift with her only sibling because of it. Her

363

conscience had driven her to apologize as soon as she managed to contact her sister, but it would take a good deal more time for her to work up the courage to face her in person.

"Let me ask you a question first," I said. "Why do you think you two became estranged to begin with?"

"I have no idea."

"Darlene told me it was because she was close friends with your second husband's first wife."

"What — did she think I stole him? That marriage was over long before I entered the picture. If Darlene implied that it wasn't, then she was lying."

"Does that run in the family?"

Judy glared at me. "What's that supposed to mean?"

"Lies of omission are still lies. When I came to see you, you told me about Gilbert Baxter's relationship with Grace Yarrow, but you left something out. I talked to him before he was murdered, Judy. He told me the rest of the story. All of it."

Yes. All right. I was stretching the truth myself, but Judy didn't have to know that.

"It was a mutual decision to split up."

She sounded for all the world like a sulky teenager defending herself to her parents.

364

Ridiculous in a woman in her seventies, but there it was. She stared out the window at the currently unoccupied bird feeder, shoulders slumped.

"Why on earth did you take up with Baxter in the first place? He was years younger than you, and unless he was a lot different back then, he did not have a particularly appealing personality."

"If you must know, I was trying to get back at my cheating husband. I went a little crazy, even letting Max think I was carrying on with other men, too, just to get a rise out of him."

"Other men? Including Frank Uberman?"

"Even him. I'm not proud of it!"

"Max Kenner must have been a real piece of work. It appears that he waited until you really did find someone else to drop that tidbit on Darlene."

Judy looked blank.

"If my theory is correct, your ex convinced your sister that you made a serious play for her husband, maybe even had a fling with him. He probably told her that the two of you met at least once at a local motel, which was actually true. Unfortunately, Frank had no idea that Max had talked to Darlene, or that she'd believed his lies, so it wasn't until yesterday afternoon that he finally got around to straightening her out."

"Good God. Don't those two talk to each other?"

"Apparently, not about you. Give your sister a couple of days to work through her guilt before you try to talk to her again. After all, she's only just realized that she was more to blame for the estrangement between you two than you were. She's got to be taking that hard."

"She always was too soft."

Despite the muttered criticism, Judy looked quietly pleased by this turn of events. By the time she left, I felt confident the two sisters were well on their way to a reconciliation.

CHAPTER 41

When I arrived at the amphitheater later that day, it was to discover that the board of directors of the historical society, all except Diego and Stacy, had come to observe the rehearsal. With only four days left until the performance, I could understand why they'd take an interest, but I could have done without the added pressure. I swear I felt their eyes boring into my back as I took my usual place at the director's table and opened my copy of the script.

Fortunately, there were only a few setbacks as we progressed. An actress was late with her cue. A costume needed repairs. One of the small children recruited to play a small child in the opening sequence dissolved into tears when he momentarily lost sight of his mother.

A more serious delay came about when Adam Ziskin reported that a wheel had come loose on the rolling set. Since his crew needed a few minutes to secure it and stabilize the platform, I called a break.

"I see all the high mucky-mucks are here," Adam remarked.

"Interesting choice of words," I murmured.

Muck led me to *mud-slinging* and *mud* made me wonder if there was more *dirt,* as in *gossip,* that I'd missed hearing about the four people sitting on the stone seats rising around us. I was convinced Darlene was in the clear, given how little contact she'd had with Grace Yarrow, but what about the others? Neither Ronnie nor Sunny had been married twenty-five years ago, so it seemed unlikely they'd have killed Grace to free a man with a birthmark from her clutches, let alone kill Baxter all these years later on the off chance that he might remember who had one.

That left Tony Welby.

Huh.

He *was* the one who'd discovered Gilbert Baxter's body. That always put someone near the top of the cops' list of suspects in crime fiction. *This is real life,* I reminded myself, *and Baxter and the mayor had dinner plans.*

Being careful not to look Welby's way, I followed Adam when he went to supervise the repairs on the set. Drawing him aside, I lowered my voice.

"Back when you were a kid, was Mayor Welby one of the teachers at the high school?"

"That's right." His attention was on the platform, as if he was itching to shove the teenager fixing the wheel out of the way and do it himself.

"Did you know him at all?"

"Naw, he'd left by the time I was old enough to take one of his classes, but my brother had him."

"The brother who was one of Grace Yarrow's classmates?"

"Right." His brow furrowed and he sent me a curious look. "Is that why you're interested? I don't ever remember hearing anything about him and Grace."

"Humor me. What do you remember about him?"

He shrugged. "He was kind of a phony. I mean, he never went to a single football or basketball game until he decided to run for office. Then he was there for every one, looking to build political support by pretending he was a big fan of the Lenape Hollow Indians."

"It seems to have worked. I understand he was elected to the state legislature."

369

"All that glad-handing," Adam agreed, and turned to look up into the rows of seats.

I was careful not to glance in Welby's direction myself, but once again I felt the sensation of eyes boring into my back. *Don't worry,* I told myself. *The mayor couldn't possibly know we're talking about him.*

"The ladies liked him," Adam said, his gaze returning to me. "Even some of the girls in his classes had a crush on him. I never understood that myself."

"Did Grace?"

He grinned. "The way I heard it, Grace Yarrow liked anything in pants."

After he went to check progress on the wonky wheel, I replayed everything he'd told me. Could Tony Welby have been more than Grace's teacher and guidance counselor? He *had* recommended her to write the pageant when, as far as anyone knew, she had minimal knowledge of history and no experience as a playwright.

There goes that overactive imagination again, I chided myself. Someone with a dirty mind could imply the same thing about Stacy's appointment as town historian. I was certain there had been no hanky-panky in that case, just run-of-the-mill nepotism. Still . . .

As I walked back to the director's table, I

thought about the story Diego's wife had told me about the coach and his pornographic pictures, and the comment Spring had made at rehearsal, and my own recollection of the teacher who dated one of his former students on graduation night. It wasn't impossible that Tony Welby had been involved with Grace, and if he had been, then it was also possible that he'd seen her as a liability when he was about to launch his political career.

According to Gilbert Baxter, Grace had been careless about what she told new lovers about old boyfriends. If Tony Welby had a distinctive birthmark, would he have panicked when he realized Baxter could describe it to the police? The possibility that they'd make the description public would surely have worried him.

I frowned, remembering what else Baxter had said about that birthmark. Grace had described it to him as being located in an intimate place. That meant only another lover was likely to see it . . . or a wife. *Welby's* wife? Could the mayor of Lenape Hollow really have killed both Grace Yarrow and Gilbert Baxter, the latter to prevent him from talking to Detective Hazlett?

Still struggling with the implications of this scenario, I made the mistake of glancing toward the audience. My eyes locked with Tony Welby's. Quickly, guiltily, I tore my gaze away from his.

He can't read my thoughts, I assured myself. *That narrow-eyed stare means nothing. He's probably just getting impatient because we haven't yet resumed rehearsal.*

"Places, everyone!" I called.

Although my heart raced for the next ten minutes, I managed to keep up a pretense of business as usual. Somehow, I got through the next hour without once turning around. By the time I did, after we called it quits for the night, the mayor and the other members of the board of directors had already left the amphitheater. I breathed a deep sigh of relief.

Overactive imagination, I told myself for the zillionth time.

Even if it was, first thing in the morning I planned to share my newest theory with Detective Hazlett. The worst he could do was laugh at me.

CHAPTER 42

In the first week of August, the sun doesn't set until around eight o'clock, but night was fast descending by the time I reached the parking area. I walked a little faster. The older I get, the less I like to drive at night. The headlights on other cars bother me more than they used to, and even in a low-traffic village like Lenape Hollow, I can easily imagine myself steering away from the glare and straight into a ditch.

Two carloads of cast members departed as I pulled my keys out of my jeans pocket and pushed the button to unlock my Taurus. I didn't hear any voices, but there was still one other vehicle in the lot, its engine idling. It was already too dark for me to make out anything but its shape.

My thoughts shifted to what I had in the refrigerator. The light supper I'd eaten before driving to rehearsal was a distant memory. Did I want something substantial, like a sandwich? Or should I go with a bowl of cereal? Or crackers and milk? My grandfather — not the one with an interest in family history, the other one — had always snacked on the same thing before he went to bed. He crumbled a handful of saltines into a tall glass of milk and ate the result with a spoon.

Smiling at the memory, I opened my car door. I'd just tossed my tote inside and was about to slide into the driver's-side seat when I heard a faint footfall on the pavement behind me and twisted around to see who was there.

That awkward movement was all that saved me from being knocked out cold. A length of pipe whistled past my head, striking the car roof instead of the top of my head. It bounced off and disappeared into the tall grass growing beside the parking lot.

With a yelp, I tried to scramble the rest of the way into the car and pull the door closed. I wasn't fast enough. My attacker caught hold of my leg and hauled me out again. I screamed for help as I hit the ground, but there was no one left to come to my aid.

Before I could do more than roll over onto my hands and knees, let alone get a look at my assailant, the old blanket I customarily spread across the car seat on scorching summer days to keep the upholstery from getting too hot for comfort was flung over my head. Powerful arms wrapped it around my upper body as they hauled me upright.

With my arms pinned to my sides, I could barely move. The more I struggled, the tighter I was squeezed. I managed to loosen a tiny bit of the enveloping material just enough to create a small pocket of air around my face, but all that did was make room for my glasses to fall off when my captor abruptly slung me over his shoulder in a fireman's carry.

My heart raced and my breath soughed in and out. I was, to fall back on a cliché, quaking like a leaf in a windstorm. *Calm down,* I ordered myself. *Think. You're not dead yet. There has to be a way out of this.*

All of a sudden, the world shifted. I was dropped, none too gently, into what I quickly realized was the trunk of a car. One heavy hand pushed my head down while the other shoved my legs inside. The sound of the latch catching as the trunk closed was one of the most horrifying things I can ever remember hearing.

Taking shallow breaths, I forced myself to lie still, listening while footsteps moved from the back of the car to the front. The driver's-side door opened. The vehicle shifted slightly as the man got in. The door slammed. When the engine revved, I was swamped with emotions, terror chief among them. Who wouldn't be terrified? Unless I found a way to escape, this was going to be a one-way trip.

I didn't have much maneuvering room, but I'd lucked out in that this was a large trunk. It was also nearly empty except for a toolbox. I discovered its location by ramming my shoulder into its sharp metal corner. Naturally, it was the same shoulder I'd landed on in the parking lot.

Feeling cautiously with one hand, I found an edge of the blanket and tugged at it until more of the fabric came free. Most of it was held down by my own weight. A series of painful contortions later, I wriggled free of the confining folds. In the process I found my glasses. One lens was missing. The other was cracked. It hardly mattered. In the blackness of the trunk, I couldn't see anything anyway.

My cell phone was in my tote bag, along with the pageant script and my wallet. I remembered tossing the bag into the car before I was attacked. With it had gone my only way to call for help. I was going to have to rescue myself.

As my eyes slowly adjusted to the absence of light in my moving prison, I felt around for the toolbox, thinking there might be something inside it I could use as a weapon. Out of the corner of my eye, I thought I saw a glow. I blinked. Had I imagined it? Twisting in that direction, I nearly cried out in relief. One small area of the trunk *was* faintly lit and what it illuminated was the release lever for the trunk.

I'd read somewhere, probably in a mystery novel, that all cars manufactured since 2000 are required to have a way to open the trunk from the inside. It appeared to be true. Further contortions made me wince, thanks to landing so hard on my right arm when I was hauled out of my car, but I didn't think I was seriously hurt. As I'd once haughtily informed my cousin Luke, I have excellent bone density.

Even if something had been broken, I'd have been determined to escape. No other option was acceptable. I continued to twist and squirm until I maneuvered myself near enough to the release lever to grab hold of it.

Waiting to pull that lever until the car slowed down enough to make escape feasible was one of the hardest things I've ever

done. I prayed we weren't stopping somewhere in the woods, where it would be easy
for him to recapture and kill me. I didn't
think so. The ride had been relatively
smooth, and even though it seemed as if it
had taken eons to work my way free of that
blanket, I didn't think I'd been driven very
far.

I tightened my grip as I felt the brakes
engage. When the car was barely crawling, I
pulled. The trunk popped open just as the
vehicle came to a complete stop. I rolled
toward the narrow opening, seizing what
might be my only chance to get away from
a murderer who'd already killed twice.

It wasn't a graceful exit. I landed on my
back on a hard, unyielding surface that
knocked the wind right out of me. It was
only dumb luck that one of my flailing
hands pulled the trunk closed again behind
me. I heard the latch catch just as the car
began to move away.

For the first few seconds, I was incapable
of movement. I was lying in the middle of
the road, so close to the car's taillights that
their brightness made me squeeze my eyes
shut.

They popped open again a second later
and I squinted through the broken lens of
my glasses at the words printed on a bumper

sticker. If I'd had any doubts about who had kidnapped me, they were instantly banished. The brightly colored banner urged voters to support Tony Welby in the next election for mayor of Lenape Hollow.

CHAPTER 43

The car continued to pull away, made a left turn at what I belatedly realized was a stop sign, and kept going.

Panic sent pure adrenaline pumping into my body, giving me the strength to roll over into a crouch and scuttle toward the nearest cover. I was terrified Welby would look out the driver's-side window and see me. When I reached a weeping willow on someone's front lawn, I ducked behind it. I was panting so loudly that I wasn't certain I'd be able to hear the sound of the car if the mayor returned to look for me.

Slowly, my breathing returned to normal and my heart stopped hammering in my ears. Nothing broke the stillness of the night. No dogs barked. No security lights came on. No cars passed by on the street. Even though I still couldn't see very well, I began to think clearly again.

What I could make out through the

cracked lens wasn't much help in getting my bearings, but I had done a fair amount of walking and driving around Lenape Hollow since my return. I felt certain that if I simply chose a direction, I'd soon spot a recognizable landmark and be able to find my way home. The first thing I'd do when I got there was call the police.

My arm throbbed. Even the slightest movement jarred it, sending shooting pains from shoulder to wrist. *Bruises, big time,* I thought. There was a tear in my shirt, crusty with blood. That was road rash, or maybe a cut. The rest of my body was one big ache. My butt and lower back hurt like blazes from bouncing off the pavement. Even before my escape, I'd probably sprained, strained, or torn assorted muscles and ligaments with all that wriggling around inside Tony Welby's trunk, not to mention the damage I sustained when I hit the pavement in the parking lot at Wonderful World.

Stop griping! I ordered myself. *You're alive, aren't you?*

I had to get to a phone. That was the crucial thing.

I could already feel stiffness setting in. If I didn't move soon, I might not be able to. Although it was a risk, I headed back toward the intersection with the stop sign. Hobbling, telling myself to ignore the pain, I put one foot in front of the other. I was limping badly by the time I covered the few yards to the corner. Thank goodness the mayor was law-abiding in most respects. He'd dutifully stopped to check for oncoming traffic.

A wave of relief swept over me when I realized I knew where I was. I'd escaped at the corner of Champlain and South Streets.

In the next second, panic returned. Had Welby been taking me to the historical society? I couldn't think why he would, but Blake Street was only one short block away. He'd have reached the parking lot behind it by now. Once he discovered I was no longer in the trunk of his car, he'd come looking for me.

Thanking my lucky stars that it was now full dark and that the moon had not yet risen, I turned and fled back the way I'd come. An adrenaline surge is a wonderful thing. It temporarily blocked out most of my hurts.

The sidewalks on Champlain Street are lined with trees — big, beautiful trees. If Welby drove this way in search of me, I'd see his headlights in time to retreat into the nearest yard and hide behind one of those thick, all-concealing trunks.

I considered pounding on the nearest door or screaming for help, but I had a pretty good idea what I looked like with my hair wild and my clothes all torn and dirty. I doubted I'd sound coherent, even if I could get someone to listen to me. I'd come off as a crazy old lady, especially if I claimed that the mayor of Lenape Hollow was trying to kill me.

Someone might call the police, but the odds were good that I'd be made to stay outside, vulnerable to attack, while we waited for an officer to show up. I'd be better off to keep moving. My own house wasn't all that far away.

There were streetlights, but they were few and far between. I couldn't see that well in any case. My glasses, bent and broken and missing that one lens entirely, were next to useless. Only the fact that I knew where I was going kept me moving forward.

The quickest way to get to 134 Wedemeyer Terrace — home, sweet home — was through backyards. I aimed my unsteady steps toward one particular residence on Champlain Street, the one that abutted the rear of my property.

By the time I reached the lot in question, I was panting again and had a painful stitch in my side. That not a single vehicle had ap-

proached from either direction did not re-
assure me. Welby wasn't going to give up.
His attack on me meant he was afraid to let
me talk to the police, just as he'd been
afraid of what Gilbert Baxter might tell
them.

I limped from the front of the Champlain
Street house to the back and headed into
the underbrush that separated that lot from
my backyard. Every ounce of energy I pos-
sessed was focused on getting myself safely
home. A few minutes later, I staggered out
of the other side of the bushes and stumbled
onto my nearly treeless property. I continued downhill, weaving like a drunkard. It's
a wonder I didn't fall flat on my face, but
somehow I made it to my back porch. Only
then did I realize that I didn't have my keys.
I'd had my key ring in my hand when Welby
tried to bean me with that length of pipe. I
couldn't remember dropping it, but obviously I had. I patted my pockets just to
make sure and found nothing but a used
tissue and a foil-wrapped hard candy.

Resting my head against the locked door,
I tried to think. It wasn't easy. My brain
was as exhausted as my body.

The sounds of a space battle, coming from
the O'Day house, told me it would be no
use trying to get Tom and Marie's atten-

tion. Even if I could climb over the tall fence separating their property from mine, I'd never be able to make myself heard. Tuesday was family movie night and the volume on their DVD player was turned up to screech.

Slowly, painfully, I lifted my head to look in the direction of Cindy Fry's house. All the windows were dark. My heart sank to my toes. Cindy and her steady, dependable husband had a Tuesday night ritual, too. They took their three boisterous boys out for pizza.

Move, I told myself. *Go around to the front.*

If I couldn't break the sound barrier to get Tom and Marie's attention, I could try another house farther down the block. It was the home of an old childhood friend. Maybe she'd —

I broke off in mid-thought and shook my head. It would make more sense to head straight for the police station. It was only two blocks away, down the hill to Main Street and hang a right. I could walk that far if I had to.

Sure I could.

It took a massive effort to get myself moving again. I dragged my weary bones as far as the footpath between my property and Cindy's. With faltering footsteps, left hand braced against the side of my garage for support, I plodded slowly along it. I doubted I could go much farther before my legs gave out on me. The distance between home and the police station, a short, invigorating walk under normal circumstances, now loomed as a journey of daunting proportions.

Back to plan A, I thought. *Get into the house, even if I have to break a window, and phone the cops.*

At the front of the garage, I felt my way along the closed and locked overhead door. When I got to the corner where the garage met the side of my front porch, I stopped, swaying a little, to catch my breath. The steps cut into the terrace were few in number, but there was no railing. The sidewalk at the top led to more stairs, the ones going up onto my porch. At the mere thought of climbing them, my thighs cried out for mercy. So did my knees, calves, ankles, and feet. My hips had stopped speaking to me entirely. My right arm was mercifully numb . . . except when I tried to move it. And my head? I didn't think I'd struck it on anything, but my mind no longer seemed capable of convincing my battered body to keep moving.

It was the sound of an approaching car that snapped me out of this dangerous inaction. I pressed myself deeper into the shadows, expecting to see headlights. There were none. There *was* a car. Its shape was dimly visible in the glow of the nearest streetlight, but I couldn't make out any details.

The vehicle slowed as if the driver was searching for a specific address. I swallowed hard when he pulled in at the curb across from my house and killed the engine. When the door opened, a shadowy figure emerged. He started to cross the street, headed straight for me.

His honor the mayor had come looking for me.

Welby carried a flashlight in one hand, but he hadn't yet turned it on. He couldn't see me cowering in my dark corner, but it would be only a matter of seconds before he spotted me. Retreat was as impossible as running up the steps. To attempt either course of action would reveal my presence, but there was another alternative.

I had to move fast and pray he didn't turn on that flashlight. Reaching out with both trembling hands, I fumbled for the catches that held one section of the porch's lattice-work skirting in place. Lifting up the hinged section sent daggers stabbing into my injured arm and made sweat break out on my forehead, but somehow I managed it

and scrambled under it and into the safe
haven beneath the porch. The latticework
settled back into place with a dull thump.

I held my breath.

Welby's shoes crunched on loose stones in
the driveway as he walked toward me.
Either he was making too much noise to
hear my movements, or he was so confident
that I could not have arrived at the house
ahead of him that he discounted any small
sound that reached his ears. When he turned
on the flashlight to navigate the steps, I
shrank back, terrified he would direct the
beam my way, but he never once turned it
in my direction. I heard him continue on
up the steps to the porch and then, after a
moment, the creak of the wicker sofa above
my head as he sat down.

He was waiting for me to come home so
he could kill me.

CHAPTER 44

I have no idea how much time passed before I dared shift my position. Crouched in the dirt and cobwebs, I flexed my cramped and aching muscles one by one. Not every body part cooperated, but I was relieved to find I still had some mobility left.

That scene on the ship in the first Indiana Jones movie suddenly made a lot more sense to me. The only place that didn't hurt was the tip of my nose, and I wasn't entirely sure that it hadn't sustained some minor damage, too.

As long as Tony Welby continued to sit on my porch, I didn't dare leave my hiding place. I couldn't risk much movement, either, for fear he would hear me. I shifted my position often enough to keep my legs from cramping and considered whether or not it would be prudent to crawl farther under the porch. As a kid, I hadn't minded spiders, snakes, or rodents, but I had no great desire to come face-to-face with any of them as an adult, especially not under these circumstances. Besides, in common with the terrace, the ground under the porch rose at an angle, leaving less and less headroom. If I tried to squeeze in under the upper end I might be better concealed, but odds were good I'd also get stuck. I stayed put and turned up my hearing aids to better monitor the mayor's every twitch.

After a while, I heard Welby get up and move around. He paced back and forth only inches above my head, sending dust drifting down on me with every heavy footfall.

A sneeze caught me by surprise. I had only a split second to muffle the sound against my sleeve.

The pacing stopped. Had he heard me? Was he coming to investigate? After an endless moment, a familiar creak reassured me. He'd resumed his seat on the wicker sofa.

Every once in a while, he shifted his weight, making me hope he'd lose patience and go away. Then all I'd have to do was wait for Cindy and her family to come home from their night out and holler for help. I could see their front lawn through the slats in the skirting.

Simple, right?

Wrong.

Welby was still there, invisible to my happily oblivious neighbors, when they returned a short time later. Two of the boys were loudly debating which superhero was more powerful, Iron Man or the Hulk, while their parents appeared to be completely wrapped up in a conversation of their own. Only the youngest child sent so much as a glance in my direction. He was six years old and failed to notice anything out of place. I tried to tell myself that was a good thing. It would be very bad for me if it was easy to spot a difference in one section of latticework.

Above my head, Tony Welby tapped his fingers on the arm of the sofa. After a bit, he cleared his throat. He shifted his weight again, making the wicker groan ominously.

Please, please, please get tired of waiting and go away.

He stood up.

Yes!

He walked as far as the top of the porch steps and stopped. Although I stretched my ears, I heard no footsteps descending, but another noise did reach me, the faint squeak as he opened my screen door. This was followed by a scratching sound.

It took me a moment to realize what was causing it. Welby had my keys. He must have grabbed them from my car, along with the blanket.

The mayor was letting himself into my house. No doubt he planned to make himself comfortable inside while he waited for me to show up.

I listened harder. The door opened. He went through it. As soon as he closed it, I meant to crawl out of my hidey-hole and go to Cindy's for help . . . if I could get my wobbly legs to cooperate. It didn't occur to me that there was an obvious flaw in Welby's plan until the alarms began to blare.

I sagged with relief. I'd forgotten about my security system. Welby didn't know the code to punch in. In a few more seconds, if I didn't answer my landline in person and tell them this was a false alarm, a phone call from the security company would summon the police.

Footsteps pounded down the porch steps and past my hiding place. A moment later, a car engine came to life. Welby pulled away from the curb, tires squealing.

I dissolved into breathless laughter. It *hurt* when I laughed, but not enough to make me stop. I was whooping helplessly, tears running unchecked down my cheeks, by the time Cindy's husband emerged from their house and headed my way.

A police cruiser was just pulling up in

front of the house when I shoved aside the latticework and crawled out of hiding. I must have looked like a cross between the witch from *Into the Woods* and the creature from the black lagoon. I staggered a few steps, lost my balance, and sat down hard in the middle of the driveway.

A young policewoman I'd met the previous year approached with gun drawn. Her eyes widened when she recognized me.

I had two important things to say to her.

The first was, "Don't let the cat out."

The second was, "You need to go arrest the mayor."

She holstered her weapon, but clearly thought I was either delirious or intoxicated. It wasn't until I was being loaded into an ambulance, about to be whisked away to the hospital to have the damage to my arm and elsewhere looked at, and perhaps be confined to a padded room, that Detective Hazlett arrived on the scene. I grabbed him by the sleeve and wouldn't let go until I was sure I had his full attention.

"Check my porch for fingerprints. I was hiding because Tony Welby was waiting for me to come home. He was going to kill me. He *did* kill Gilbert Baxter. *And* Grace."

Hazlett's response was a curt nod. "I'll take care of it."

I hoped he wasn't just humoring me. I didn't have the strength to keep hold of him any longer. Before I could add any details to back up my claims, the ambulance attendant shut the doors between us.

I closed my eyes.

It's possible I felt asleep from sheer exhaustion.

CHAPTER 45

Four days later, the amphitheater was three-quarters full for the one and only performance of the quasquibicentennial pageant. Since no one booed or walked out, I considered the production a rousing success. Afterward, the younger cast and crew members headed for the local pizza place to celebrate. We old fogeys adjourned to my house. Calpurnia, outraged by the invasion, initially hid out in my office. Later she crept downstairs to investigate and ended up sitting on my lap.

Since everyone seemed to be having a good time, I stayed put on the loveseat and let the sound of a dozen cheerful conversations wash over me. The last time the house had been this crowded with people I'd been thirteen and celebrating my birthday with an assortment of classmates. It had been my one and only teenage party to include both girls and boys.

Two of the attendees on that occasion were again present — Darlene and Ronnie. To my delight, Darlene was chatting amiably with her sister. I'd spotted Judy at the start of the pageant, sitting in the audience with her sister and brother-in-law, and invited her to join us. She'd been reluctant at first, but I'd pointed out that she already knew most of the other guests.

The remaining members of the board of directors of the historical society — all but the one currently in jail — were present and accounted for, along with their spouses. Even Diego had come. He and I made a good pair with his leg in a cast and my arm in a sling.

The mayor had been caught two days after he tried to kill me, attempting to board a flight out of Stewart Airport. He was charged with kidnapping and attempted murder and denied bail. My claims, wild as they'd sounded, had been backed up by the fingerprints he'd left behind on my front porch.

Someone sat down on the other end of the loveseat, and I looked over to see John Chen smiling at me. He nodded his head toward the wall across from us. "The old fireplace was there, yes? I looked it up in my files. If you want to open it up again, the job shouldn't be too complicated. You'll probably want to have the chimney lined, though."

"I remember pretty green tiles," I said. "Do you suppose you could find some like the originals?"

"I imagine I could." He reached over to stroke Calpurnia's head.

"She'll enjoy a nice fire on a winter's night," I said.

After he left to browse the hors d'oeuvres, I contemplated the wall in question, imagining it as it would be in a few months' time. It was a pleasant fantasy — a fragrant applewood fire burning in the hearth, myself curled up on the loveseat with a cozy mystery novel. There would be an afghan over my knees and a cat at my feet.

When the doorbell rang for the umpteenth time, I didn't get up. Someone else could let in the latecomer. It wasn't until a sudden silence fell over the wrap party that I turned my head and saw Detective Hazlett standing in the archway between my living room and the hallway.

"Trouble, officer?" Ronnie asked in her grande-dame voice. "I'm quite sure no one filed a noise complaint."

So was I. I'd taken the precaution of inviting all my neighbors to the party.

397

Hazlett spoke directly to me. "A moment of your time?"

"Is this something you don't want the others to hear?" I continued to stroke Calpurnia's fur, hoping to level out the spike of anxiety Hazlett's sudden appearance had caused. The only thing I could read in his facial expression and body language was a vague disquiet, but for one awful moment, I was afraid he'd come to tell me that the case had fallen apart and Welby was about to be released from jail.

"Perhaps you could step out onto the porch?"

"I'll take that as a yes. Excuse me, folks."

I stood, moving slowly and stiffly. At my age, it takes a while to recover from bumps and bruises. I took my drink with me.

The level of noise rose to its former volume as soon as we left the room, but I doubted that would prevent Darlene and Ronnie from trying to eavesdrop.

"How's the arm?" Hazlett asked.

"I'll live."

I hadn't broken anything, but I had pulled several muscles. Temporarily soothed by a generous infusion of rum and cola, the worst of my aches and pains were in abeyance. I made myself as comfortable as possible on the cushions of the wicker sofa while the detective settled into one of the matching chairs.

Since the pageant had been performed at midafternoon, it was still early evening. Our celebration was more happy-hour cocktail party than a late-into-the-night affair. By eight, everyone would have gone their own way, off to have a late supper if they weren't too full of finger food. I rather thought Darlene, Ronnie, and Shirley might linger after the rest had gone. Depending upon what Hazlett had to say, I hoped I'd be able to satisfy their curiosity.

He cleared his throat. "It looks like your theory about Welby's relationship with Grace Yarrow was right on the money."

"He confessed?"

"No, but the evidence is mounting against him. He'll be charged with her murder and that of Gilbert Baxter. I thought you'd want to know."

"No chance of him getting out, then?"

Hazlett shook his head. "You don't have to worry about that."

I half expected him to leave once he'd delivered this news. When he didn't, I was emboldened to ask for details.

"I shouldn't be telling you any of this." Hazlett's voice was gruff.

I smiled to myself. "If anyone complains,

399

you can tell them I beat it out of you."

His bark of laughter sounded sweet to my ears.

"So he seduced Grace when she was in high school? He was what — in his thirties?" I took a long swallow of my drink.

"There's some question as to who seduced who. Whom?"

I waved off the question. At this precise moment, correct grammar was the least of my concerns. "Did someone confirm it?"

"Yes. Welby's wife."

"She *knew*?"

Hearing the disgust in my voice, he grimaced. "You've never met Mrs. Welby, have you? Let's just say that back when this all started, she shared her husband's ambition. She was willing to turn a blind eye to his affair so long as no one else knew anything about it. According to her, it continued, on and off, from the time Grace was a junior in high school until shortly before she allegedly left town. Mrs. Welby claims she never suspected that Grace had been murdered, and that she was glad when she heard the news of her departure. When the body was found, she still wasn't suspicious of her husband. She thought she was living with a philanderer, not a killer. And before you ask, she also claims she never confronted him

400

about his extra-marital activities. According to her, he didn't know she was aware of his relationship with Grace Yarrow."

"Grace was a minor. Mrs. Welby was living with a sexual predator."

"Some people are good at justifying what they want to believe. My guess is that she'll now play the deceived spouse to the hilt."

I pondered that for a moment. "I'm surprised she talked to you at all. When everything you've just told me becomes public knowledge, she won't be seen as a sympathetic figure."

"It was finding out that Baxter was killed to keep him quiet about the birthmark that pushed her into talking to me." A faint smile made the corners of his mouth twitch.

"Baxter said it was . . . distinctive."

"You could say that. Apparently, it resembles a question mark when the location is in a, er, resting state, but when it's, um, erect, it turns into an exclamation point."

It was a good thing I hadn't yet taken another sip of my drink. As it was, I choked on a laugh.

"It's not in a place where just anyone might see it," Hazlett continued, avoiding my eyes, "but since Baxter was planning to report everything he knew to me, Welby was desperate to stop him before anyone else

401

heard the description and put two and two together. It's possible his wife isn't the only woman who would have recognized the birthmark, but she was probably the one he was most worried about."

"Talk about overreacting! The affair took place decades ago. Why would he assume his wife would leap to the conclusion that he murdered his lover?"

"Mrs. Mayor wasn't the job she signed on for. That's no secret. Welby's political career wasn't supposed to bring him back to the same small puddle he started out in. He couldn't trust her to stick by him if there was any kind of scandal."

"So he killed Gilbert Baxter and then came after me." I'd been puzzling over that ever since. "He must have read something into the expression on my face after I talked to Adam Ziskin. I suppose he remembered that Adam was on the stage crew for the bicentennial. If he knew Adam was involved with Grace, he must have thought he knew the same thing Baxter did, and that Adam had shared that information with me. Talk about paranoid! Do you suppose he meant to kill Adam, too, just to be on the safe side?"

I could imagine it all too vividly. Footsteps in the dark. A length of pipe swung at an unprotected head. I'd been lucky. If Welby's first attempt to dispose of me had succeeded, he'd have cracked open my skull. Had he intended to leave my body where it fell, in the hope that people would think I'd been the victim of a mugger?

"We may never know the whole story," Hazlett said. "Welby has lawyered up and isn't admitting to anything. It's only thanks to you that all his crimes are finally catching up with him." His lips twitched. "You'll remember that we found several partial fingerprints on that scrap of paper caught under Grace's typewriter. One of them is Welby's."

"So he did set up a rendezvous with her, and when she met him at the historical society, he murdered her."

What Grace could have revealed about him would have killed the political career he was about to launch. Since he couldn't trust her to keep her mouth shut, he'd killed her and hidden her body, confident it would never be discovered.

"I guess we know now why he wasn't enthusiastic about reviving the pageant. I'm surprised he didn't try harder to stop the repairs at the historical society."

"He couldn't make too much of a fuss without calling undue attention to himself,"

Hazlett said.

I thought back over my encounters with the mayor. "That wasn't his biggest problem."

"Oh?" Detective Hazlett asked. "What was?"

I took another sip of my drink. At that moment, I felt very much alive and was just tipsy enough to imagine I was being witty.

"He'd developed bad habits," I said, "both in his manner of speaking, and in the way he dealt with those he saw as a threat. He just couldn't stop *repeating* himself."

A RANDOM SELECTION FROM "THE WRITE RIGHT WRIGHT'S LANGUAGE AND GRAMMAR TIPS"

BY MIKKI LINCOLN

If you want less trouble keeping to a budget, you should make fewer expensive purchases. Less refers to value, degree, or amount. Fewer refers to something you can count.

Be careful not to lose the loose change in your pocket.

Don't overdo during strenuous workouts if you are overdue for a checkup with your doctor.

The blonde has blond hair.

When writing on stationery, one is usually stationary.

When you breathe you draw in and expel your breath.

A healthy person usually prefers to live in a healthful environment.

The principal stockholder forgot his principles when he tried to make a killing on the stock market.

The nurse's aide came to the aid of the patient by helping him pour a glass of lemonade.

I remember the '60s. I wore a 1960s' outfit to a costume party.

Always spell out century references, and remember that the sixteenth century encompasses the fifteen hundreds.

Half an hour from now, on the half hour, there will be a number of half-price items on sale.

The rule is to use *a* before words that start with consonants and *an* before words that start with vowel *sounds,* so that old television commercial got it right when the actor said, "It's an herb, Herb."

From whence is redundant. Whence means

from what place.

A character can grit her teeth when speaking, but for an author to write, *"Go away,"* *she gritted.* is just plain silly.

ACKNOWLEDGMENTS

For this novel, which will be my sixtieth traditionally published book, I am grateful to many people, but especially to my husband. By the time *Clause & Effect* is in stores, Sandy and I will have celebrated our fiftieth wedding anniversary. For much of my career, he has been the "spouse with health insurance" so necessary to the survival of most writers. He has also been my beta reader for almost every one of those sixty books. I can always rely on him to tell me when I get something wrong.

One of the characters in *Clause & Effect,* that of Shirley Martin, the librarian at the historical society, is based with deep affection on the real Shirley Martin, longtime reference librarian at Mantor Library at the University of Maine at Farmington. I worked there as a library assistant at circulation for several years and Shirley was an inspiration on both a personal and professional level. With the permission of her widower, Robert Martin, I named the character in her honor. Sadly, Robert also passed away, just a few months after his wife's death, but not before donating funds in her memory, and in memory of the cats who were their cherished companions over the years, to build a new wing at a local no-kill animal shelter.

Once again, Tom and Marie O'Day, who won naming rights to their characters at an auction at Malice Domestic, play a role in the story. Fred Gorton was my grandfather's name. All other names are random and the characters who people this story are entirely fictional. If you think one of them is based on you, you are wrong.

One additional thank-you goes to Eileen Dreyer, the source of the true story that inspired the location and description of my villain's telltale birthmark. Yes, she did use the real version in one of her novels. I altered it slightly for mine.

ABOUT THE AUTHOR

Kaitlyn Dunnett grew up in the Borscht Belt of New York state, otherwise known as the Sullivan County Catskills, the area she writes about in the Deadly Edits mysteries. These days, Kaitlyn lives in the mountains of western Maine with her husband and cats and can be reached through her website at www.kaitlyndunnett.com.

The employees of Thorndike Press hope you have enjoyed this Large Print book. All our Thorndike, Wheeler, and Kennebec Large Print titles are designed for easy reading, and all our books are made to last. Other Thorndike Press Large Print books are available at your library, through selected bookstores, or directly from us.

For information about titles, please call:
(800) 223-1244

or visit our website at:
gale.com/thorndike

To share your comments, please write:
Publisher
Thorndike Press
10 Water St., Suite 310
Waterville, ME 04901